CW01021637

CRIMINAL PURSUITS

CRIMINAL PURSUITS

Edited by
Samantha Lee Howe

In Aid of POhWER

First published in 2021 by Telos Publishing Ltd,
139 Whitstable Road, Canterbury, Kent, CT2 8EQ, UK

Telos Publishing welcomes feedback
feedback@telos.co.uk

Criminal Pursuits © 2021, Ed. Samantha Lee Howe

Cover Art © 2021, Martin Baines
Cover Design © 2021, David J Howe

ISBN: 978-1-84583-193-6

The moral right of the authors has been asserted.

British Library Cataloguing in Publication Data. A catalogue
record for this book is available from the British Library.

This book is sold subject to the condition that it shall not by way
of trade or otherwise, be lent, resold, hired out or otherwise
circulated without the publisher's prior written consent in any
form of binding or cover other than that in which it is published
and without a similar condition including this condition being
imposed on the subsequent purchaser.

Contributing Authors' Copyright Information

'Changeling' © 2021 Bryony Pearce

'Flesh of A Fancy Woman' © 2019, 2021 Paul Magrs. (First Published in *The Book of Extraordinary Historical Mystery Stories.* Ed. Maxim Jakubowski. Mango Publishing Group.)

'Dangerous Women' © 2021 Sandra Murphy

'The Travellers' © 2021 Maxim Jakubowski

'Nights On The Town' © 2021 Sally Spedding

'Blindsided' © 2021 Caroline England

'The Victim' © 2020, 2021 Awais Khan. (First Published in the Blink Fiction issue of *The Hindu,* 2020.)

'The Way of All Flesh' © 2015, 2021 Raven Dane. (First published in *Tales of the Female Perspective.* Chinbeard Books, 2015.)

'And Here's The Next Clue …' © 2008, 2010, 2021 Amy Myers (First published in The Crime Writers' Association anthology *M.O.*, Ed. Martin Edwards. 2008. Comma Press. Also in *The Mammoth Book of Best British Crime*, Ed. Maxim Jakubowski, Robinson, 2010 (US edition Running Press)

'The Trap' © 2021 A A Chaudhuri

'The Caveman Detective' © 2021 Rhys Hughes

'Faceless Killer' ©2018, 2021 Christine Poulson (First published in *Ellery Queen Mystery Magazine*, March/April, 2018)

'Slash' © 2021 Samantha Lee Howe

'The Good Neighbourhood' © 2021 Paul Finch

CONTENTS

ABOUT POhWER

What do crimes have in common with human rights breaches? They both involve human dignity, occur without warning and threaten our safety. Both the victim of the crime and those experiencing human rights breaches will feel helpless, voiceless and frightened.

I write this introduction as we come out of a global pandemic where often individual human rights and entitlements were not necessarily upheld and many protections were eased to fight the Coronavirus. I write as the CEO of POhWER (which stands for people of here want human rights), the UK's largest independent advocacy, information, and advice charity. We exist to empower people to uphold their human rights in public institutions and services.

Wherever you are in this world reading this book, you will have your own identity and life experience. Your own identity and circumstances will be unique. You might live with disability, mental health, identify with a marginalised community or you may even live a life of privilege. You will feel, sense and know where you stand in terms of your own human rights. Your own country might champion human rights and make you feel like an equal in society. Your own country may not and you might be facing persecution and discrimination. Your lifestyle might be criminalised, your voice to fight for rights may not exist.

Some of you may live in what you perceive to be a place where human rights protections are very good. Have you asked yourself the question – who are those protections for? Are they protecting just you? What about people from different ages, genders, race or ethnicities, sexual orientations, living with disability or mental health, lacking mental capacity or those locked up in institutions such as care homes, mental health facilities or prisons. Is everyone around you living freely and as equal members of your own society?

No matter who you are and where you live, your rights matter. Empowering yourself with information, advice and advocacy can help you to know your human rights. POhWER was established in 1996 by a group of ordinary individuals who were tired of people treating them poorly who wanted to address the imbalance of power in our society and empower others to uphold their human rights.

I am a pragmatist and a realistic. Often I feel like a disappointed idealist in my line of work. Crime will always exist as will discrimination and unequal treatment. Both are abuses of power. My own leisure reading includes other-world pursuits, crime and the supernatural. I read to forget and to escape the sadness and strife I see within POhWER's work. My leisure reading and love of crime and the supernatural allows me to re-charge and to bring my best self to work the next day in our collective fight for human rights.

Meeting Samantha Lee Howe in 2020 was a gamechanger. She helped me to see through fresh eyes how relevant POhWER's work was not only to people living in the UK but globally. I am so proud to call Sam a friend, a POhWER patron, and to see how she is using her own position to help advocate for the importance of POhWER's work. Samantha has been the driving force behind this book – pitching the idea, commissioning the book, editing and writing her own story. Samantha's introductions to the writers in this book made this incredible charity project possible.

I cannot express the deep gratitude I feel for the writers – Bryony Pearce, Paul Magrs, Sandra Murphy, Maxim Jakubowski, Sally Spedding, Caroline England, Awais Khan, Raven Dane, Amy Myers, A A Chaudhuri, Rhys Hughes, Christine Poulson, Samantha Lee Howe and Paul Finch. They have given their time to enrich us with these incredible tales and have donated the royalties from this book to POhWER. A very warm thank you to David and Stephen from Telos

FOREWORD

Publishing who took on this amazing project in aid of POhWER. I thank my lucky stars every day that you decided to support POhWER, when I am well aware there are so many other great organisations you could have worked with. On behalf of our POhWER colleagues, trustees and beneficiaries: a very warm thank you for your generous contribution.

A special thank you to my POhWER colleagues without whom this project would never have happened: Penny Bodger-Yates who introduced me to Samantha. Tony Kildare, Tim Jarvis, Ben Baxter, Louise Large, Emma Jenkins and Fiona McArthur-Worbey who patiently worked through the details with me and shared the vision on the impact of this project.

400,000+ benefited from POhWER's work this past year. Purchasing this anthology helps us to expand our reach, help more people and further our work to serve millions who are slipping between the cracks of public services.

Thank you for your support dear reader. Grab a cup of tea, curl up in your favourite chair and enjoy this wonderful book.

Helen Moulinos
Chief Executive, POhWER
August 2021

To learn more about POhWER's work visit us at
www.pohwer.net

CHANGELING

Bryony Pearce

I knew it was you, the first moment I saw you.

Not just because you were the right age, or because John's gold-flecked, brown eyes were staring at me from your face but because, when you reached for your muzzy, I could see the patches of white on your fingertips. Vitiligo. John has it too.

The woman you are with does not have it. Nor does the man who came to pick you both up. The man she kissed after she clipped you into your car seat. Those are not your parents.

'Are you all right?'

The young woman who has approached me is with a toddling boy, his fingers sticky from the strawberries she has been feeding him, his cheeks crimson from the spring chill.

'I mean ...' she swallows. 'You've been standing here for a while. Are you with one of the children?' She shuffles awkwardly, then remembers that she's here as self-appointed child-protection officer and straightens. Meets my eyes dead on.

She's been in the periphery of my attention, and it's obvious she knows most of the parents here. She worked out that I was alone a little while ago. If I was a man, or if she was, she'd have marched straight up to me and would be outright accusing me of creeping on the kids. But we're both women, so instead we do this dance.

'No.' I smile and touch my hollow belly. 'No, I'm not with any of the kids.' I duck my head, shyly. 'I will be in a few months though ... all being well.' She follows the flicker of my eyes, to my fingertips, which are stroking my stomach.

It never quite recovered after the birth, still a bump where the muscles haven't knitted back together, where the pointlessness of dieting and sit-ups has left a mark.

'You're pregnant?' She lights up. 'When are you due?'

'It's early days.' I almost believe my own lie. I *want* to believe it, but I know I can't be carrying. John hasn't touched me in months. 'I'm a bit scared, to be honest.' I meet her eyes and tell the truth. 'Watching the children reminds me why I'm going through with this.'

'I understand,' she looks at her son, who has picked up a stick and is poking it into an anthill. 'This is such a great age.' She bends down and retrieves the stick, which is drifting towards his mouth. 'This is Nicky.' She picks him up and settles him on her hip. 'Say hi, Nicky.'

He looks rebellious, then buries his head in her neck.

I smile. 'Hi, Nicky.'

He wriggles and she puts him down. Immediately he flees towards the sandpit. 'I'm Tash.'

'Anna.' I hold out a hand and she shakes it, her gloved fingers warm against mine.

'Well, if you want to know anything about the baby years, I'm your go-to.' Strands of her hair catch in the breeze, and tickle her nose and neck. She has one eye on her son, one on me. 'I have three little sisters and I was a nanny before I had Nicky. I can't remember a time I wasn't around babies.' She laughs.

One of her friends, who has two children here, a baby in a pram and a little girl on a swing, looks at her with a raised brow and she gestures. It's all right. The friend turns back to her conversation, absently pushing her squealing daughter with one hand. I am no longer a threat.

I say something dangerous. 'That little one who just left was so well-behaved … if mine turns out anything like that, I think I'll be okay.'

Tash laughs and takes the bait. 'They're not all that easy, you know, but you're right.' She leans closer. 'That's Kai. I've never seen him fuss and, to be honest …' she lowers her voice. 'It's just so wonderful to see. I know the family. They had such difficulty conceiving, if anyone deserves an angel-baby, it's Lissa.'

'She couldn't have children?'

If I wasn't sure before, I am now. And I have your name: Kai. It isn't the one John and I gave you, which honoured his dad but, despite myself, I do like it. I don't want to like anything she has imposed on you, and yet …

'When she got pregnant, we had a huge party. Cake on the picnic tables, music, an entertainer for the kids.'

Pregnancy can be faked.

Did she see me first, and fake her pregnancy to match mine? Or did she decide to fake the pregnancy, then take a baby born at around the right time? If you had been born a week earlier, or later, would I be here with you, and she the childless interloper?

'You're all friends?'

'Well, when you're in the park day-in, day-out … Lissa used to nanny as well, we both came here with our charges, that's one of mine, over there.' She points to a much older boy. He's sitting on a bench with an iPad, nothing around him snatches his attention from the screen.

'Shouldn't he be in school?' I tilt my head.

'He's been sick.' She sighs. 'To be honest, his new nanny is a bit …' she tails off. 'But I can't help, he won't speak to me anymore, he resents Nicky. … Anyway, I've been coming here for a few years now. It's a nice crowd. I could introduce you.' She takes a step towards her friends, but I shake my head.

'Not today …' I bite my lip. 'If the pregnancy doesn't work out, I don't want to have too many mummy friends – people I'd have to explain things to.'

'Are you worried about losing the baby?' She drifts nearer, her expression sympathetic.

'I lost one before.' Again, the truth. My grief must be reflected in my face because her own eyes fill with tears.

'I'm so sorry.'

'No, it's -'

'This must be terrifying for you.'

'I just … want to hope.' I touch my belly again, where I carried you for too short a time.

You were three-weeks early. I missed out on that feeling of being too pregnant. Of being desperate to give birth. Of drinking raspberry leaf tea, eating pineapple and curry. Awkward sex. Sometimes I still feel you kicking, popping bubbles that wake me at night, making me think you're still inside. Then I remember that you were stolen from me, and my pain is an open wound.

'If there's anything I can do … anything at all.'

She seems a good person, but I can't help loathing her.

All those times she's been with you in the park – she's spent more time with you than I have – and she hasn't even noticed that you don't rightfully belong to her friend. Doesn't *everyone* know that vitiligo is genetic? It's obvious you are out of place. Yet, no call to the police. No report that her friend has a stolen baby. I could have had you back months ago. *Months.* But it's been down to me. Down to me alone to search every park in the city, until I found you.

I press my lips together. 'I'll be okay. Thanks.'

'Well, it's lunch time,' once more she looks at her friends, who are drifting towards the picnic tables. 'A few of us are staying for a picnic, making the most of the fact it isn't raining. You're welcome to join us.'

'Oh, I don't think -'

'Lissa and Mitch drove to the deli – they'll be back in a bit with a few nice things and there's bound to be extra.'

They're coming back? I had been certain you were gone for the day. But I could see you again. Perhaps even spend time with you … if I let myself be drawn into the group.

It's a risk. If I emerge from the trees, Lissa might recognise me. It could frighten her off. It depends a lot, I suppose, on how closely she stalked me when I was pregnant.

I've cut off my hair since, it's gone from almost waist length, to hitting my chin; I couldn't bear all the strands I was losing after the pregnancy. My face too, has lost its pregnancy pouchiness. I touch my cheek, my temple: the bones in my face are sharp now. John has been begging me to eat, saying he hardly recognises me.

My clothes are different too. While I carried you, I wore maternity dresses, soft things, items I thought a good mother would wear. I pictured myself bare-footed in them, baking cookies as the material swirled around my ankles. Now I am back in my old uniform: black trousers, roll neck jumpers, long camel coat.

My breasts have sagged, the milk you never had a chance to try, dried up.

I have sunglasses too, that I can slip on.

It has been almost a year since she saw me last. I am not the same as I once was. I think it is worth the risk.

'All right,' I say, 'if you think no-one will mind.'

I reach into my pocket for my glasses and my fingertips touch the other thing. I flinch, as if I'd forgotten it was there, slip my glasses on, and step into the light.

'Everyone, this is Anna. Anna's having a baby. Anna this is everyone.' Tash waves an arm, satisfied that she has adequately introduced me.

There are five women sitting at, or standing, around the picnic tables. One is changing a nappy on her lap as if she's done it a thousand times. She waves with one hand, the other holds a baby wipe. I wonder if I would have become so expert. 'Tamara. Hi and congrats,' she says. 'Don't squirm, Addie.'

A very pale, very young, girl, is breast-feeding in the only corner with some shade from the bright noon. She has a brilliantly blue shawl wrapped around herself, and she looks up at me through eyes that are blank with exhaustion. 'Hi,' she whispers. I wonder how old she was when she fell pregnant. How old the father is? I wonder why Lissa didn't take *her* baby. Perhaps the timing was wrong. I can't tell how old the infant is under that bright shawl, the only splash of colour on her.

17

A singularly round woman with a ridiculous puff of hair is emptying a bag into the centre of one of the tables. Tupperware after Tupperware emerges, and the containers are opened with small flourishes. Apples, strawberries, brownies, sandwiches, sliced meat, cheese.

'Gosh, you're so good, Leanne,' Tash says, reaching over her for a brownie. Leanne preens, but Tash rolls her eyes at me behind her back.

The woman with the two children, the one who I think must have tossed a coin with Tash to see who was going to come and speak to me, is watching me with narrowed eyes. She keeps looking at my stomach, where my coat is belted perhaps a little more tightly than it should be.

'How far along are you?' she says, leaning forward. She reaches for my stomach.

I jerk back and Tash puts a hand on her friend's shoulder. 'Leave her alone, Saira, it's still new and I promised her we wouldn't bite.'

Saira sniffs and glances at her baby, asleep in his pram, as if my very presence is a danger.

'Don't worry,' Tash whispers. 'Saira just doesn't like strangers.'

'Shut up, Tash,' she says, frowning.

I stand awkwardly, simultaneously centre of attention and on the edge of the group. They've known each other a long time, these women, bonded over feeding and nappies, childhood illnesses and vaccinations. They form a country I've never visited; the borders were slammed closed just as I arrived, gasping and bleeding and expecting to be welcomed.

My breath shortens. I am about to tell Tash that this was a mistake, and retreat back to the trees, when a familiar car pulls up at the entrance to the park.

Lissa jumps out, with a bag in her hand. 'Pasties and sandwiches from the deli,' she calls.

'You'd better have eclairs in there too!' Tamara puts her hands on her hips.

'Extra just for you!' She talks as she bends down to

unclip your car seat. 'Kai's spark out,' she says, with her head half in and half out of the car. She clips the seat onto the pram her husband has pulled from the boot. 'Thanks.' She kisses him. 'Come and get us in a couple of hours.'

He waves at the women in the park. 'Having a good time, ladies?'

'We love you, Mitch!' Tash yells and Saira laughs.

I only have eyes for you. You are fast asleep, tucked under a striped blanket, similar to the one I'd bought for you and which is still neatly folded in the centre of the cot I will not allow John to dismantle.

Your hair is lighter than I'd expected it would be, it was dark when you were born, plastered to your skull in sticky commas. But it's been so long, that of course your eyes and hair have changed. I missed watching your eyes every day, waiting for the colour to settle, I missed it when your baby hair fell out and was replaced.

When you were born, your legs and arms were long and skinny, as if you were a grasshopper. I missed it when your limbs fattened and grew strong enough to support you. I missed the moment you rolled for the first time, the days you crawled, stood, took your first steps. I missed your first word.

Hatred makes me retch, but I reach into my pocket and touch the item I have been carrying with me, as if it's a talisman. It calms me down.

'Crikey, morning sickness. What a nightmare!' Tash reaches into a tupperware. 'Quick, have a cracker.'

I can't think of an excuse not to, so I take it and nibble as Lissa hands out deli food and you shift in your sleep, your fingers curling and uncurling. I can't take my eyes off you.

'He's a cutie, isn't he?' Tash says as she fixes a plate for Nicky. 'I mean they're *all* lovely, but Kai is something special.'

'Aw, thanks, Tash.' Lissa grins. 'He really is, isn't he?' She glances at me. 'Hi, I'm Lissa.'

I have to tear my eyes from you. 'Anna,' I say. I regard her through my sunglasses. She doesn't look like a monster.

She is wearing a pair of bootcut jeans, trainers, a red top

and a black coat. Her brown hair is in a low ponytail. She is smiling at everyone, her skin clear, her blue eyes bright. There is a small scar on her temple that the cold air has made white.

I can imagine her in a nurse's uniform. I assume that's how she did it, somehow swapping a dead child for mine. There must be all sorts of checks, but at the same time midwives have long shifts and people don't always pay enough attention if they are distracted by a crisis. And they must have temporary staff in all the time, covering illness, or maternity leave. Perhaps she even worked in the hospital, briefly. I clench my fists.

It doesn't look as if she's had a moment of regret. She looks happy, healthy, not a care in the world.

Does she think of me at all – the woman whose baby she stole? Does she wonder how I'm getting on? How I'm *surviving*?

She blinks at me and I realise that I am staring, my jaw set. 'Sorry,' I say, with a forced laugh. 'I'm trying not to throw up.'

She frowns and Tash snorts. 'She's pregnant, Lissa!'

'Oh, right, how awful for you.' She smiles at Kai. 'It's worth it though, isn't it Tash? Every moment of backache, every second of nausea.'

As if she'd know. Rage almost knocks me off my feet, grotesque tentacles winding around my limbs and making them shake, as all the women nod their agreement.

'Leanne had hyper ... hyper... God I can never remember, Leanne what is it?'

'Hyperemesis gravidarum.' Leanne sits on a bench, eating a biscuit. 'Like Kate Middleton. Didn't feel much like a Princess though. Took me a year to put the weight back on.' She shudders. 'Mark wants another one.' She looks horrified. 'I said I'll have to forget the last time first.'

Saira is watching me. I can feel her. She isn't as accepting as the others. She isn't fooled.

'Do you mind if I sit down,' I whisper. 'I'm feeling a bit ...'

Tamara shuffles along, creating a space. 'Quick, you do look like you're going to faint.'

I sit down, I am right next to your pram now. I can smell you.

They all eat around me as I hold my cracker. They hand food to kids, wipe noses, change nappies, break up battles. Somehow, they manage to eat too, with babies on their laps, or holding bottles. They giggle and chatter and swap children with one another and I sit on my bench, damp wood under my thighs, feeling cold and empty and increasingly furious with every passing heartbeat.

I only want to watch you, but Saira hasn't taken her eyes off me and I don't dare glance your way for more than a moment at a time. Snatched seconds.

Before I know it, leftovers are being put back into boxes, babies are being swaddled and put into prams and children are told to enjoy their last few minutes of play.

'You're leaving?' I look at Tash.

She nods. 'Leanne has to work this afternoon. Tamara has an appointment with the health-visitor. Saira and I are going into town.' She smiles at me. 'You're welcome if you …'

'No thanks, honestly. I should get back myself.' I look at Lissa who is checking her texts with a frown. 'What about you, Lissa – are you busy?'

'Not in the slightest.' She smiles. 'Mitch just said he's going to be late to pick us up though.' She gestures at the phone. 'Typical.'

'I'll stay with you,' I say immediately. 'I mean, if that's all right.'

Saira stiffens but I ignore her.

'I don't have anywhere important to be,' I insist.

Lissa looks a little awkward. 'Don't be silly, you've only just met me. You don't want to keep me company while I mope.'

I smile at her and it feels like a rictus. 'Actually, I've got questions about being a mum. You could answer them for me. You'd be doing *me* a favour.' The words almost stick in my throat.

Lissa puts her phone back in her pocket. 'Well, all right then. Mitch will be here in forty minutes, so you won't have to put up with us for too long.'

Tash gives her a quick hug and picks Nicky up. 'It was really nice to meet you, Anna. We'll see you again?'

I nod and remain unmoving as the group shifts towards the park gate. Some of the kids trail behind, trying to get one more swing, or one more turn on the roundabout. One of the babies starts to cry.

Lissa leans on the picnic table. 'It's always like this. You'd think this place was utopia. None of the kids want to leave.'

Now there are car doors banging. Saira and Tash are sharing a lift. Saira looks back at us, then waves at Lissa.

'Call me later,' she shouts, unsmiling, and Lissa nods.

Tamara sets off walking, her stride lengthening as she vanishes out of sight. Leanne and the teen mum head for the bus stop.

'It is a lovely park,' I say. 'All those trees at the back.'

You are still asleep, and I feel safe looking at you now. In fact, I think it would be strange if I didn't.

'There's a nice walk around if you fancy it.' Lissa rises to her feet and stretches. 'Do you want to take a lap? It'll keep Kai asleep a bit longer.'

'Yes,' I say. 'That would be lovely.' I stand with her and she takes hold of the pram.

We start to walk.

'So, tell me, how do you get him to sleep?' I ought to know, and it kills me that I don't.

Lissa looks at you with so much love that I want to hurt her. She has no right.

'Kai's an easy baby. Tea, bath, book, bottle, bed.' She snorts. 'Worst case – a walk in the pram or a trip in the car with his daddy.' She rotates her shoulders as if they're sore.

'He wasn't always that easy. He had a touch of colic when he was little, but honestly, I've seen a *lot* worse.'

'What about food – what are his favourites?' We're at the tree line now. Shadows fall over us, and the scent of pine and rotting leaf mulch mingle in the air. The swings creak behind us and I turn, thinking someone else has arrived, but the park is quiet. It'll fill up again after school. For now, it's just us and the wind.

I step onto crackling leaves.

The pram wheels roll into the gloom, snapping twigs, and Kai murmurs in his sleep. As the sunlight abandons us, Lissa shivers and she pulls her coat closer around her.

Just ahead there is a pile of branches. Someone has tried to make a den. I almost expect a growl to emanate from beneath, but it is quiet here. Even the birds have fallen silent at our presence.

'He'll eat pretty much anything,' she says, still walking. 'But his favourites are avocado and banana, or chicken and mango.' She takes another step. 'We're really blessed. Sometimes I think he's almost too easy, especially when I see some of the others, but I suppose we had our own hard times before the birth. Getting pregnant, you know.'

'I don't,' I say. My fingers edge into my pocket. 'Not really.'

'Lucky you.' The path meanders. There are brambles across a fence, and holly in a corner. Spines and thorns.

'Yes. We decided to have a baby and there it was the next month, a positive test.'

'Do you know what it is yet?' She looks at me. 'Of course not, it's too early. Do you know what you want?'

'A boy,' I say it unequivocally. 'Who looks like John.'

'John's your husband?'

I nod.

'My husband's best friend at uni was called John.'

The path here has been covered by mud and our footsteps are muffled, the pram wheels making a shushing sound. Kai snorts and starts to snore.

'Do you live locally then?' Lissa asks, never taking her eyes from your face.

I don't answer her, instead I pull it out of my pocket. It belongs to John; he went through a phase when he thought he might whittle. Ridiculous really. I don't think he even remembers that we have it.

I slide the cover off. The knife gleams in what is left of the light. Or at least it does for a short time.

You never even wake.

I leave the blood-spattered pram in the park and carry you to my car. I have my own pram at home and a car seat all set up. We bought it when I was pregnant, and I wouldn't let John get rid of it. I knew I'd find you eventually.

I strap you in with some difficulty. You are still dozy, and you want the woman you think is your mum. '*I'm* your mummy,' I whisper. 'Don't worry, I found you. I'm sorry it took me so long.'

You cry all the way home. Perhaps you are hungry. I park, take you out and carry you into the hall. You are hot in my arms, your face wet with tears.

'Everything is going to be okay,' I say.

I don't have any milk. I didn't know that today was going to be the day. We can do an online shop tonight. In the meantime, I have a banana in the fruit bowl. I offer it to you, but you smack it away with angry little fists.

You resist when I try to cuddle you in the nursery, and I have to clench my fists and remind myself that this isn't your fault. It's hers'.

I wasn't expecting this to be easy, I'm not a fool, but I thought that you'd know, instinctively that you were mine. I thought you'd remember somehow, the smell of me and the sound of my voice. I start to sing, the songs I sang to you when you lived inside me. It makes no difference, you cry louder.

'Abi, what's going on?' John is standing in the hall, staring at me, his face is pale. 'Whose baby is this?'

'He's ours.' I hold you up for his inspection, but you kick and yell. I roll my eyes. 'He'll settle in soon, then you'll see. Maybe if you take him for a bit.'

'If I … take him?'

'Yes, John.' I sigh. 'You can't expect me to do *everything*. You're his dad so you have to get involved. Remember, we agreed – fifty-fifty.'

'Yes but …' He grips the doorframe as if his knees can't hold his weight. I suppose this would be a bit of a shock. I knew you were coming home; he didn't.

'I told you I'd find him.' I touch your face.

John comes carefully into the room. 'Abi …' he clears his throat. 'Abi, Dylan died. We buried him.'

'He didn't. That was someone else's baby. They replaced him at the hospital.'

'You can't still believe …' He swallows. 'Where did you … find him?'

'The park, out by Northampton Square.'

He kneels down in front of us. 'Maybe I *should* take him for a bit.'

'Okay.'

I let John scoop you up. As soon as he does it is even more clear to me that you are his son. You have the exact same-shaped face, even if yours is red and swollen with tears. The same nose, the same jaw, the same hair. And then there's his skin.

'You can't deny him,' I say, with a laugh.

John shakes his head. He murmurs something to you, something comforting, and you stare at him, your tears halting. You touch his chin, and he bounces you a little.

'The park out by Northampton Square,' John says. 'It was on the news just now. They found someone …'

'She shouldn't have taken our baby,' I snap.

John shudders. 'Abi, there's something I need to tell you.' He looks as if he wants to put you down, but then he tightens his hold on you. You put your head on his shoulder. I wish I could take a picture. Father and son, reunited at last. There are tears on John's face, he must be so happy!

'Do you remember me talking about my friend from university, Mitchell?'

I shake my head. 'Why tell me this now? We should be concentrating on our baby.'

'Just listen.' He rubs his face. 'Mitchell and his wife, Lissa, they couldn't get pregnant. He asked if I would donate sperm.'

My ears start to ring. I laugh, as if he's joking. As if I can drown out the sound of his lies with my own hysteria.

He waits until I fall silent. We stare at one another and I stiffen. 'You didn't though.'

John just nods. 'Lissa got pregnant just over a month before you did. I was going to tell you, but there didn't seem to be a right time and then ... Dylan died and how could I tell you he had a half-brother? That I donated sperm to someone else and their baby was okay when Dylan wasn't.'

'Don't lie to me!' I leap to my feet. 'Give me my son.'

John shakes his head. 'He isn't yours' Abi.' He half turns, as if protecting you from me.

'He is.'

'He's not.' He retreats into the hall, taking his phone from his pocket.

I stand up. I can't believe he's taking you. That he's on her side. That he would lie to me.

I still have it. It's in the pocket of the nursing chair, where you couldn't get to it. I take it out with trembling hands. I have to protect you, protect us, even from John.

ABOUT BRYONY PEARCE

Bryony Pearce is the multi-award-winning author of nine young adult novels. Her debut adult domestic noir, *The Girl on the Platform*, came out in 2021 and will be followed by *Little Rumours* in 2022. She also writes short stories which have been published in science fiction anthologies.

When she isn't writing, Bryony teaches others how to do

so. She is a reader and mentor for Cornerstones and The Writing Coach, she teaches a creative writing course at City University and she visits schools, festivals and events doing creative writing workshops and courses.

If you would like to know more about Bryony and her work, do visit her website: www.bryonypearce.co.uk or follow her on Twitter or Instagram @BryonyPearce or TikTok @bryonyvpearce, she loves to meet readers!

If you are a reviewer, do request copies of her new books from Netgalley.

FLESH OF A FANCY WOMAN

Paul Magrs

'You always was a scrubber, Lily Mahon,' my Patrick laughed at me and I swear down I could have gutted him then and there. I had nothing to lose, did I? I'd been drawn in to his hideous pit of bloody awful horror and it was everything I could do to keep control of myself. I just glowered at him and kept on scrubbing, didn't I? Whatever else was I going to do?

He'd brought us into disaster, like everyone said he would. Deep down I'd always believed in him and so I always defended him. I wouldn't let no one say a word against my Patrick. He was perfect in my eyes, even when he wasn't.

And I would always do anything for him.

So that was why.

So, there I was – scrubbing out the master bedroom of a bungalow in Bournemouth. Floor to ceiling. Skirting boards. All the fixtures and fittings and the bedding and the furniture and all that. He'd got it everywhere, the dirty little bastard.

Oh, I'd have loved a weekend in Bournemouth. A little bungalow like this. A couple of days away, somewhere I could catch my breath and stretch my limbs and feel like he cared, just for a bit.

But it wasn't me he brought here, was it?

Just his bleeding floozies.

Red and brown and scabby and reeking like something

out of hell. That's what that bungalow in Bournemouth was like. You see, by the time I got there, things had been rotting for a little while. Rotting down like compost does and it stank to high heaven behind that door. I was horrified enough at what Patrick had done, but somehow... making a muck of that lovely seaside cottage. Making it stink like that. Well, that seemed just awful to me. Obviously, not the worst thing he was guilty of. But it was like added insult to injury, you see. That's what it was. That stink! I've got it in my nose right now, when I think of it.

The stink of his fancy woman. Lying there in Bournemouth. Like she hadn't a care in the world. Well, she hadn't, had she? Not anymore.

The details are gruesome, dear. Do you want to hear it all? I bet you've heard everything, haven't you? You've heard it all before. Here, let me fetch us another drink, old mother. More gin. They water it down to nothing here. It's hardly gonna get us pissed, is it? But I need to whet my whistle if I'm gonna tell you more.

Here, watch my bag, old woman. Keep an eye on that Gladstone bag, me old duck, will you? Don't open it, though! Don't touch that clasp! Not if you don't want a shock like what I got. I felt such a fool. Standing in the lost luggage office at Waterloo Station. Well, I almost screamed. I had my neighbour with me, Mrs Turton, and she nearly screamed as well, and she ain't no softy. She's had as hard a life as I've had, nearly. But I wouldn't go prying in that bag if I were you, dear. You won't say no to another gin, will you? Hang on, I'll be back.

And then you'll read my fortune, won't you? When you've had another tot. You'll tell me what the stars hold. I'm hoping it's something good. I could do with an upturn in my fortunes. The past week's been bleeding awful.

It began with his good jacket. I know I shouldn't go poking my nose in, but I do. I've lived seventeen years as his wife and I know when he's up to no good. Though he said he'd been away at the races, there was more to it, I knew. And Mrs Turton from next door was round for a cup of tea and she said there weren't nothing wrong with it. Just going through his pockets in case there was money in there. I brushed his jacket and felt through the pockets with impunity. And that's when I found the ticket.

'Oooh, treasure,' said Mrs Turton. She spooned the gloopy sugar from the bottom of her teacup and sucked it with relish.

The ticket was for the Cloakroom at Waterloo Station.

'What's he left in safekeeping there, that he couldn't bring home?' I wondered. My curiosity was piqued and my neighbour was egging me on.

'Let's go and find out,' she kept saying, crunching her way through all the biscuits. 'You've got your suspicions about him. He's probably nicking stuff. He might be nicking stuff from you!'

'Huh, I've got nothing,' I laughed. 'He took anything what I had years ago and flogged it off.'

Mrs Turton – she's a bored old soul – works on me and winds me up all evening. And the fact that Patrick doesn't come home until one in the morning, reeking and not telling me anything – makes things even worse.

The next morning me and Mrs Turton catch the omnibus up to Waterloo Station. 'Good girl,' the old ratbag commends me. 'Best to grasp the nettle. Best to find out what's really going on.'

When we get there it's all a-bustle and a-swarm and a great big echoing marble hall and I wonder: how did I end up sneaking around the edges of my husband's life? I'm investigating him. I don't trust him an inch, do I? Then I'm queueing at the desk and the young man there is examining the ticket and looking up to study Mrs Turton and my good self. We both look respectable, don't we? We don't look like no kind of disreputable trollops. I'm a decent wife, concerned about things. Mrs Turton smells of brandy a bit, but she's bad with her nerves.

The young man makes a meal of being officious and in charge. He goes over to the little lockers and the board displaying all the tiny keys. Then he finds the right door and unlocks it. He pulls a face. There's a smell. No, more than a smell. A right stench.

It's a Gladstone bag. It was once Patrick's dad's. It was something he was always proud of. Polished smooth with use. Old, soft leather. Like butter, it felt that soft. His dad was supposed to have been a doctor, but I doubt it. Safecracker, probably. Housebreaker. That would be more likely.

The young man plonks it down on the desk and his face is all curdled and grim. The bag really hums and Mrs Turton cries out. 'Good heavens!' she gasps and wafts her hands.

'Take it away,' the young man says. 'We've been thinking we could smell something funny in here.'

It's an infernal stench. A smell out of hell. I'm ashamed to pick the baggage up and take it out of there. I'm ashamed that people on the omnibus going home are going to think it's something to do with me.

'Open it up!' Mrs Turton keeps urging all the way home to Peckham Rye. 'Have a look inside!'

But I won't. Not till I get home. I'm not opening this thing in public. It'd be like setting off a bomb. Let's wait till we're back in my parlour, with all the windows open and away from prying eyes ...

And then comes the bit when Mrs Turton turned against me. Honest, she hasn't spoken to me ever since that moment. We were in my parlour and she turned on her heel and walked right out of there.

'I want nothing more to do with it,' she said in this thundery voice. She put down the glass I'd poured her. Drained it first, of course. 'I've had my trouble, Lily. I've had an awful lot of bother in my life and I don't want no more. You, ducks, are on your own.'

Then Mrs Turton was gone. My front door slammed.

And I was alone with that Gladstone bag.

And its contents.

The silk lining was ruined. It was black with blood. And there were rags inside and you could see what they were covered with.

Clarts. Muck. Gobbets of flesh.

I was reminded of chopping up scrag end and the worst cuts of meat for a stew. Even with the stench rising up to meet us when I opened that bag I was thinking of food. But that's obvious, I suppose, because the only time I ever saw meat like that it was supposed to be food.

Not this. Not this.

Not the remains of a fancy woman.

Because I figured it out. Soon enough. I was only seconds behind canny Mrs Turton in the figuring-it-out stakes.

This was human remains. Just a lot of bloody rags and some gobbets. When I dug around gingerly in those filthy recesses I saw some other bits, too. Ah yes. That was human all right.

I snapped the bag shut and I went to be sick. The gin fumes were making it worse. When I came back, the gin fumes made it better again. I poured a glass or two, turned up the wicks of the lamps and sat waiting for Patrick to come home.

The Gladstone bag still sat on the dining table. Fastened shut, but that fetid, almost shitty smell still seeped out and tainted our living room.

And it set Patrick's red nose twitching when he came in, late that night.

'Christ, is that the drains?' he snarled at me, bursting through the door.

'No,' I said. I must have given him a deadly look because he stepped back, one look at my face. I'd been drinking all evening, I admit it. And my look must have given him pause for thought.

Then he saw the bag on the table and realized what the source of that reek was.

'Ah, fuck,' he said. 'What's that doing here …? How did you …?' His face darkened with anger. 'What have you been doing, Lily Mahon? You been spying on me?' And he raised those pan shovel hands against me, like he had done so many times in the past.

Now I guess I got real reason to fear them, haven't I? They don't just administer slaps and stinging blows. They deal death blows, don't they? My insides thrill with horror and … yes, excitement, too. Cos now I know. My hubby. My beloved of seventeen years. Now I know what you can do. 'You been chopping women up,' I tell him, and that halts him in his tracks. 'Who was she? Whose bits were in that bag of your old dad's?'

Do you know what he told me, old mother? Here, have the rest of mine. Steady your nerves. Yeah, this is scary stuff, I know. You need a gulp just to take it all in. But don't get too pissed. I still want my fortune telling. Don't go insensible now. I want you to hear the rest of this.

He said, 'Ah, that's just dog meat, dearie. Don't you worry about that. It's a little racket I been involved with. Just a harmless little deal. Dog meat – I been bringing it from the knackers at the races, you see? Bringing it back to town. It's ruined Dad's old bag, but the stitching were going anyway. I didn't know what else to put it in. And then it stunk so badly afterwards … I didn't know where to put it. So when I went through Waterloo, I thought, I'll leave it in a locker and get it cleaned later. But that's all it was, my love. Just dog meat. Plain old dog meat.'

'Patrick,' I told him, and the air was going smeary and swimmy with the lateness of the hour and the wicks burning down. 'You take me for a fucking fool, don't you? I've had seventeen years with the wool pulled over my eyes while you've done everything and anything you wanted.'

'Dog meat, my dear! It's dog meat! It's horseflesh that's been in there! That's all!' He gave a loud, boisterous laugh, like the bastard didn't have a care in the world.

Funny, it was the laugh that made me more scared than anything. I thought: you can even convince yourself that you've done nothing wrong.

'Patrick,' I said. 'We ain't got no fucking dogs. Why'd we need horsemeat for 'em?'

Then he laughed long and hard at his foolish, gullible, ignorant wife. 'I was selling it, wasn't I? I sold it to them who *has* got dogs. And a tidy few quid I made, as well. It ruined the bag but I made a few quid. That's life.'

'Patrick,' I said to him. I was keeping tight grip on my sanity and what I had seen in that bag. I knew I had. I knew he couldn't tell me fucking otherwise. 'Patrick, there's an ear in that bag. And it ain't no horse's.'

I made him tell me everything.

That's how I came to be in Bournemouth.

He told me he couldn't do it by himself. He'd got in too deep. He couldn't get the place clean at all. There was still evidence everywhere.

He only had the place on lease till the Tuesday.

'And you've always been a scrubber, ain't you, love?' he asked, with this snide little giggle. I thought – ooh, you're chancing it. By then I was up to my elbows in the scabby grime and gore.

But what could I do? I could never refuse him anything.

I made him sit down in that glorious front room of that bungalow and tell me the whole sordid tale. There was a picture window. A picture window looking at the beach. Oh, my heart wept for the sight of that. Why did he never think of me? When he was bringing fancy women here? Why did he never think: Lily'd like the view from here. I should bring her, some time.

Well, now he has. And now we sit here, knee to knee and he confesses:

'I can deal with it when they come on too strong. Usually, I can. But this one. She was like a fucking steamroller, Lily. She wouldn't take no. She was all, let's run away to the continent together. Fucking Europe. I never heard the last about Switzerland and Paris and Madrid from her. She had all kinds of poncey friends abroad and she said she could run away any time and live with them, and she wanted me to come too.

'Well, I played along for a while. I was enticed a bit, and my head was turned. But I was always coming home to you, Lily. You know that, don't you? And when that one talked about divorce and setting me free and getting all the papers and a proper solicitor, it fair turned my stomach. I thought: she's building up her part. She tried to get me to get myself a passport, just like she had. Badgered me to fill out the forms. Well, there were unforeseen difficulties there. She didn't know that moving around and names and stuff, that they're all a bit difficult for me with my past and everything.

'I know you understand that, Lily. You understand everything about me.

'And then came this Bank Holiday Weekend and she turns up at Waterloo and she's beaming and extra lah-di-dah. She's pleased with herself and I can't work out why. By then it was on the wane for me. I promise that, Lily. She was looking old to me, and boring. And all the talk that used to thrill me with its sophistication – about opera and pictures and fancy restaurants and that – it was getting on my wick, to be honest. I thought: you're no better than me and my Lily. You've just read a few more library books and been to a few more galleries and you married money with your first bloke and that don't make you any better than the scrubber you are. Beg pardon, Lily, no offence.

'So then she started on how she was up the duff. Yeah,

I know. It was a cruel blow. Here, don't cry, Lily. Please don't cry. I couldn't stand that, on top of everything. I've caused enough upset. But I thought – yeah, don't that just put the tin hat on it. She goes and gets herself pregnant. She knew – she absolutely knew that she was rubbing it in. I'd told her you was barren. I told her there was no hope. And there she was. Easy as anything. Showing off, really. Stood where you are now. Soon as we arrived on the Friday night. 'I'm expecting our child, Patrick!' Like I was gonna be glad. Like I was gonna jump up and change everything round. Like I was gonna start dancing to her tune. Yeah, she thought she'd won.'

Ah, you'll need a tot more gin for this bit, I think, old mother. You don't mind me calling you that? You see, I lost my own over ten years ago. Patrick said it was for the best. And it was so peaceful, her just slipping away in her sleep like that. But when there's bother, I do miss her advice and her comforting.

This was the hardest bit. Getting rid of what was left.

A lot of Emily Kaye he smuggled away in his Gladstone bag. Piecemeal. Gradually. On the train back and forth to Waterloo.

How he kept from screaming and going out of his mind, I don't know. He can be quite steadfast, methodical. He can be a good little worker when he tries.

He'd get a carriage by himself. He'd pull the little curtains on the corridor. Then he'd work quickly. Up went the window. Whoosh went the wind. Shriek went the engine and the whistle. He unclasped his father's leather bag and he'd bring out a piece of Mrs Kaye at a time.

And then he'd chuck her.

Off she'd fly! Bit by bit!

Bye-bye Blackbird!

A long, elegant forearm, tossed into a hedge.

Her thigh (which one?) flung into the depths of a

forest.

A field full of meadowsweet and larkspur got a smooth, pale shoulder.

A bagful of guts was dropped in a canal.

I can't imagine what he went through, steeling himself to do these awful acts.

But he wasn't caught. He was brazen. And no one even noticed the disposal of Mrs Kaye.

Here, don't choke. Don't gag.

And don't go. Please don't go yet. I'm sorry. I know … I understand that this is hard stuff. Even on a strong stomach like yours, old mother. But I'd like you to stay to the end. Hear the last of it. Then I'd like you to tell me my future.

I want to know, you see, whether it was all worth it.

He isn't a monster, you know. The most tender bit, the most heartbreaking bit – that's coming up now. You see, the unborn child – he wasn't such a brute that he threw that from the window of the train, along with the rest of her. Now, the little child he kept for a day or two. Like a little fairy child, delicate in its squashy bag of stuff. He kept it for me to see, which was thoughtful, I suppose. It looked like a little pixie or a gnome, all curled round. We both looked at it and imagined that it was ours.

Then, in a special little ceremony we took it out into the bluebell woods near that cottage by the sea and we buried it a few feet down under the flowers. It was really quite moving.

When we was back indoors we took stock of how much was left. Mostly it was dirt. That, I could deal with.

But it was the question of the head, you see.

Not something I'd thought of, but of course, he couldn't go chucking that out of the train. What if someone had recognized her? When he explained I thought – oh yes, it's obvious, isn't it?

He'd put her in the grate and tried to set a match to her, to burn her face off, kind of thing. But that hadn't worked out for some reason. It turned his stomach.

'You must help me,' he said, in his most helpless voice.

'I'll put her in the river,' I promised him. 'She'll sink. She'll go all the way down to the bottom. Especially if we stuff her full of beach pebbles and rocks. We can't throw her in the sea because the tide will bring her back. But if I take her into town in that bag … I'll go down to the river and drop her in. Some quiet dock. Some nasty little corner where the water's black and oily and bobbing with all kinds of jetsam and the like. No one will notice one more bit of trash.'

'Oh, please, oh please,' he begged me. 'Just get her out of my sight. Those eyes keep following me. I can't stand her face. Once she's gone, that last little bit – when you've done that, we'll be able to start again, Lily, don't you see? All the mess will be gone and we'll be free to live our lives with no interference. Now, go on. There's a train back to London at half past six.'

And so there was.

And here I am. Drinking gin in the closest parlour I could find to the river. We're right on the front here. It's all clabber and clarts outside this door. Just a few steps away and it's the scummy heartsblood of the city, flowing past us in the twilight. That's where I'm gonna drop her and then she'll be gone for good. We've stuffed her good and proper to make sure she won't float. That would be awful, wouldn't it? To set her free and step back and watch and then she didn't sink? I dunno what I'd do then.

Do you want to see her? Do you want to look at her face? Maybe you could say a little prayer or something? You've got a nice face. A kind expression. It might be nice if the last face that looked at her was a kindly one. Someone who meant her no harm. Here, I'll undo the clasps. Sit this way, facing away from the room. Don't let anyone else see. You can come with me, in a minute, if you want, and watch me drop her in the river? It might be quite emotional. Of course, I'll stand you another drink first.

Also, if you'd do that thing? Would you read my fortune? I'd love to know. I need to find out. I'm staking everything on this. My life … our lives … Patrick and mine … they're gonna get better, aren't they? Now that we've got rid of his fancy piece. We're gonna be happy in the time we have left? Tell me it's true, won't you, old mother …?'

ABOUT PAUL MAGRS

Paul Magrs brought out his first novel in 1995 when he was 26. He has lectured in Creative Writing at UEA and at MMU. In 2019 he published his book on writing, *The Novel Inside You*. In 2020 Snow Books republished his Brenda and Effie Mystery series of novels. He lives and writes in Manchester with Jeremy and Bernard Socks.

DANGEROUS WOMEN

Sandra Murphy

I love waking to the soft caress of Egyptian cotton sheets on bare skin. I savoured their touch, knowing it would be the last time, for a while. Today, I'd start my new job. Today would be made up of a lot of 'last times' and 'for a whiles.'

I stared at myself in the full-length mirror. An extra half inch to pinch at the waist, compliments of too many pina coladas. No matter, it would be easy enough to subsist on salads and sensible meals, for a while. I'd miss the sweetness of the drinks more than the rum. I went through twenty minutes of yoga, followed by half an hour's meditation on the deck, careful to stay in the shade. A tan wouldn't sit well with my job. I was going to miss the mist of salt on the breeze and my skin. With a sigh, I went inside, coloured my coppery hair a dull shade of brown, showered, and packed.

I made the two o'clock flight to St. Louis with no problem. I was lucky — no crying baby, no chatty seatmate, and enough leg room to be comfortable. At the airport Enterprise kiosk, I picked up my rental car, a small, non-descript thing I'd keep for the duration.

The drive to a medium-to-large-sized town about an hour away, was pleasant enough. I drove past the office, just to get my bearings, before going to the one-bedroom apartment I'd rented furnished, sight unseen except for the online photos which weren't far off from reality. At least the living room wasn't all sharp-cornered wood laminate and plaid upholstery.

A mom and pop restaurant on the same block provided me with a meal of roasted chicken, tender green beans, baby potatoes, and a decent glass of wine. I went to bed early and managed to fall asleep, despite the polyester-blend sheets.

At 8:30 the next morning, I presented myself to Margaret, the executive assistant to Ben Johnson, CEO of Johnson, Inc. Margaret turned me this way and that, checking my outfit of a frumpy navy skirt suit and matching shoes, off white blouse buttoned high enough to make me feel strangled, and low-key makeup. She announced I would do. We discussed my duties and hours, then I spent the morning filing contracts, invoices, and letters.

Ben strolled in about eleven. I was introduced as 'Reva, my new assistant' and was worthy of barely a glance. 'Margaret, make a lunch reservation for two at Pierre's. Ask if the chef will make that fish thing I like. 12:30, as usual.'

He went into his office and closed the door.

'How much work will he be able to get done before leaving for lunch?' It seemed to me, Ben was a little lenient about his work ethic.

'He putts. I work.' Margaret made a face. 'And now, you'll work too.'

'He's in there putting?' I almost said I couldn't believe it but then, of course, it was entirely fitting with his personality. Let the little people work, take the credit, the glory, and the money.

While Ben came in late, took three-hour lunches, and schmoozed clients over dinner, Margaret and I were expected to go out, eat, and be back in half an hour. Given how crowded the elevators were any time after eleven, not to mention nearby restaurants, Margaret and I brought peanut butter sandwiches from home, because they didn't need to stay cold. She finally convinced Ben to spring for a dorm sized fridge, used, so we wouldn't get food poisoning. I overheard Margaret's pro-fridge campaign.

'You spend more on one lunch at Pierre's than this fridge costs. Besides, this way I'll be in the office in case "awkward phone calls" come in. Reva wouldn't know what to say. Unless you want me to give her a list?'

Ben caved pretty quickly after that. The phone calls were from women he'd dated and told he was getting a divorce. It was surprising how many of them believed him. When they got clingy, he told them his wife had hired a private detective and was having him followed. He'd be in touch when the divorce was final. Liar. He was already divorced.

On Friday, I managed to answer one of the awkward phone calls while Margaret was in the restroom down the hall. Ben was too cheap to spring for an office with a bathroom. 'Why pay extra for that? I'm not here that much.' He got that right.

'Well, LeeAnn, he's not here, really. No, I don't think giving him a message would help. Yes, I understand. No, I can't talk about that here in the office. I guess but … of course. No, it wouldn't work. That's a much better idea. You do that. Thanks for calling, bye-bye.'

Margaret heard the last part as she came in the door. 'Who was on the phone?'

'Somebody named LeeAnn. She wanted to talk to Ben. She gave up though.'

'One of these days, he's going to meet somebody he can't con,' Margaret said. 'I just hope I'm there to see it.'

'I do too.'

The food is good at the mom and pop place but tonight, I needed a change. I stopped at the pizza joint a block from the office. 'Do you deliver to the Belmont Apartments over on 10th Street? No? That's too bad. I've got a pretty nice place there, on the second floor in the back where there's no street noise. Guess I'll take a medium cheese and pepperoni to go then.' I paid the man and left, almost bumping into a woman sitting at one of the small tables as I dropped the receipt in my purse.

Businesspeople are always saying you have to have goals and a plan to achieve them. In my mind, I had a goal and the beginnings of a plan. Now to put the whole thing in motion.

Monday morning, Margaret was already behind her desk when I arrived.

'Hey, am I late or are you early?'

'I'm early. Ben had a breakfast meeting and needed his notes,' she says. 'Like he can't open a file drawer and look for the label that says Donovan, Marvin? I don't know why I keep working here. I could retire, go somewhere warm, learn to knit maybe. Or learn to just sit and think. Or not.'

'How much vacation time do you have coming?'

'Vacation? I've heard the word before, somewhere.'

'How much?'

'Six weeks. I haven't taken it because the last time I went out of town, Ben called me on Day Three and said the temp was messing everything up.' She sighed. 'I thought he meant the cheque book and filing or contracts so I rushed back. She'd made a reservation for lunch for Ben with the girlfriend du jour *and* told the most recent dumpee, he was eating at Alfred's. There was a cat fight and Ben had to pay the damages.'

'I thought Pierre's was his favourite lunch spot.'

'It is now. He's barred from going back to Alfred's.' Margaret smiled. 'I went to brunch there on the following Sunday, just to get the inside scoop on what happened. My server was an out of work actor. I swear I laughed so hard, especially when he got to the part about flying watermelon chunks, I thought he would have to Heimlich me. He so loved telling it to somebody who knows how Ben can be and getting to act out all the parts, he treated me to lunch.'

'Write down the address and the guy's name. I'll splurge and go this weekend. Come along if you want.'

Margaret phoned and said she had an emergency, she was fine, but couldn't make lunch. She'd explain on Monday. I ate alone and had a lovely chat with Chad, the actor/server. I was careful not to have food in my mouth while he re-enacted what he called "Ben's Restaurant Wars". I had the eggplant parm. It was excellent.

Sunday, I was back at the mom and pop place. 'Reva, if you hear of a job, would you let me know?' Adriane was mom and pop's daughter.

'I thought you loved working here. Who wouldn't, surrounded by so much good food?' I pointed to the soup, salad, and garlic bread special.

'I do, but I've done this since I was fourteen. I'd like to try something different, something that's not food. I mean, I'll probably inherit this place and do it until I'm like ninety. I'd like to try other things now and come back to this because I love it, not because it's expected, know what I mean?'

'I do. Okay, if you could have any job you wanted, no limits, what would it be?' I expected her to say a backup singer for a band, a runway model, or a veterinarian. She surprised me.

'Don't laugh. This is off the wall. I always thought I'd make a great spy. Not the Bond Girl kind but one who's in disguise, like an office cleaner or a secretary.'

'Stealing company secrets? That's risky and illegal.' I took a sip of my wine. She laid my order in the window to the kitchen.

'Not stealing! No, like Erin Brockovich. Finding out someone's doing others dirty and making a difference by getting proof, so it stops. Stupid, right? Forget I said anything.'

'You'd have to know about accounting, how to read contracts, have a smart phone to take clear photos and hide them in the cloud or wherever, in case you were caught.'

'I went to junior college and took business accounting classes, management, that's my degree. I could totally do it. I handle the books here, take care of the rental agreement, deal with vendors and all that.'

'Hey mama, is it okay for Adriane to sit and talk to me while I eat?' I yelled back to the kitchen.

'*Si*, is okay. I bring you tiramisu for dessert. Make room.'

On Monday, Margaret was as angry as I'd ever seen. 'What happened? I was worried when you couldn't come to dinner. I loved Chad's version of what went on with Ben and the

"Fighting Honeys".'

'My sister Trisha, you've heard me talk about her, she fell down the stairs. She had to have surgery. She was alone and frightened and I wasn't able to be there for her.'

'What happened?'

'Ben happened. He called with an emergency, told me I had to help him, there was a big business deal involved. I came over here and it was nothing. A "lost" contract that was right where it was supposed to be. I was ready to leave to be with my sister but Ben insisted I stay in case the gal he pegged for his next girlfriend called while he was out with the departing one. Of course, she didn't know she was departing, not until they were ready to leave the hotel room he'd had me book—under my name.'

'What happened with Trisha?'

'Since I wasn't there, she made them postpone the surgery until the doctors insisted. She was in a lot of pain. She's still in the hospital but will be coming home soon and needs care. I don't know what to do.'

'Is she married?'

'No, I'm all she has. She took care of me when we were children. What am I supposed to do, hire a nurse and leave her with a stranger?'

Margaret maintained her anger until Ben arrived hours later.

'Margaret, make lunch reservations for me at Pierre's. Tell them the fish was too salty last time. I'll have the prime rib today. Rare.'

'If you can press the little numbers on your phone to call your girlfriend, you can damn well press them to call and make your own lunch reservations.' Margaret followed Ben into his office and slammed the door. Luckily, she was mad enough to be loud and I could hear every word.

'You made me come in to work for no good reason. Like an idiot, I came over here. I'm done working sixty hours a week and getting paid for forty. I'm done doing your work and getting no recognition, no raise, no respect. I have six weeks' vacation coming and I'm taking it, all at once. With pay. Starting this minute.'

'Now, now, Margaret...'

'Don't you now, now, me!' Margaret's voice went up an octave. Maybe two.

'Look, I know you're upset but I did need you here. I'm sure your sister is fine. Your anger probably stems from hormones, although well, given your age, I'd think menopause. Have you seen a doctor? They have good drugs for this, I understand. My mother takes them.'

'*Your mother?*' Margaret's voice reached levels only dogs could hear. 'I am not your mother. Come to think of it, as of this moment, I'm not your executive assistant. I am leaving. You will sign a cheque for six weeks' vacation pay at twice my usual rate. You will not protest unemployment or extended benefits. You will write me a check for severance pay. Should I want it, you will give me a glowing recommendation. You will also give me a sizeable cheque for retro bonuses. Are we clear?'

Ben was stupid enough to laugh. 'Why the hell would I do all that? You walk out that door, you can't come back. No money goes with you.'

'Really, Ben? Let's not forget how long I've worked here and how one of my strengths is keeping good notes. I know how many girlfriends you've had. I have their names and phone numbers, updated as necessary. I have copies of receipts for jewellery, hotel rooms, lunches, all your bank statements, business and personal. I know every move you make and I have it all on paper. Give me what I want or I start making phone calls, starting with your ex-wife who would just love to take you back to court.'

I heard a choking sound and headed for the door, afraid Ben was strangling Margaret, but then I heard her speak. 'I'm glad you agree. Write the damn cheques and make them sizeable. Don't even think about stopping payment.'

'This is blackmail.'

'No, it's wages earned. Blackmail only works if you have something to hide.'

Two minutes later, the office door opened with such force it hit the wall and the knob left a big dent. She stopped at my desk. 'Come with me. Your skills can get you a better job than this.'

'I can't.' I pitched my voice to carry into Ben's office. 'Maybe Ben will give me a promotion. I won't do the job as good as you did but I'll try.' In a softer voice, spoken right into her ear as I hugged her goodbye, I said, 'Be at my apartment tonight, eight o'clock.' I stared into her eyes and was quiet. She got the message, nodded, and left the office for the last time.

That night at eight o'clock, Ben's entire existence changed and he didn't even know it. Yet.

'I know you're wondering why I called you here. I've always wanted to say that.' I smiled. 'Let me introduce each of you. Margaret was Ben's executive assistant until late this morning. Chad used to be Ben's server, when Ben was allowed to eat at Alfredo's. Chad is also a fine actor and those skills will come in handy. Adriane aspires to be a spy. And last, but certainly not least, this is LeeAnn, one of Ben's um ...'

'Castoffs? Duped girlfriends? Suckers? Take your pick.' LeeAnn was understandably bitter.

'LeeAnn called the office one day and suggested we meet. I stopped for pizza and made sure she overheard my address so we could make plans without ever having been seen together. I'm here on behalf of Ben's wife who's also Margaret's friend, Jackie. He dumped her, left her homeless, and almost penniless. She's been staying at my house,' I said. 'Margaret, you said one day Ben would meet someone he couldn't con and you hoped you'd be there to see it, right?'

'You bet. That lowlife deserves everything bad that could happen.' Margaret hadn't gotten over her anger yet.

'Now's the time and I'm the one who will make it happen, with your help. Together, we're going to take down Ben Johnson and Johnson Inc.' I took a deep breath. 'Are you in?'

I looked each one in the eyes as they nodded. 'Here's what we're going to do.'

Our plans were relatively simple. Ben was lazy. He signed any paper Margaret put in front of him and didn't bother to read it. I convinced him Margaret had taught me everything. For every real contract, I added two fakes, tying Ben's business to companies that didn't exist. They were blatantly fraudulent and borderline illegal. I also got him to sign cheques made out to cash or to okay bank transfers. Margaret was in charge of all the creative paperwork. She was so inventive.

Adriane got a job as a cleaner at the newspaper's office building. She was able to 'share' some of the fake paperwork with a reporter she befriended, after getting him to promise to hold the story until she gave the go ahead. Chad and LeeAnn were chomping at the bit to get to the Big Finish when they were needed.

I was surprised to find, with Ben's unwitting cooperation, I was able to drain every account he had, leaving only enough for day-to-day expenses. I'd told him the money would earn interest by switching to another bank.

'See, Margaret never thought of stuff like that. You're good for the business, Reva.' He reached to pat my butt but then given how frumpy I looked, pulled back. Good thing.

I called another meeting. 'LeeAnn, you're up. You've got the flyers ready to hand out and have contacted the other dumpees? Chad, you're ready too?'

'I wish I didn't have to wear a black suit and white shirt. Tres' boring!'

'Just remember, you are not to say you're a federal agent, just look the part. All you need to do is convince him he's in big trouble.' I hesitated. 'Adriane, are you sure you want to do this? I'm afraid of your mom. She'll never feed me tiramisu again if she finds out.'

'Don't you worry. Your tiramisu is safe.'

'Then Operation Pulverize Ben Johnson is a go.'

Monday lunchtime, LeeAnn and the rest of Ben's Rejects, as they'd named themselves, picketed in front of the building. Their placards read 'Liar' 'Cheat' and 'Womanizer.' LeeAnn handed out brightly coloured flyers with Ben's photo, captioned, 'Avoid this man at all costs.' Men dodged the women; women took extra flyers for their co-workers.

Meanwhile, Chad, dressed in his 'tres' boring' black and white, was in Ben's office, discussing improprieties in the bookkeeping.

'Look, I don't have any idea what's going on. First, there are all those women downstairs. I think you should arrest them, for defamation of character, namely mine. I have no idea what you're talking about with bookkeeping errors. My executive assistant recently went on family leave and her assistant has been doing the work. Maybe that's what happened.' Ben followed his usual business practice; if something good happens, take the credit, if it's bad, blame the 'girl in the office.'

'I see. You're the CEO and you're blaming the office employees?' Chad frowned and wrote in his notebook. 'Claiming you were unaware?'

'No, no, I'm sure it's just a misunderstanding. Give me a little time to find out what happened and fix it.'

'That seems reasonable. I'll be back tomorrow. Nine o'clock. I expect answers.' Chad stood and adjusted the cuffs of his suit. 'There's no excuse for shoddy bookkeeping, sir.'

'No, you're right, of course. I'll get it fixed, I promise.' Ben was sweating even though the temperature was a cool 60 degrees.

As soon as Chad left, Ben was yelling for me. 'What the hell, Reva? Get this straightened out. The last thing I need is some government agency breathing down my neck. I'll be at Pierre's if you have to reach me. I need a drink.'

'Yes, sir. It will all be taken care of before you get back.'
And it was.

Ben's American Express card was declined at Pierre's. Then the Visa, the Mastercard, and even the Diner's. He was forced to pay cash, barely leaving him enough for cab fare to the office. In the lobby, he tried to withdraw cash via the ATM. Each transaction was met with "Insufficient Funds".

When Ben arrived upstairs, he found the building maintenance man scraping Johnson, Inc. off the glass in the door. The office was bare down to the light bulbs. The door to the safe hung open, showing empty shelves. 'Where's my furniture, my beautiful desk, my paintings? The jewellery's gone! What are you doing?'

'Boss sez you're behind on the rent so you're outta here. Dunno about the rest, some guyz showed up, sed they was takin' the furnichure in loo of money owed. They looked connected, if you get my drift, so I dint argue. Some hot babe left this note for youse.'

Margaret, her sister Trisha, LeeAnn, Adriane, and Ben's ex-wife, Jackie, each held a paper umbrella-topped pina colada. Chad would join us in a few days. Mom and Pop were in the kitchen making a dish that involved angel hair pasta, fresh vegetables, and a sauce so light, only the taste was there.

'Tell it again, Reva.' Jackie grinned. 'I can't get enough of this story.'

'We started with three — Jackie, who'd been wronged, Margaret who'd been used, and me, who could help. The rest of you, and Chad, joined the fight. LeeAnn trashed Ben's personal reputation by handing out the flyers and sharing what a louse Ben was. No woman would date him after that. Chad put the fear of government oversight into him. Adriane passed on the fake documents to a reporter who wrote a blockbuster article, timed to break that same day. Margaret and I cancelled his credit cards, emptied his bank accounts and the office safe where the jewellery was stashed, put the money in her name, offshore, even sold the house. He signed the contract without even looking at it. His car was repossessed. We left him with the clothes on his back, just like he did Jackie after the divorce.'

Margaret passed slices of tiramisu and offered more pina coladas. 'Tell Jackie about the note you left. It's a classic.'

'The maintenance man gave it to him. It said, 'You screwed, screwed over, and screwed up the women in your life. The name Reva is of Hebrew origin, meaning 'to tie, bind, trap, snare.' We have taken what is rightfully ours. Revenge is sweet.'

I was back where the sheets are Egyptian cotton, the sun shines every day, and the mist of salt on the breeze caresses my skin. I was surrounded by friends, new and old.

There was only one thing left to do.

'A toast,' I said. 'To dangerous women!'

ABOUT SANDRA MURPHY

Sandra Murphy lives in St Louis, Missouri, in the heart of the US. Her tales have appeared in anthologies such as *The Book of Extraordinary Amateur Sleuth and Private Eye Stories, The Book of Extraordinary Impossible Crimes and Puzzling Deaths,* and *The Book of Extraordinary Historical Mysteries.* She's the editor of two anthologies, *A Murder of Crows* and of *Peace, Love, and Crime: Crime Fiction Inspired by the Songs of the 60s. From Hay to Eternity: Ten Devilish Tales of Crime and Deception* is a collection of her oddball stories, ranging from humorous to mysterious to creepy.

TRAVELLERS

Maxim Jakubowski

We had built an extension to the house, to shelve away thousands of the books which had spread like wildfire hills across our rooms over the previous decades. Call me a hoarder if you will, but it breaks my heart to part with a book. Or a CD. Or a DVD. I never agreed to graduate to streaming or downloading my voracious appetite for culture, I fear. A proper contrarian.

While moving the piles into the new room, which we now called the library – not that the rest of the house was book-free by any means even after we had filled the new locale – I came across many lost pages, volumes I had forgotten I owned and also countless folders stuffed with the daily bulletins from several of the cruises we had been on. One of them also revealed a set of photographs taken at our dinner table on Magellan on the occasion of our first ever cruise; which had taken us across the Baltic, covering the Nordic capitals and also Tallinn and St Petersburg.

With terrible memories of being violently sick on countless occasions in my youth while regularly travelling between London and Paris on the Channel ferry, I had once sworn that when I grew up I would never voluntarily set foot on a boat again and had held firm until an advertisement in *The Guardian* for a Baltic cruise caught my attention. D had never been to Scandinavia, although I had done so on various occasions on business, and we had both been eager to visit St Petersburg for ages. The offer was attractive and we agreed to book. Forty-eight hours prior to departure I visited our local chemist on Brent Street and stocked up on sea sickness pills.

Which, of course, we never used. I probably still have a lifetime supply of them should anyone be interested! We thoroughly enjoyed the cruise and in the years that followed undertook many more. We roamed the Caribbean, explored China and navigated down the Yangtze River, even once sailed halfway round the world, taking nearly three months to reach Sydney, where we stayed a week in a boutique hotel off Bondi Beach before flying back to London, swept down Dutch canals and the Danube. To be fair, we were not your usual species of 'cruisers' and seldom interacted beyond politeness with other passengers. More comfortable unsocially spending our time together both on board and on land.

The photos were only six years old but, God, how we looked so much younger. Different. Her hair was lustrous and swept back, she wore her pale blue jacket and skirt outfit from that fashion store in Covent Garden in one of the photos, and in the other, taken on a separate evening, an embroidered top with swirling lace patterns which conjugated perfectly with her smile and offered a hint of cleavage. A minute gap between her top front teeth that I had always found profoundly endearing was unveiled by her smile to the camera. I was wearing a dark blue tie against a similarly pale blue shirt and a beige jacket, looking dapper as hell. Not the real me at heart; these days I mostly live in T-shirts and jeans.

My heart skips a beat seeing her in the photos.

Fuck, she was so beautiful.

Last week, she didn't recognize one of our grandchildren in another photo that had been sitting on a shelf in the front room for longer than I recall. She hasn't washed her hair for weeks and has acquired this terrible habit of scratching herself. Her legs, her nose, her scalp. Last night, she left the bedroom to go to the toilet down the corridor, and I was woken by her fumbling in the room next door, got up and found her standing like a deer in headlights having again forgotten where the upstairs toilet actually was. We've lived in this same house for 45 years. There are days when her mood swings take over. One moment she is needy and in constant need for a kiss, a cuddle, an embrace and then just a few minutes later a distorted memory from our past rises to the surface of her mind and she has to argue wildly with me about things which either do not matter or happen to be false memories. I try to be patient, but sometimes I just can't hold my irritation back, and feel guilty for hours afterwards for my lack of compassion.

This is what dementia does.

She has become the ghost of the woman I once knew, struggling in self-denial against the ravages of the illness.

Once she was the most gorgeous woman I had ever come across, and I couldn't believe my luck when she didn't turn me away from her bed. What did she see in me? Two years later we were married.

How we travelled!

We lived in Italy, where the fog swept down daily through the valley at the point which the motorway between Milan and Venice ran. The small village where we lived only showed a movie once a week in the local church, and every foreign movie was dubbed, so we had to drive an hour or more to Milan to view something with subtitles or in English. I still remember how there was always a break halfway through the film, always when you least expected it. Attending, for work purposes, a trade conference in Venice, we visited the casino on the Lido, where the security guard wouldn't initially allow her in as he didn't believe she was of age until she presented her passport; she was actually 29. He blushed, while she was delighted to be considered still so young in appearance.

We had children.

We had grandchildren.

We once flew back from Mauritius and floated above the Sahara. Looking through the windows of the plane cruising at low altitude, witnessing the endless sand dunes shimmering like a sea of sand, ever in motion, wave climbing over wave, a mineral ocean in constant flux, alive, slithering, boiling, a vision that has never left me.

At sea for over five days between exiting the Panama Canal and reaching the islands of French Polynesia – Nuku Hiva, Tahiti, Bora Bora – watching the endless vistas melting into the distant, curved horizon, experiencing the sheer magic of human existence on a planet so full of water and unexplored depths, the calm, but undulating sea like a repository of profound knowledge, watching through the porthole in our stateroom, feeling small and unimportant in the eyes of creation and literally stranded voluntarily in the middle of nowhere.

Memories bubbling up again: another year in our journeys, the Viking Sky seemingly moving at a snail's pace through the becalmed Stockholm Archipelago in bright summer sunlight, slaloming lazily in low gear around its 24,000 islands, D on the balcony, topless, her breasts tanned and still high and firm on offer to the cloudless, untroubled sky, long blonde hair cascading down to her shoulders.

On the photographs taken at the 8pm dinner sitting on Magellan her smile is luminous, as if she has not a care in the world, ignorant of the future, barely bothered by her already erratic memory, and blaming it on absent-mindedness.

Some photos exist, scattered around the house, in folders, albums, orphaned between the pages of books. Others are, I have no doubt, purely nested in my imagination, that simulacrum of memory that feels ever so real and treacherous. A naked beach in Jamaica or maybe it was in the south of France when we drove every summer down to the Languedoc, but then cameras were not allowed there, so why do I picture the images and scenes so clearly? Us standing proudly, feet moored to the warm sand, our skin tanned, our genitals shaven one morning in an act of amused compliance to the fashion of the day and initially feeling like plucked chickens, more naked than nude, and in no way sexual descendants of Adam and Eve in the Garden of Eden.

This morning, she lingers in bed while I come downstairs and work on the laptop, labouring through edits. I hear her steps on the landing and abandon my work mid-sentence to check up on her. She looks at me from the top of the stairs.

She appears to be standing in fog, as if unsure of where she is. She looks at me, opens her mouth and out come foreign words, the language she was born with and which I can barely understand. It's almost half a century since she left those distant shores but something inside her damaged brain must have clicked and she tries to communicate with me through the barrier of the years. I have to remind her several times during the course of the next few minutes that I cannot understand what she is attempting to tell me, until it dawns on her after our frantic cross-purpose conversation what she is doing. Later, realization sweeps over her, and she begins to cry and I have to hold her in my arms and console her. I dread the inevitable day when she will not even recognize me.

Lazily drifting down the placid Yangtze River, passing through the gorges that rise on both sides of the boat, peering out for the tombs carved into the mountain side where souls sit forever and holding our breath, in awe again of the sheer power of nature, I turn towards her, seeking her eyes out. Her glasses have turned dark, but I recognize how pensive she is and imagine we might be thinking the exact same thing.

On an ill-thought through vacation to Mauritius, during the wrong season when the light fades too early in late afternoon and the evenings are idle and interminable, we swam in the infinity pool that rose above the Indian Ocean, and watched in communal silence as the sun climbed down the line of the horizon, a fleeting vision of gold and fire drowning in savage splendour.

She spends the day as if wrapped in a curtain of mist, aimless, forlorn. She falls on her way home from the newsagent where she had picked up today's *Guardian*, broken her spectacles and suffered a bad cut to her face, which will leave a forever scar across her cheekbone. One day she walks by our home, having temporarily forgotten which house, which front door, is ours, wanders past it and is chaperoned back by a kindly passer-by who returns her to nr. 95 after she confesses she is lost. Yet another visit to A&E. On another day, not long after, she slips while going down the stairs and badly bruises her ankle. Hospital visit. No break but damage to the soft tissue inside her left foot. For three weeks she has to use a lightweight metal crutch to shuffle along and blank out the pain.

New Orleans had become our adopted city. The smell of beer in the gutters of Bourbon Street; the festooned balconies; bougainvillae in bloom spreading through the treillis with its odorous trail of honeysuckle and sun; the glossy green leaves and delicate white blossoms of the magnolia trees, an endless feast for the eyes and the senses. New Year's Eve on the balcony at Tujague's watching the ball drop on the facade of the Jax Brewery to trigger the fireworks exploding on the barges in the nearby, wide Mississippi. The crawfish boils releasing their spicy aromas, the fat, greasy oysters on their bed of ice, followed by gumbo; gospel brunch at the House of Blues on Decatur, just across from the dusty warrens of Beckham's Bookshop over the street where I would spend hours hunting down collectibles through a maze of spines of all colours and textures.

On our last overseas trip – now, sadly, already a couple of years ago – she has a moment of blind panic at the e-gates at immigration at Heathrow on our return, forgetting where she is, unable to scan her passport in the scanner and raises a terrible fuss with security staff rushing to the affray. I have to reassure them. 'She has Alzheimer's,' I explain quietly and out of her hearing before she is escorted through and we can finally make our way to the luggage hall where, of course, our suitcases are almost the last to emerge on the conveyor belt.

The world, our world, is no longer what it used to be. Gone is the Water Margin on Golders Green Road, the Ganges on Gerrard Street, that couscous restaurant in Paris off the Boulevard Saint Michel, the cavern-like bodega in New York where they served seafood tacos, the sushi place on 13th Street. Somehow, I am beginning to associate all the eating places which we can no longer go to with mental images of her anchored in the beauty of the past.

She walks like an old woman, hesitant, slowly, dragging her heels, wading through unseen molasses. In a room in which we have lived several decades, she points at some photographs on a shelf and asks 'Who is that?' and I have to remind her it's us when we were younger, or point out which grandchild is which. On a regular basis now, she enquires where our children live, even though both have respectively been in New York and Chorleywood for years and we Skype weekly.

Yesterday she woke up in the middle of the night, wishing to go to the toilet and began wandering through the house, walking downstairs and setting off the burglar alarm in her daze. The screech of the alarm must have woken up half the street by the time I rushed down in panic and cancelled it, finding her in tears and totally disoriented.

In Tahiti, in a large mall in Papeete, I bought her a necklace of black pearls and got my currency conversion rate wrong and paid ten times more than I thought. By the time I realized, we had sailed away and were already heading for New Zealand.

She wanders through the house, picking things up and moving them to small hiding places. Keys disappear. Jewellery is secreted in drawers and promptly forgotten. She cannot bear for anything to be thrown away and even sometimes busies herself going through the domestic rubbish to retrieve items I had disposed of; empty plastic bottles, food containers, foil wrapping, packaging. Every Friday morning, I purposefully rise early to slip downstairs and furtively dispose of all the unnecessary clutter of items I can find before the rubbish collection van arrives around eight a.m. or we would be swamped. There is no point arguing with her; she always protests that any given item could always be reused given the right opportunity. So, I deceive her on a weekly basis, knowing that by then she will have forgotten what she had spirited away.

We honeymooned in Desenzano on the shores of Lake

Garda, following a brief stopover in Nice on the Côte d'Azur where I had to go on a training course. As I watched her against the background of the still, green waters bordered by snow-topped mountains I remember thinking she was the only woman in the world and that she was just too good for me, her long blonde hair falling to her shoulders, slim but wonderfully curvy, and with a smile so full of intelligence that could have happily led me to eternal damnation. My father on our wedding day had predicted to his pals that the marriage wouldn't last a year. We proved the bastard wrong.

It's silly what you remember at times like this, sorry for yourself and with anxiety burrowing through the pit of your stomach. The lentil and barley soup at Veselka in New York on the street full of Ukrainian businesses, the sizzling, chargrilled oysters saturated in an herb butter sauce at the Acme Oyster Bar in New Orleans where you had to earn the right to eat by queuing for ages outside, the boiled tongue at the Dostoyevsky Restaurant in a suburb of Cologne. I keep on booking further trips in hope, and end up cancelling them like clockwork when the time comes and am no longer sure whether we will ever travel again. I blame it on Covid 19 but, in truth, I'm not sure whether she will ever be in a condition to travel anymore, recalling with horror the time she went AWOL in an airport in Texas on a stop-over returning from New Orleans and it took nearly three hours to find her with the help of officials. Since then, I stand at the door every time she has to go to the toilet in a public space, store, restaurant, airport, waiting for her.

It happened to her mother, she once told me, the same way until the day she visited her at the care home where she was being looked after, and was no longer recognized.

It will be a sunny day, I know, when I will come to her and she will look up at me, her grey eyes full of questions, the ghost of the woman I have loved, and she will say 'Who are you?'

I will then know we will never travel together again.

I will walk to the bathroom with my heart thumping.

Open the medicine cabinet where so many pills have accumulated over the years, prescribed for my blood pressure, her thyroid, the arthritis in her joints. The surgery renews all our prescriptions electronically every two months, an automatic process, even when certain medications are no longer required and we have quite a collection. I'm aware which ones should be taken with caution, the painkillers required for a past illness or another.

I will puncture the blister packs and spread the pills in the hollow of my hand and give them to her tonight as a replacement for her normal cocktail of medication. She will not know the difference. I've already researched the matter online. I know it will be painless. She will die in her sleep.

Her suffering will be over.

Only for me to be left with the guilt.

It's a fair exchange.

ABOUT MAXIM JAKUBOWSKI

Maxim Jakubowski worked for several decades in publishing and later owned the Murder One bookshop. He has written 20 novels (including 10 under a collaborative pen name, several of which made the *Sunday Times* top 10) and 5 collections of short stories. He is recognized as a major expert on popular fiction and reviewed crime for 12 years each for *Time Out* London and *The Guardian*, and won several awards in the mystery and SF & fantasy field. He is also a major editor of bestselling anthologies, and has been translated widely. He is currently Chair of the Crime Writers' Association. He lives in London.

NIGHTS ON THE TOWN

Sally Spedding

Thursday 5ᵗʰ November 2015. 8.30 a.m.

'It'll end in tears, son. Just you wait.'

Mammy's words still stung like those jabs the school nurse gave us to protect against Rubella and God knew what else. Except the sins of the world. And this same warning had come at *my* expense, on *my* phone if you please. On her frigging birthday.

'That tart of yours is bad news,' she'd added before I'd slapped the phone down. The woman who'd been the main mast in my life. Who'd often known what I was thinking before I did.

Damn you.

I pulled out of Dream Kitchens' empty forecourt and joined the heavy traffic on the Pontarddulais Road. If lucky, I'd have forty minutes of my lunch hour with Donna Marie Davies over at the DVLA. The woman I should have met when *my* dreams still seemed reachable.

12.30 p.m.

Fog from nowhere. Thick and sulphurous, showing no signs of lifting.

Bejesus.

Not bonfire smoke or some retard burning tyres. This lot hovered just below windscreen level, making all the familiar landmarks and street furniture disappear. A Royal

Mail van overtook me, grazing my wing mirror, forcing it inwards.

Bastard.

This car symbolised my success. The first thing my customers saw when I turned up to plan their perfect kitchen, to spiel the spiel. Normally, I'd have given chase, but not with six points already on my licence. Not with almost nil visibility …

I pulled over into what I guessed was a lay-by, but was in fact, a pavement filled by two women pushing large buggies. Yelling and screaming, they bashed on my passenger side door, but I moved off sharpish. Donna Marie and her smooth, shaved legs with their gold ankle bracelets, her sexy smile, was waiting.

2.10 p.m.

Back in my office on the fifth floor of Anchor House, overlooking Swansea's dock area, I'd phoned her to say that the lunchtime weather hadn't been my fault. But instead of being understanding, there'd been a sulky silence that stayed with me during what seemed like an endless afternoon. That fog too, had hung around and later there'd be bonfires and bangers. After all, this *was* Guy Fawkes night. Poor sod *he* was.

I was angry. Pissed off. Even Siân, my secretary kept out of my way while I tried to firm up deals with various wholesalers still pushing for rich pickings in time for Christmas. Mike Spence of Wood Works over in Morriston, for example. Still as hard as nails.

'You won't beat three grand on six cupboards, eight feet of worktop and the rest,' he said on a less than perfect line.

'Two five,' I argued. 'Or it's not worth me getting the van out.'

'Sharp today, aren't we? What's up?'

'My shrinking bank balance, that's what. You've taken the mickey too long. I've been loyal to you, remember? So get stuffed.'

I banged the receiver down and stared out at the murky scene where normally one could catch a glimpse of the bay and Port Talbot's flames beyond. Mrs Griffiths in Landor had bleated on about her new kitchen-diner I'd measured up a fortnight ago. Then Mr. Watkins in Sketty wanting those top-of-the-range beech units in by the time his wife got back from South Africa. Oh, I knew the histories. The ins and outs of marital discord. So I spent the rest of the afternoon brown-nosing suppliers I'd stupidly dropped in favour of Wood Works.

4.35 p.m.

Things weren't looking good, and I stood to lose twenty grand from both these orders. Never mind being taken to court over unfulfilled contracts …

'Fancy a cuppa?' Said Siân, but her brown eyes beneath her dark fringe, were focused on that same window. 'Before I go home, if that's alright. It's bad out there.'

'OK. Better call these two punters now.' I passed her Mrs Griffiths' and Mr Watkins's details. 'Keep them dangling.'

'But the fog's getting worse. For a start, that big crane's not visible, and it'll take me ages to get back to Neath.'

I'd got the hots for Donna Marie alright, and every second since Siân had left the building with her car's little red fog light glowing like some evil eye, had added to my blood heating up. Yet my jacket felt cool. Cold even, as I slipped my arms into its sleeves. No lining – not on something I wore day in, day out for workshop inspections and those tight eejit clients who'd try beating me down to some rock-bottom price they'd seen on TV.

'Can't do it for less,' I'd say to them before leaving. Nearing their front door. My file of dreams sweaty under my arm. 'Quality never comes cheap.'

'OK. Let's talk.'

Exactly what I'd planned for Donna Marie, but with fun first. The kind that left me dizzy, disorientated. Away with the fairies …

5.20 p.m.

Fireworks already. Their glittery colours staining the fog, as I nudged along Kingsway amongst home-going traffic. I turned up my Audi's heater to take the growing chill out of the car I'd bought new just a month ago, from the proceeds of a pub re-fit down in Llanelli.

Mother Mary…

I was in the wrong lane, and already on the turn-off for the waterfront, executing a full, risky circle. Late already. In my mind I pictured a pissed-off Donna Marie hanging around in the DVLA's foyer, checking her phone. Her glossy mouth in a pout. Maybe even thinking of her ex who'd just landed a job in Dubai, laying sewage pipes under the sand. I'd spotted a photo of him lurking behind one of me in her wallet when we'd last been to the Mandala disco in Victoria Street. And that got me thinking how his name had cropped up quite a few times of late. But – and I admit this with some difficulty – I'd stayed buttoned up. You see, as a kid, I'd been told never to cry …

The DVLA building rose like some giant tombstone from the dark fug. But why no lights from any of it windows? And just to see it there so stark, so dead, reminded me of my Granny's grave back in Meath. A place that even on the brightest day, seemed shrouded in grief.

'Just get me there,' I said to my soft, perforated pigskin steering wheel. 'Before it's too late.' Then my left hand stroked the top of the dashboard – smooth and cool like Donna Marie's skin, especially between her thighs. And just to feel it under my fingers made me want her even more.

Meanwhile. beyond my car's windows, a kind of war was in progress, with comets, bangers, sudden, hidden blasts that could have been The Blitz all over again. I could hear the home goers' angry revving and hooting, till some speeding cretin gave me a hefty nudge from behind.

Damn!

Normally, I'd have got out, my hunting knife at the ready. Given them a fright. But not then, because as if by some miracle, the traffic suddenly thinned and there she was. Donna Marie. My 'other woman' waiting. Smelling of someone else …

Saturday 5th November 2016. 9.20 a.m.

Christos Zaroudi stroked the glistening, thirteen-month-old, black Audi Quattro so many times, it could have looked odd. But of all the cars he'd seen at the Swansea Valley Autos' showroom, this was by far the most alluring. He'd also sat on its granite-coloured leather driving seat for perhaps longer than he should, and, in the deepening smog outside, already taken it for a slow dance along Valley Way.

All good. Until the moment of no return.

'Any deals on the price?' he asked the sales girl hovering nearby. A shapely blonde with the name *Clare* scripted on her badge, and the remains of a significant bruise under her left eye. 'Seeing as I'm paying cash up front.'

She twiddled with her calculator. 'Can't give it away, much as I'd like to, but say twelve grand. That's three off our original quote *and* Glass's Guide.'

She then gestured towards her desk where a single white rose stood rigid in its slender glass vase next to her open computer. Having sat down opposite her, Christos retrieved his Parker pen and a new, bulging wallet perfectly matching the Audi's steering wheel. His pulse rate was up. He was too eager. In love with that car after only forty minutes. Play it cool, he told himself. Step by step …

While she photocopied his driving licence details, Christos glanced over to where, beyond the Accessories Special Deals display, some thoughtful interior designer had created a small lounge area complete with black leather sofas and a TV showing scenes from Washington's State Penitentiary where Westley Allan Dodd was about to be hanged. However, it wasn't scenes of noisy protestors that held Christos' attention, but the hulk of a fleshy-faced man in his late forties, wearing a cheap, navy suit, who almost filled one of the sofas. Glaring his way.

'Sign here, please, Mr Zaroudi.' The salesgirl's voice made Christos start. 'So we can sort out your warranty and servicing package …'

His pen hovered for a moment over the designated space before beginning to write. The inside of his mouth felt suddenly dry as chalk while dead leaves drifted into the showroom when its automatic doors slid open.

He glanced up.

That same man was outside, walking away. His distinctive shape merging with the dark November morning.

'Are you alright, Mr Zaroudi?' asked Clare staring at him. 'Can I fetch you a coffee?'

'I'm fine, thanks.'

But he wasn't. Especially having checked his signature. Who the Hell was Declan O'Rourke? And why had his own normally sloping handwriting become upright and squashed as he gave an unfamiliar address in Brynmill, almost as if someone else's energy was powering his pen?

9.35 a.m.

Christos had explained to the salesgirl that his strange lapse in concentration while writing his signature, was due to jet lag. A long-haul flight originating in Sydney, which had only landed at Heathrow the day before.

She'd seemed happy enough with this explanation and completed the rest of her form-filling, occasionally looking up to give a wide, reassuring smile. Either the smile of someone with a hefty commission coming her way. Or fear he might jump ship?

'You having any fireworks tonight? She asked, passing over the warranty for him to sign.

He shook his head, unwilling to reveal he'd been a singleton for four years, with an ex back in Athens where they'd worked for the same firm of architects. Then he noticed this warranty was only valid for one year, not the three so loudly trumpeted from the showroom's display units.

'How come?'

'I've really no idea.'

She then pushed back her chair, stood up and clack-clacked over to where another suited woman – this time, a red-head with a less generous mouth – was drinking coffee from a Styrofoam cup. Both joined him and stayed standing. Just as he would with a prevaricating client. Subtle pressure to seal the deal. These sales people were trained in it from day one.

He needed a nice car. They needed a sale. They'd soon picked up on his longing, and even the glistening Audi 90 outside the showroom's main window, seemed to be winking at him like a beautiful guy on the pull. Moreover, someone who'd already attached himself to his heart.

'Has it ever been in an accident?' Christos persevered, dreading the answer from both the suits standing even closer together, whispering. Colluding, maybe?

'No way,' said Clare, whose bruise seemed to have grown bigger, darker. She looked affronted. They both did. 'We've a reputation to maintain. Why not let our Servicing team reassure you?'

He checked his Rolex, realising he had a large watercolour sketch to finish for a fellow Greek coming to live on the Gower. An important and timely commission. A step up for his practice; bucking the downward trend.

'I've too much on,' he said finally. 'But I'd like the car

radio re-tuned before I settle up.'

'Sure. No worries.'

With that top-of-the-range radio fixed, the saleswomen separated and Christos, wondering which personal number plate to order, followed Clare outside towards the Audi's already purring engine. However, something about it made his pulse slow down, for he could have sworn that the same, big, shadowy figure in a navy suit, was behind the wheel, and had given her no smile of recognition, but rather, a glowering death stare.

5.20 p.m.

Christos felt more than a little strange, but put his recent hallucinations down to overwork and jet lag. Building up his Delphi Design practice in Walter Road and opening a new branch in Sydney had taken its toll, yet there'd been something familiar about that bulky, navy-suited male who'd sat in this very seat. His big hands folded over that same wheel ...

Not so the strange signature and address which had slipped from his pen almost eight hours ago. He'd puzzled over them until late afternoon and, despite the tricky driving conditions outside his drawing office window, was tempted to visit Brynmill and find out more. Failing that, examine the electoral roll.

Don't be a bloody fool...

Yet within minutes, he'd left his nearby lock-up and joined the early evening rush-hour traffic, filtering first into the inside then outside lanes.

Brynmill proved to be a settlement of tall, mostly grey terraced houses, some converted into B&Bs or offices, all with views over the bay. Christos was about to turn off towards it when all at once came a voice from nowhere. Hard, sharp and angry, in an accent he couldn't quite place.

'Pull over right now! You're going the wrong way for a fucking start.'

'What do you mean? Who the Hell are you?'

Christos' foot left the accelerator. He'd been listening to Chopin on radio 3. The tinkling piano keys lightening his mood. He should be happy, having just taken possession of the best-looking car he'd ever owned. And at twenty-seven years of age, that was quite something ...

He switched off the radio and, as he did so, checked his rear-view mirror.

'Do as I say, Mr Zaroudi,' that voice went on. Now with a more dangerous edge, making him tighten his grip on the wheel. Also his resolve to keep going. 'You've got one minute.'

'For what?'

'*I* give the orders. Pull over.'

'No way.'

He'd just parted with a serious amount of money. He wanted to enjoy his special present to himself in his own way.

'You've had forty-three seconds already. Forty-four, forty-five...'

An Irish voice, maybe? Hard to tell ... Still counting ...

'Get lost.'

Then, with a sudden lurch inside his stomach, Christos fully recognized his companion.

That same navy-suited figure filled the passenger seat. *His* passenger seat, delivering the smell of smoke, diesel and Lynx aftershave, plus a noticeable drop in temperature that seemed to stretch his own olive-coloured skin even tighter over his bones. This was crazy! How in God's name had his intruder got into the moving Audi in the first place? And why?

'Time's up.'

Definitely an Irish voice.

Christos touched the brake. 'What d'you mean? Get out! This is *my* car, got it?'

'Wrong. She's still mine.'

Still mine?

Christos shivered. What the Hell did that mean?

'I've just paid up,' he argued. 'Got the paperwork, the ...' His tongue seemed frozen against his teeth as the car surged forward towards the next roundabout and set off the way he'd come.

'I'm stopping in the next layby,' Christos finally announced, pumping the brake to no effect. 'So whoever you damned well are, get out. Or ...'

'What?' The hulk challenged.

'I'll call the police. You've been stalking me since this morning.'

A sour laugh followed, bringing a distinct whiff of beer, while the speedometer showed double the urban speed limit. Christos prayed there'd be no traffic lights on red. No other obstruction.

Help me, Mama ... Help me Iesus ...

His brakes weren't working.

From inside his mac, he pulled out his cell phone, just as the fog hanging over Singleton Park began to thin, and a firework display from the university's campus, arced its twinkling stars into the sky.

'I'll have that.' The bigger man was too quick. Too strong, and seconds later Christos heard its casing splinter against the tarmac. He was trapped by something he'd never experienced before. Not only fear, but what seemed an almost superhuman force.

The last time he'd used this road had been to Port Eynon in

a hired Toyota to remind himself of how, if his latest project there won the prestigious Royal Society of Architects' Domus prize, he could return to Heraklion a wealthy man. Open yet more outlets. Buy his Mama a decent house and perhaps, with this beautiful, black beast imported to grace those sunlit streets, even meet a new soul mate. A guy who wouldn't try to change him ...

Slow down ...

The handbrake was useless too, and the sign with MUMBLES WELCOMES CAREFUL DRIVERS came and went. Something out in the bay winked its lights then vanished.

The overweight intruder leaned closer. That beer smell stronger. Also, something new. The coppery taint of dried blood

'I'm Declan O'Rourke,' he whispered. '*I* signed for her this morning, remember?'

Holy Zeus ...

'But *I* signed again,' Christos countered, trying to keep his place in the road.

'Not the copy she kept.'

'Who? The blonde with the bruise?'

A cynical chuckle followed.

'If you like.' Then under his breath, 'the slut.'

In the glare of oncoming car lights, with the speedometer rising, Christos wondered what he meant and saw in close-up that block of a face in every pock-marked detail, from its shifty blue eyes narrowed to black, to the thin, twisted lips.

No ...

He heard the sudden click of all four doors locking around him, making his bowels turn over. Next, a blade jutting from that huge fist, then perfume stronger than anything he'd known. Sweet, cloying, eking out from behind his seat. He'd always hated incense whenever his widowed Mama had made him attend Heraklion's local church as a kid. He'd sneezed then and sneezed now.

Another glance in his mirror ...

My God. Clare?

Was it really her, filling that small glass oblong? Dark-haired this time, not blonde, but those same features, the lip-glossed mouth and that huge, spreading bruise.

Then, as quickly as she'd appeared, she was gone.

5.56 p.m.

All I remember is my wheels screaming as my real woman hits a traffic island then veers to the left where a solid stone wall bordering the Court Hotel looms up just beyond her shattered windscreen.

At least she's mine again. No thanks to Donna Marie Davies, my betrayer.

Several dark, greasy curls lie on my lower arm while the rank stench of blood and body fluids still leak from the boot. His and hers...

Suddenly, a knock on my window. My eyes snap open. A cop in a fluorescent cagoule is peering in. Old enough to be the dad I'd not seen for years. I lower the glass. Take in the blue, spinning lights on an empty, chequered car behind him. To my left, dog walkers are crossing the mudflats towards the sea.

I'd had a dog once. Less trouble than bitches every time. Especially the human variety, hell-bent on revenge.

'You alright, sir?' He quizzes. 'I could arrange an ambulance.'

'I'm fine. Not a scratch. Now, if you'd excuse me, I've an important client to see ...'

'You were all over the road. Could have been a nasty accident. And we don't want another one here like last year's bonfire night, do we? An Irish man and a young woman killed outright, remember?' The Fuzz sniffs and pulls a face, adding years to his features. 'Any passengers lying low?'

Not any more.

'No, sir.'

'I'd still like to check the boot.'

My prayer to the Virgin Mary takes three seconds, then I add, 'I fit kitchens. There's just cupboards and stuff in there.'

Meaning the gay Greek and that heartless tart who'd dumped me as if I'd been nothing more than a pizza wrapping for the wind to blow away. She, who, since then – bruise and all – joined the sales team at Valley Way Autos to flog my car to someone else. So, this time, only a total write-off will suffice.

'Up to you.' The Fuzz gabbles into his two-way then stands back to peer at my number plate. 'Hey, that's a bloody big coincidence,' he adds. 'Curiouser and curiouser …' His last words before my foot's hard on the accelerator. My heel grinding against the mat's deep pile, leaving that little rip-off town behind us. Those blue lights, spinning, fading …

Wind from the sea soon disperses the bad smells and lifts that stiff's girly curls from my suit, as my fingers caress the cool, pigskin steering wheel and once again, intense joy is king. Claiming every part of me while the road up beyond Caswell Bay becomes narrower, and the nearside verge a soft cushion beneath my wheels, as my real woman's take-off into the night bears us all towards the churning waves below.

ABOUT SALLY SPEDDING

Born near Porthcawl in south Wales, my family's turbulent European background and my own experiences and observations of places and people influence my crime/thrillers, short stories and poetry, involving duplicity and betrayal. How human beings don't change but gradually reveal themselves. I studied Sculpture at Manchester and St Martin's, London and having won an international short story competition, was approached by an agent.

Wringland and *Cloven* were published by PanMacmillan in 2001 and 2002 in a two-book deal. *A Night With No Stars*, then *Prey Silence* (both published by Allison&Busby) and *Come and be Killed* Severn House) followed. Next in 2012 was *Cold Remains* and *Malediction*, (Sparkling Books) then *Cut to the Bone* featuring a psychopathic but beguiling schoolboy, of interest to Virago at the time, it was optioned for a feature film in 2020. *How To Write a Chiller Thriller* (Compass Books) came out in 2014 and *The Yellowhammer's Cradle* in 2016 and *Behold A Pale Horse* in 2020. Endeavour Media (now Lume Books) are currently publishing five of my backlist titles as ebooks and paperbacks.

An active member of the CWA since 2002, Mystery People and recently, Crime Cymru, I was the CWA's Wye Chapter convener, and in normal times, enjoy meeting my readers at book fairs, literary festivals and crime/thriller events. Assessing manuscripts for the CWA has seen debut writers become published, and is useful in editing my own work. My short stories have won awards and been widely published including in many CWA crime anthologies. The latest, 'Run Rabbit Run' (in *The Book of Extraordinary Historical Mysteries*) and 'Rosy is Red' (in *The Book of Extraordinary Amateur Sleuths and Private Eyes*) are published by Mango (USA) edited by CWA Chairman Maxim Jakubowski. *Strangers Waiting* (bluechrome) my short story collection, includes that eponymous story which won the H E Bates Short Story Prize.

In September 2018, Richard Foreman of Sharpe Books signed a Contract for seven of my crime chillers. Firstly, *The Nighthawk*, set in the eastern Pyrenees, features newly-retired DI John Lyon from Nottingham who, while on holiday, really shouldn't have strayed off the beaten track. Now available as an ebook and paperback. Second in this trilogy is *Bloodlines* set near Poitiers, then *Death Knell*, set in 1920's rural Norfolk. *Downfall*, the first in my wannabe gendarme Delphine Rougier quartet, is set in the flat Sarthe department, where dark secrets linger, and danger lurks at every turn. *The Devil's Garden* was published in January this year. After *Blood at Beltane* came *Fatal* published in February 2021, and the last, *Fin du Monde* has just appeared.

My poetry has also won awards and been widely published in the UK and abroad. Two poems were recently included in the 25th edition of *Atlanta Review* edited by Agnes Meadows, and 'Seizure' will be published by the Black Spring Press in *Best British and Irish Poets 2019-2021* on 28th September 2021. I also adjudicate national and international writing competitions, including the International Welsh Poetry Competition three times, including last year. My late husband was the renowned artist Jeffrey Spedding, and we spent part of each year in the eastern Pyrenees where he worked on his commissions and I on my books. Where timeslips still seem to occur …

Sacrifice, my poetry pamphlet, was published by Hedgehog Poetry Press last November.

https://www.sallyspedding.com

BLINDSIDED

Caroline England

'So what was your highlight of the day?' Dan asked, shovelling in a surprising amount of pasta at our favourite Italian.

Dan was the fortunate by-product of my marriage to Marcus, which had imploded a year previously. Marcus was now with Monica, and even Dan agreed the 'M&M sprog' had been 'pelted out' with indecent haste.

Though he'd once been Marcus's close mate, he'd remained loyal to me. With his non-stop chatter, his tattoos and piercings, he was the very best and brightest company, as well as the most unlikely of surgeons.

I had to consider his question for a moment. 'Not sure if *highlight* is the word, but I spent a considerable part of it fending off a childhood friend.'

'Fending? Sounds intriguing.'

'Not really. It's just ...' I thought back to Sally as a twelve-year-old: *Best pals forever, Harri* ... 'She can be a little ... cloying, I suppose. But she's always been consistently lovely too. She wants me to go to a reunion.'

He pointed a fork. 'Got it. Your posh boarding school.'

'Hmm, I'm not sure "posh" is the word. Sure, we wore boaters and grey suits on a Sunday, and...' I delicately patted my mouth with a napkin. 'Woe betide if we forgot to take one of these – duly laundered – to meals, but the teaching was pretty dire and once we were locked up it was more like Victorian deprivation than privilege. No central heating, mice, disgusting food. Chapel every bloody day.

And silence for hours. In lines, at meals, in prep.'

Undoubtedly at the thought of staying quiet for more than a minute, Dan looked appalled. 'And your parents *paid* for this? They could have got it free at Her Majesty's Pleasure.'

'Absolutely.' I laughed. 'I served the time without even doing the crime.'

'So this friend —'

'Sally.'

'Your teenage bestie, I take it?'

I thought about that one. 'Eventually.'

He narrowed his eyes. 'I'm smelling a rat. So there was a bit of elbowing and jostling for position at first?'

Dan wasn't a paediatrician for nothing, but I didn't take the bait and fortuitously the waiter appeared to clear our plates.

'So what was yours?' I asked. 'Your highlight?'

He crooked his little finger and I chuckled.

'Not again!' I said. 'How very disappointing for you.' Dan didn't have a current boyfriend, so it must have been a one-night stand. 'A first – thing – in – the - morning disappointment?'

'I wish; even a weenis would be better than the current drought. Nope. Here's a clue: it's an organ which has negligible value to the human body.'

'Ah, so definitely not a penis, then.'

'Correct. But though this finger-shaped pouch might seem innocuous …' He did an explosion motion with his hands. 'It can become swollen and rupture. If it bursts, a pocket of pus often forms in the abdomen which requires immediate surgery to remove the bugger and clean the abdominal cavity.'

'Why thank you for such a lovely image.' I pushed away the dessert menu. 'Still, it's a good subject over dinner if you happen to be on a diet.'

But Dan was now on song. 'I'm talking about an appendix.'

'Yeah, got that.'

'And if the patient gets peritonitis, namely inflammation of the peritoneum, it can be extremely dangerous if left untreated.'

I raised my eyebrows. 'A wild guess, but did a dashing surgeon somewhere in this vicinity remove a child's appendix today?'

'Yes, an appendectomy. Not to be confused with an appendicostomy ...'

Did I really want to know the difference? I took a breath to ask, but Dan was still speaking. 'And for females, perforation can cause additional problems such as scaring, tubal infertility, ectopic pregnancies and so on. It can even be life-threatening.'

'So the patient was a little girl?'

'Yup.'

'Well done you. You love your job, don't you?'

'Yup.' His lips twitching, he scooped up the pudding menu. 'It has to be the vanilla panna cotta with caramelised orange, don't you think?'

Clearly still on the 'pus' visuals, he mischievously peered over his glasses. But my thoughts had moved on.

'So coming back to *your* girls ...' he said, as though reading my mind. 'I think you should go to this thingy. Get out and about and stop dwelling on the M&Ms.'

'Well, if the doctor says so, then patently I should.'

'I'm serious. Show them how successful, beautiful and talented you are despite the dire teaching and deprivation.'

'Hmm, and single and childless.'

He lifted his eyebrows. 'Well you know my offer stands. Buy a turkey baster and I'm all yours.'

'OK, I'll think about it.'

He made to stand. 'Even better than pud. I'm all for it.'

I laughed. 'I'll think about the *reunion*.'

'Good. And while you're there, steal a valuable

painting, etch your initials on an antique or do something dreadful. You've served the time; you might as well do the crime.'

Sally was amazed when I said yes on the phone.

'What? Really?' Then a pause. 'You do know this one's at Willowdene?'

Over the last two decades there'd been all sorts of get-togethers, some in the main building of the school, others in various pubs, towns or cities dotted around the country, and I had attended a few in the early years, but I'd never joined the annual event in our 'house', the small mansion we'd lived in from eleven to eighteen. The old property wasn't owned by the school anymore, but the kindly proprietor opened her doors and invited the 'old girls' in to reminisce for an afternoon each May.

Though 'fun' wasn't the accurate word, I still used it. 'Yes, I know. It'll be fun.'

'Fantastic! Tell you what, why don't we find a way of travelling together? We'd have longer to catch up on our news and dissect old times, and negotiating the country roads will be quicker with some company.' She laughed. 'And it would be nice to have a drink or two without the kids pestering me.'

It was a subtle hint for me to drive. 'OK. I'll have a think and give you a buzz back.'

'Brill! I'm so excited to see you, Harri. So astonished and pleased you've said yes.'

I was fairly astonished myself, but I always saw things through once I'd made a decision, so it was just a question of the logistics. After I'd mulled the idea of company for the journey, I determined that would be a good plan, so I made the call but ended up chatting -- or maybe just listening – for another good hour to more exuberant tones: it would be great fun to see each other after so long; quiff a glass or two of champagne; the speeches and awards were such a hoot; yes, one of the old walks was an excellent idea; meeting at Edensor village was a good midway point; we'd have to resist stopping for a naughty cream tea; though if we were starving after our hill tromp …

I wryly shook my head when I finally put down the phone. We'd pretty much covered our crowning moments of the last few years. Would we find more to 'dissect' in two weeks?

Though I had travelled via the thin – and very muddy – Derbyshire lanes and roads, I ended up meeting Sally at the local train station. I was a few minutes late, and in truth I had stopped at a carwash to get rid of the dirt on the bodywork and tyres of my new car, but I knew not to tell Sally. I'd always been a perfectionist, a touch OCD, and she'd be sure to mention something from our childhood that would grate.

That was the trouble with boarding school; for seven long years we'd slept in the same dormitory, eaten, had lessons, hung out together; showered in adjacent cubicles, cleaned our teeth in adjoining sinks, so we knew each other – or at the least the girls we'd been – far too well. Sally was lovely, a really sweet friend, but she'd never been the brightest in the tool box and sometimes she could be inadvertently tactless.

'Harri!' She was now holding out her thin arms. 'I was starting to think you'd changed your mind, but here you are!' She nodded at my gleaming Nissan GT-R. 'Is this yours? God I wish, but with a hubby, the twins and only two seats …'

I fixed a smile. 'Come on, hop in. A champagne greeting, I believe. We don't want to miss out on a glass.'

The journey took all of ten minutes, but Sally didn't immediately climb out. Her expression concerned, she studied me with those huge brown eyes.

'You've never done this one before …'

'I know, but things change. I thought it was time.'

She nodded. 'Great. It's just … well, afterwards I realised it was me who'd encouraged you to come today. I'd hate to you feel uncomfortable or just do it for me.'

'It's fine.' I squeezed her hand. 'I'm actually doing this for myself.'

'Oh, OK.'

We made our way down the steps to the heavy front entrance. Though still painted black, the corroded ram knocker had been replaced with the features of a friendly lion. I made to use it, but the door was opened.

As I stepped over the threshold, I didn't know what to expect. Smell, I suppose. That old tang of mould, damp plimsoles and body odour; and whatever revolting concoction Miss Philips would simmer for hours on the hob for her cats. And, of course, cold; I expected it to be freezing, to see a cloud of my breath precede me. But the hall was fragrant, warm and bright, the rows of name pegs, strewn hockey sticks and wellies long gone. A huge bouquet of roses sat proudly on a morning table, adorned with a plaque: *From the Old Girls of Willowdene House.*

'Arranged by Petra, no doubt,' Sally muttered. 'I wonder if she's already here.'

Petra. I inhaled to say something, but a gaggle of voices interrupted. 'Harriet Billington, is that really you?' 'Oh, and Sally MacDonald.' 'Wow, look who's turned up.' 'Harri Billington! Our famous friend …' The welcome committee had spotted us.

Already anticipating the thrust of the conversation, I followed Sally into what had once been a dormitory but was now a beautiful drawing room looking out to the pristine gardens. I managed to hover, sip my champagne and listen to the chitchat for a while, but when comparisons of wealthy husbands and flourishing progeny set in, I meandered to the large bay window. Seeming to appear from nowhere, I was joined by a tall elderly lady with a cloud of white hair.

'Harriet Billington, I take it?' she asked. 'Known as Harri?'

'That's me. And you must be Miss Watts. I love what you've done with the house. It's beautiful.' I gestured to the glass. 'And this view is stunning.'

She smiled. 'It is indeed. You can see One Tree Hill in winter. I believe you girls used to go there on walks.'

'Yes, we did. Two by two in a crocodile. Woe betide if anyone broke ranks.'

'One had to be sure of one's best friend, then?'

Picturing Petra, I nodded and took a breath, but Miss Watts interrupted.

'You haven't been before, so let me give you the tour. The others have seen the house many a time.'

I had wanted to look around and absorb the memories by myself, or perhaps with Sally, but a smug voice piped up from the central cluster.

'I can beat that. I popped my fourth three weeks ago. A home birth too.'

'You're joking? You look so fab. Petra won't be impressed that you've caught up with her current record. She'll be dragging poor Nigel to bed the moment she gets home tonight…'

'Yes, that would be lovely,' I said, taking my host's proffered arm.

It wasn't Lucy or Eniola, Holly or Kushi's fault that I didn't have children. And in fairness to them, they'd never grilled me or given me loaded sympathy at the other reunions. Indeed, they'd seemed to assume I'd chosen to put career before kids. Though they'd talked incessantly about their offspring, they had managed one or two questions about my job, and they'd appeared to be a little wistful about what they might be missing in the workplace. Which, of course, was nothing. I had spent my entire adult life pursuing my career as a celebrity lawyer with ease and panache, but all the while yearning for a baby, a child that never came.

Infertility had ultimately destroyed my marriage to Marcus; not only our inability to conceive, but the apparent lack of reasons for it. We'd foolishly never had investigations nor tests, but silently blamed each other instead. As things turned out, that hadn't been fair on Marcus. His Monica had fallen pregnant two minutes after their affair began and a whole series of random lovers hadn't done the job for me, so I knew the 'fault' was mine, even before that stunning, eye-opening meal with Dan.

I followed Miss Watts up the spindled staircase. I had spent all those years here but had never noticed how elegant or ornate it was before. Nor how handsome the high ceilings, picture rails and cornices were. On the landing we stopped at the first open door. I steadied myself before peering in, but still the words I'd expected immediately rushed back.

Miss Philips needs some milk, Harri …

I felt the old lady's eyes on me. 'This is the dormitory you remember the best, I see,' she said.

I nodded. The room was now a sophisticated double bedroom. But when I was eleven, nearly twelve, it had housed six beds and lockers.

'Your first year away from home, I believe,' Miss Watts commented. 'It must have been a wrench, to say the least. Four new girls – you, little Jane Evans, Sally and dear Petra. Eniola was deputy and Lucy head of dorm. Am I right?'

She must have seen my look of surprise. 'I've been welcoming the old girls for some years now, Harriet. I have a great memory and I'm a very good listener.'

The echo came again. *Miss Philips needs some milk, Harri …*

As though hearing it too, Miss Watts cleared her throat. 'How lucky you were to share a dorm with Petra. Such fun, or so I hear, and a lovely young woman. I do look forward to our chats every year.'

I smiled automatically. That's what everyone always said.

Sally caught up with us then. Slightly breathless, she squinted over my shoulder. 'How's it going?' she hissed. 'Does it take you back? You know, to that night?'

Though Miss Watts' head slightly twitched, she busied herself straightening the heavy drapes.

'That night?' I asked.

'You know, when Petra …'

'Oh *then*.' Despite the tingling in my fingers, I shrugged. 'I hardly think about it really.'

'But I thought that was why …' Her face pink and slightly sweaty, Sally looked eager for approval, but Miss Watts had returned.

'We'll see you in the garden later,' she said to Sally in a somewhat dismissive tone. Then slipping her arm back into mine, 'Ready to continue our tour, Harriet?'

I had all but forgotten about the procedure until Marcus mentioned it one day after a whole afternoon in bed, lazily making love.

'You have a very fine scar, just here. It's hardly visible, but I can feel it,' he'd said.

I'd almost told him the story then, but it had seemed too silly to mention. We'd been young girls taken away from a normal childhood; it had been play of a sort, a tussle for friendships and dominance in an unreal world. Besides, I hadn't liked the thought of admitting to any weakness: I was a successful career woman who took no prisoners, so how could I admit to being one myself?

I can't remember who'd started it; perhaps it was me, maybe it was Petra. She was undoubtedly the Queen Bee and we were all in awe of her; I certainly adored her, proud to call her my best pal. And it was a just a joke, a laugh: whoever happened to be the last person in any given room would be trapped by the weight of three or four giggling girls on the other side of the door. But only for moments, no harm done.

And then something happened, something changed in the blink of an eye. Without rhyme or reason, Petra was no longer my friend. From then on it was just me who was trapped both in Willowdene and the main school; in the classroom or the music room, the toilets or the gym. Even in the chapel with Jesus on the cross staring down with a frown. Wedged in by a small table or chair, it wasn't funny. Claustrophobic panic took over; I'd be late and in trouble.

'Oh, you've decided to join us, Harriet,' our form teacher would say. 'What should we do about Miss Tardy today? More lines, or perhaps you'd like to sit outside Miss Robinson's office and explain the mystery to her?'

Though everyone tittered, I knew better than to tell tales. Instead, I became withdrawn and fearful, unbearably afraid of being the last person in the room, any room. And that's when the tummy aches started.

When we arrived in the kitchen, Miss Watts turned, her face luminous. I glanced around too. She was right to be pleased: the cupboards, units and drawers were clearly bespoke and painted cream. The old oven had been replaced by a handsome range, and a huge dresser was adorned by china crockery and ornaments. The sun streamed in through the French doors, but I felt the chill.

Miss Philips needs some milk, Harri ... She's asked you to get it.

My host gestured to the small room at the back. 'You remember the larder.' It was a statement, not a question. 'And it's still one to this day, Harriet. The stone is so thick; I really don't need a fridge.'

Stepping to it, she lifted the old latch and opened up. From the glossy home baking, cheeses and cold meats, an aromatic aroma escaped, I imagine, but all I could smell was the stench of Miss Philips's cat food.

Her expression shrewd, Miss Watts tilted her head. 'Look dear, you'll be pleased to see it has a light switch on the inside these days.'

I swallowed and nodded. Nothing seemed to escape this perceptive old lady.

I'm told the pain of childbirth is overwhelming, but that once over, it's soon forgotten. Well, it's something I'll never know, but I do understand the point. In the pitch black and locked inside the larder, I had already been terrified. But then the horrendous stomach ache had taken over, crippling me with such pain that I'd fainted.

It turned out that the tummy problems weren't just nerves, but a grumbling appendix which finally perforated when I was in that freezing box. Yet as debilitating as it was at the time, the actual memory of that acute, indescribable pain vanished. Miss Philips was alerted, I was taken to the local hospital and rushed in for emergency surgery. As rumour spread through Willowdene, then the whole school, I became something of a star and grew rather accustomed to all the visitors, the cards, the presents, the good wishes. I went home for a period of recuperation, was madly spoilt by my worried parents, then I returned to school. And everything was fine; by some amazing miracle, my dark days had passed and my popularity reinstated. All my class and dorm mates – including Petra – were both cordial and admiring. The unfortunate episode was forgotten, but Sally was my best friend now.

'Shall we?' Miss Watts said, stepping to the French doors and opening them.

A fragrant breeze and hum of chatter filtered in. Joining her, I looked out to the immaculately cut grass and the spectacular, sun-lit Derbyshire hills in the distance. In groups of two or three, pockets of girls from other years had gathered on the side terrace. I didn't know them all; maybe some weren't married or didn't have children. Perhaps others were too timid to join the central hive, or didn't think it seemly to constantly brag about their wonderful good fortune and picture-perfect bloody lives.

I was fully aware my emotions were irrational. The loathing which frothed in my belly was jealousy; simple as that. Those mothers had something I deeply yearned for and couldn't have. But it was the unfairness that made me so frustrated and embittered. From a 'posh' private school whose *raison d'être* was to generate half-educated young women who'd marry well and have children, as many as humanly possible it seemed, I was randomly the only 'old girl' in my crowd who hadn't conceived. But two weeks ago, I'd discovered it hadn't been a quirk of fate after all; I'd accidentally unearthed a *reason* for my infertility and this had finally helped me to shape the deep resentment, give it form and meaning and a purpose. There was finally something I could do to get closure.

The gentle wind was blowing Miss Watts's thin hair. She deeply inhaled. 'Sweet pea, gardenia and lilac. Can you detect them?'

I smiled. 'I couldn't pick each out, but the garden smells and looks wonderful. You've done an amazing job.'

As we watched, Eniola darted from group to group, clearly asking a question which was met by the shake of heads.

My elderly friend cupped her ear. 'She's asking if anyone's heard from Petra. It's so unlike her to be late.'

'Perhaps she's stopped off *en route*. Back in the day her mother took us out for a cream tea in the village of —'

'Edensor.'

'You don't miss much, do you?'

'As I said, I'm a good listener.' She circled her watch crystal and frowned. 'Three o'clock. Petra should be here for her usual —'

'Speech?'

I framed it as a question, but I knew the Queen Bee's star turn was more elaborate than that. Petra had told me about her 'award ceremony' during our long telephone chat two weeks ago. Prizes for this and that – for travelling the furthest, hitting a milestone marriage, any notable achievements and, inevitably, the most children. She'd deserved to be taken out for that alone, but when I'd done the necessary, climbed from my Nissan and peered at the blood pooling around her smashed head, I'd kept my last words to the point: the tummy aches I'd ignored because I was too frightened to complain about her bullying, the 'explosive' imprisonment at her hands and the ultimate outcome of my ruptured appendix – my miserable, barren life.

The penultimate image of Petra's face now flashed behind my eyes. Clearly pleased to see me, she'd beamed, lifted her hand and dashed over the country lane to the spot we'd agreed to start our walk. I remembered how much I had once loved her then. But I'd already made my decision; I had to *dissect* the memory to finally get closure.

So I stamped hard on the accelerator and absorbed the satisfying thud.

The sound of Miss Watts's voice broke my thoughts. 'Sorry,' I said. 'I was miles away.'

I hadn't really looked at her properly before, but her eyes were cloudy and unfocused. Yet she still gazed at me as though reading my mind. 'It's a tale I've heard often.'

'Sorry?' I said again, not following.

'Apparently you were trapped in the larder for some considerable time. A sturdy padlock and a missing key, I believe. The fire brigade came, and an ambulance. Then the police …'

Shocked, I glanced at the old wooden door. I had always assumed it was simply shut by the latch on the outside. I'd been unconscious, so had never known about the padlock, let alone firemen and police. But the news was good, very good. Locking in by padlock and 'losing' a key was considerably more evil than a five minute prank. I'd done the right thing by *dispatching* Petra, and this old lady was somehow giving me vindication, a pardon.

'But what a night it must have been, Harriet! You're part of the lore of Willowdene House. It's discussed every year. The burly firemen cutting through metal, the police officers giving the girls a good talking to, Miss Philips' search of every dormitory locker …'

She stepped outside, so I followed.

'Though the key was never found, I've heard a few versions of who hid it,' she continued. 'Yet things are never as they seem. We get blindsided by the first person to jump in with their version and we believe what we're told.' She tapped her ear. 'But over the years I've developed a talent to hear beyond the words. Something akin to a lie detector, which makes me a rather good judge of character. Leaders tend to get the blame, but more often than not it's the timid follower, patiently waiting in the wings to get what they want.'

With a beam, she held out her arm. 'Help guide me down these steps will you, dear. I know the inside of the house like the back of my hand, but without sight, the outdoors can be full of surprises, even dangerous ones at times.'

Taking the A roads and a motorway, I gave Sally a lift home.

Her gaze wide and concerned, she spoke after a while. 'You're very quiet, Harri. Was everything alright? Not too traumatic or bring anything back?'

'No, it was ...' Did I get the closure I craved? I swallowed. 'It was fine.'

'Golly, I'm so glad you're OK.'

It was an echo of her words the morning I'd returned to Willowdene after my recuperation. Of course, she was already my saviour for reporting my larder imprisonment to Miss Philips, but she was also the first to make a fuss, the first to kindly give me a 'welcome back' magazine and box of chocolates, the first to offer her hand on the crocodile walk.

Seven long years of intense friendship. And yet what did I know about this once chubby and teased 'best pal'?

Her words flashed in again: *Petra says Miss Philips needs some milk from the larder, Harri.*

As though she'd said them now, I glanced at her, finally certain of one thing: Petra hadn't snapped down that padlock and hidden the key; this woman had. Groping for reasons, I returned my gaze to the windscreen, but all I could see was Petra, her life seeping from the deep gash in her head.

Petra says Miss Philips needs some milk from the larder, Harri.

Petra says ... Yes, the prefix Sally had so often used. Meek little Sally, the follower, who just did what she was told. But also occasionally: *Harri, it was Petra who* ... Quietly, stealthily; whispered so softly I barely heard it.

Why? Why on earth did she do it? Was it an excuse to enact the nasty things she'd wanted to do anyway? Or to turn me against Petra? Or was she insidiously plotting to become my …

Best pals forever, Harri.

ABOUT CAROLINE ENGLAND

Author of psychological thrillers *Beneath the Skin*, *My Husband's Lies*, *Betray Her* and *Truth Games* as Caroline England, and *The House of Hidden Secrets* and *The House on the Water's Edge* as CE Rose, Caroline likes to write multi-layered, dark and edgy 'domestic suspense' stories that delve into complicated relationships, secrets, lies, loves and the moral grey area.

Drawing on her days as a divorce and professional indemnity lawyer, she loves to create ordinary, relatable characters who get caught up in extraordinary situations, pressures, dilemmas or crime. She admits to a slight obsession with the human psyche, what goes on behind closed doors and beneath people's façades. She also enjoys performing a literary sleight of hand in her novels and hopefully surprising her readers!

Caroline has also written *Convictions* and *Confessions*, a legal drama series under the pen name Caro Land.

Website: http://carolineenglandauthor.co.uk
Twitter: https://twitter.com/CazEngland
Facebook: https://www.facebook.com/CazEngland1/
Instagram: https://www.instagram.com/cazengland1/

THE VICTIM

Awais Khan

On a stormy July night, the kind of night when you sweat despite the rain, I was hurrying home, careful not to let the pot of biryani rice slip from my wet hands. The rain wasn't showing any sign of relenting, and I was afraid of the water seeping into the pot. Not that my brothers would mind. They weren't the generic, sister-beating kind, no, they were obedient, hard-working farmers, if at times a bit sulky and petulant. They were just normal younger brothers whose sole aim in life was to eat – and get their sister married as soon as possible. That was the responsibility our parents had left them – not to eat their way into an early grave, but to get their long-suffering older sister married.

I was twenty-three years old on that July night, almost a spinster, but I couldn't be happier. I had a man who loved me, and wanted to marry me. Well, he wasn't exactly husband material, being married (gasp!) to someone already. But he was allowed to take on another wife, thankfully, and I was happy to play second fiddle. At least, I'd be getting him in the bargain, half or full I honestly didn't care, nor did I exactly have the time to care what with cooking and cleaning after three younger brothers. He had already asked me, and I'd said yes without an ounce of hesitation. I wasn't a prude. I'd had sex numerous times and was proud of it. With more than one man. All those furtive trips to the wheat fields, the generous smiles I bestowed upon those young unsuspecting boys, they were all a means to an end. For I was a healthy young woman with healthy urges. Why should I resort to pleasuring myself when I had hordes of men, with hot blood coursing through their veins lusting after me, pleading to fulfil my every desire? Why should any woman limit herself? Well, maybe I was a bit modern for the people in my village, but I swear none of the men I lay with had any objections. They were always happy to oblige. If they called me names in the privacy of their homes, that was their prerogative. The bastards needed to sleep at night, didn't they? And besides, I had no qualms taking on their sins in addition to my own. I wanted to see how many sins I could hoard before the time for retribution came.

Needless to say, it came sooner than I had expected. Anticipating an eager welcome for myself, the eldest sister who had so lovingly brought in food to celebrate monsoon, I was nonplussed to see their grim faces when I entered the hut. I have to admit, I didn't sense danger then, not even an iota of it, or else I would have run for the hills. Instead, I put on that lopsided smile of innocence I had perfected over the years, and enquired as to what was wrong.

'You are what's wrong,' the oldest of my brothers, Aslam, said. Or spat, considering the amount of spittle that came flying from his mouth and landed on the earthen floor.

'Either speak or spit, Aslam. Where are your manners?' My voice was calm. After all, what was there to fear from my own brother?

'Jamal was here moments ago.' That was Rashid, the youngest of the three. He rose from the bamboo wicker chair and advanced toward me. 'He was looking for you. Do you know him, Baji?'

The first current of fear sliced through me, then. I confess, it was unlike anything I had ever felt. When my parents died, I had felt something akin to grief, the kind where your heart threatens to burst its dams, unleashing ugly waves of anger and sorrow. My eyes had remained dry, but I was told that was grief too. Well, who am I to doubt anyone's word? Maybe it was grief, after all. But this, this was something alien like a hot branding iron going through my skin, only its touch was icy ... glacial.

'Who is Jamal?' Lying was second nature to me. I'd

fooled my brothers this long. Why not a little longer?

'So, you don't know him?' Aslam asked me.

'No.'

'Then, why would he come looking for you, Baji?'

'That's something you'll need to ask him, Aslam.'

I didn't care much for his tone, and I told him that much.

'My tone offends you?'

'As a matter of fact, it does. Now do you want to eat or not?' Despite that unknown sensation of fear coursing through me, I stretched myself to my full height. My brothers aren't very tall, so it seemed like I was looming over them. I hoped they'd be cowed into silence.

No such luck.

But if I had ever let luck dictate my life, I wouldn't be where I am today. I ignored both my brothers and busied myself with the food. To think, I was still carrying the pot. I dumped it on the table, and prised off the lid. The scent of basmati rice hit me then, washing away some of the fear with it.

'He said you have agreed to be his second wife.' Aslam again. 'Second wife! How long have you been sleeping with him for him to make such a filthy offer, huh? You would stoop this low?'

I pretended not to have heard, but that earlier uneasiness had returned, niggling my dry throat. They were trying to make me feel worthless. I put my foot down – literally. I stamped the heel of my khussa on the stone floor.

'If you believe all the nonsense you hear from people, you will be a very sad lot, I assure you.'

'He was surprised we didn't know,' Aslam continued. 'He called us a poor excuse for brothers.'

Jamal, you bloody fool. If I had any doubts about Jamal actually being here, they were rudely dispelled. This was so like Jamal – cocky and self-assured.

I leaned back from the pot and straightened myself. The smell was making me feel sick now. These were my brothers, for crying out loud. If I couldn't be honest with them, then with whom?

I took a deep breath and turned around. 'Look, there's something—'

I never got the chance to complete my sentence. Well, that's not entirely true. I remember completing the sentence, only the words got lost as the melting skin filled my mouth.

At first, there was no pain, only irritation that Shabbir, my middle brother, had taken this long to make an appearance. Then I saw the bottle in his hand, a satisfied smirk on his face.

This happened when I was trying to finish speaking. And then the realization hit me, or should I say burned into me. The pain, oh the pain. That was all my mind was capable of registering at that time, the nerves sizzling as they wracked my body with currents of pain, my vision blurring, my mouth going slack as my lips melted right off my face, trailing somewhere down my chin.

Somewhere over the din of my muffled screams and panic, Shabbir's voice filtered into my head.

'Serves you right, whore!'

For what, I wanted to ask. But, of course, I was in no position to ask anything. I was melting alive, if that is what you call getting bathed with acid. All of this occurred to me later. At that time, all I could do was stagger toward the door, half-blind, my mind reeling with pain. All I can remember is that I foolishly ran my hand over the half of my face that had suffered the brunt of the acid attack. My hand came away with folds of skin, my fingers singeing with the remains of the acid. Since then, I haven't had any fingerprints on that hand.

Jamal told me I made it all the way to his house at the end of the street, but I think that I just collapsed somewhere in a ditch, because I do recall some respite from all the burning. Although my nasal passages were burned clean through, I somehow remember the rancid taste of piss and feces in my mouth. Has a bunch of human waste ever saved anyone's life? Well, I like to think that it saved mine. That filth was like a balm on my flaming face. In any case, it was Jamal who took me to the sad excuse of a hospital the village had.

Far from having a surgeon present, the village doctor didn't even have the basic supplies to combat my burning skin. He just resorted to applying some ointments. Cursing him inwardly, I passed out.

And here I am now, sitting on a stool in front of the mirror, watching what had once been a passably beautiful face reduced to this mess. Well, if I sort of cover half of my face with the scarf, holding it in place with a bit stuck in my teeth, I can pass for an unremarkable woman. I am blind in one eye now, so it isn't like I'm missing much in terms of vision if I cover that part of my face. After operating on my face, they managed to restore at least a certain smoothness to the skin. Make no mistake, I am not flattering myself. I'm just stating the facts. The skin has an oily sheen to it with blotches of dark colours swirling around. A human rainbow.

I try to smile – try being the important word here. All I can manage is an ugly curve of my non-existent lips. I cast off the dupatta and throw it away. One side of my head is bald. I lean forward, looking at myself closely, almost admiring every abnormality I have been bestowed with. If looked at separately, each anomaly has a certain beauty to it, almost like art. It was as if my face was a blank canvas that night, and Shabbir's hand an artist's easel as it laid waste to me.

'How many times have I told you not to mope in front of the mirror?' Jamal stands in the doorway.

'Do I look like I am moping?' I shoot back, angry that he has seen me moping. 'When have I ever moped about anything?'

My good eye, the one that escaped the acid, shines bright with unshed tears, as if making up somehow for the one in absentia.

Jamal holds up his hands. 'Hey, hey, don't start on me, okay? I just don't like to see you like this.'

I sigh. The funny thing is that despite everything, Jamal married me. I mean, he didn't have to, especially not when I looked like this. I'm someone else now, inside out. Ever since moving to Lahore, I have discovered the joy of YouTube and found many women who have suffered the same fate as myself. Their bright smiles and optimism don't fool me one bit. Staged, all of it. I know exactly what it feels like to have your face robbed away from you. I see the way those kind society ladies cringe when they see me. They're good at hiding it though, for some of the victims hardly notice. They're bored but kind-hearted housewives out to do some good in the world. But I see that involuntary cringe, the averted gave, and that makes me want to stab them with something sharp. I didn't ask to look like this, and I certainly didn't ask for their help. What makes them think they can come prancing into the privacy of my home and ask all these invasive questions about my life, nodding and shaking their heads at the right moments. I've tried to catch them off guard with tricky questions, but they're so meticulously coached that they don't falter. I see them wrinkle their nose at the tea I serve them, the way they pretend to sip at it before setting the cup down. The way they sit on the edge of the seats ready to make a run for it, as if my damaged face is a contagion that could catch them if they're not careful.

'And what happened to your brothers?' they never fail to ask me.

What do you think, I want to shoot back, but I refrain from doing that. Jamal tries his best, but he has another family to feed, and with a job as a secretary's assistant at some useless office, it means that he can barely make ends meet. So that's where I come in, feeding my story to these rich society ladies, making sure I cry at the correct times, holding my scarf to my one working eye, leaving them to gape at the other obliterated one.

I once caught one of them taking my picture from her phone. She thought she was being discreet, but I could see the camera reflecting off her reading glasses. It almost made me laugh.

Jamal picks up my scarf from the ground, and covers

my head with it. 'Why do I always find this on the ground?' he asks, holding up an edge of the scarf. 'A dupatta is a woman's jewel.'

'I must look a fright without it, so I'm not surprised you grab every opportunity to cover me with it.'

Jamal rolls his eyes. 'Please—'

'Am I that good in bed that you're willing to overlook this face? I mean I had no idea. I think I deserve a standing ovation for my sexual charms.' I spread my arms. 'Hideous old me saddled with poor, handsome Jamal.'

I can tell that he wants to hit me. But the question is, where. I see him hesitate, and I smile in triumph. He always makes the mistake of thinking I'm too weak, and I let him. He is ever so careful not to touch any of the damaged flesh, bestowing all his kisses on the other side of my face. He thinks I don't notice, but I notice everything. If there is one thing this mutilation has brought me, it's perspective. That is how I deduced the true feelings of those repulsive society ladies. The old me would have lapped up all the attention.

Jamal's face is red with repressed anger. I want to play with all that fire, but I don't.

'Quit feeling sorry for yourself,' he manages to choke out from between tight lips. 'I am sick of this pity party. I work all day to put food on the table, and what do I get in return? Contempt?'

I want to remind him about who really puts food on the table (me!), but I let it go. Another feather in my cap. I neutralize my face with a subtle smile, and turn toward him.

'You're right, of course. Don't mind me, I was just being silly. Let's have dinner and I can tell you all about my interview with those society ladies today.'

That always brightens his mood. His mind equates the ladies with money, and why not? I have a wad of five-hundred-rupee notes nestled in my bra, a gift from the ladies for the interview this morning.

After Jamal slithers off me that night, I run a hand over the damaged part of my face. It never ceases to amaze me that

I don't sweat from that side. My entire body may be as slick as a seal's, but this part of my face is the same as always. It used to creep me out, but now it just fascinates me. I think of my three brothers, and wonder if they ever think of what they've done. I lie to the society ladies when I tell them that they regret it.

The truth is that they're rather proud of it. In the end, they just got away scot free. Nobody charged them for committing this crime as it had been done in the name of honour, and by the time I was lucid enough to talk about the incident, my anger had cooled.

At first, the anger had festered in me for weeks as I battled the pain and disbelief. I wanted to carve out their faces with a knife and feed their eyes to the crows. I wanted to rip their chests open and smash their hearts of stone, for I was convinced that they didn't – couldn't – have human hearts. What kind of brothers could inflict such unimaginable pain on their own sister? There were times when I questioned my own behaviour and rationalized my brothers' actions, but no matter how much I tried to humanize them, the fact remained that they were animals, savage beasts who had ruined me for life. But in the end, family is family. No matter what. My father would have been proud of me for forgiving them.

A solitary tear escapes my good eye, and I rudely rub it away. 'Do not feel sorry for yourself' – this was something I had promised myself the moment I had seen my swollen bandaged face in the mirror for the first time. A storm had raged inside, but I was determined not to let out a single tear from my good eye, and much to the surprise of the doctors and Jamal, I had succeeded. But, sometimes, that traitorous sadness just seeps in like cold into the bones.

Just as I am nodding off, Jamal starts snoring. I give him a good kick in the shins. I giggle as he wakes up with a yelp. I bet his good first wife would never dare. That's why she's in the village and I'm in the city, sleeping by his side, making love every night. There is no room in this world for the weak.

This deformed, defiant mess of a woman has somehow

trumped that normal and deferential wife Jamal has left behind in the village. That in itself is a victory.

The society ladies have managed to get their hands on some kind of plastic surgeon. The fat one – Shabnam – enunciated the word plastic very carefully as if I were an idiot. 'P-l-a-s-t-i-c surgeon. That's a doctor that fixes faces. He works in America, but he's visiting Pakistan and we have convinced him to take a look at you. He's pulled off miracles, I tell you.'

Pfft. Gone are the days when I used to believe in miracles.

There was a pause during which I realized that Shabnam was waiting for me to offer some sort of thanks. The conceited dear, bless her. Out of curiosity, if nothing else, I said my thanks, and quizzed her more about the doctor. She went on and on, dutiful as ever.

It's a farce, an elaborate scheme devised to exploit the pockets of these poor ladies, but I'm not too worried. If the doctor shares some of the spoils with me, I'm completely willing to go along with the lie. I'll even amp up the makeup to make the improvements look convincing.

I smile as I shift myself away from Jamal, nestling my face deep into the pillow. Being damaged goods isn't all that bad.

ABOUT AWAIS KHAN

Awais Khan is a graduate of the University of Western Ontario and Durham University. He has studied Creative Writing at Faber Academy in London. He is the author of the critically acclaimed bestseller, *In the Company of Strangers* (published by Simon & Schuster, Isis Audio and The Book Guild). *No Honour*, his second novel, is published by Orenda Books. He has given lectures on creative writing at Durham University, American University in Dubai, Canadian University in Dubai, United States Educational Foundation of Pakistan etc.

His work has appeared in *The Aleph Review*, *The Hindu*, *Missing Slate*, *MODE*, The News International, *Daily Times* etc.

He has appeared on BBC World Service, Dubai Eye, Voice of America, Cambridge Radio, Samaa TV, PTV Home, City 42, SpiceFM etc.

He is represented by Annette Crossland at A for Authors Agency Ltd London.

THE WAY OF ALL FLESH

Raven Dane

London October 1940

Celia was oblivious to the visceral reek of blood, flesh and offal and the large kitchen of her seventeenth century Islington townhouse was no stranger to butchery. The white marble slabs had known many great, bloody haunches of beef and pork for the lavish feasts of the past. A woman's work was never done, she smiled to herself as she separated ribs with her cleaver with practised skill and accuracy – and strength. She was not a brawny woman nor in the first flush of youth but each swing brought the wide knife clean through flesh and bone.

The sonorous tones of a chiming grandfather clock in the hallway reminded her she needed to change for work. There was a war on and her driving skills were needed urgently. Removing her gore-stained apron, she tidied up her afternoon's butchery and cleaned herself up with the usual sense of irony. At the end of her night on duty, her appearance would be far more bloodied.

The blackout had already begun as she carefully negotiated the narrow steps down to the street in the gathering gloom but to her annoyance, her neighbour, an interfering busybody of a man offered to help her. 'Mind how you go, Miss Stephens,' reaching out to take her heavy tapestry carpet bag, 'no need to struggle with that.'

It took all her carefully acquired personal skills to remain polite, squeezing out a grudging smile from her pale, plain features.

'Mr Benson, you are as always so gallant. But this is

nothing, just some clothes for when I go off duty. I'll be carrying around much heavier things during the night.'

The reminder of her wartime voluntary occupation made the man shudder and with a polite tip of his hat, Benson disappeared into the night with hurried footfall. *Damn the little wretch*, Celia cursed to herself, he was always snooping around, she could see him hide behind twitching curtains every time she left her home, day or night. Too old to fight, yet young enough to contribute, why wasn't he doing something else for the war effort? To make her mood worse, leaving home after nightfall and the blackout was totally out of character for the man. Celia fumed as she threw the carpet bag onto the front seat of her car and drove off, curbing a strong impulse to run down the interfering neighbour. The nightly bombing would start soon and Benson usually preferred the comfort of his private air raid shelter built in his garden, damn the man for doing something different that night.

Still in a foul mood, she arrived at the ambulance depot where she would exchange her old Austin Seven Swallow for an ambulance. In a city already crowded with ghosts, Celia could move unseen, unnoticed and unremarkable against a hellish backdrop of human carnage, blazing buildings and chaos. Nothing made the woman stand out, she was small, middle aged, an already dumpy figure made shapeless by her navy boiler suit uniform, her gender further disguised by an over large civil defence beret pushed down over her short brown hair, still bobbed in the women's style of the 1920's. Later if or more likely when the German bombs fell from the sky, she replaced the beret with an equally unbecoming tin helmet. People ignored her, which was exactly how she liked it.

With casualties so high, the movement of an ambulance driver was never questioned, Celia had the freedom of a Blitz blasted London and she had never been happier. Most nights now, she ferried the dead and the dying to morgues and hospitals, casualties of the bombing. Though not all of them were victims of the Blitz. Sometimes she added to the death toll from the Nazis with victims of her own choosing. War was most convenient, it had turned London into a personal playground for Celia Anne Stephens, spinster of the parish, allowing her full rein to act on her most savage impulses and get away with them.

Not complete bodies though, Celia had realised early on that even in the nightly madness and horror, order ended up on the winning side. There was always a bureaucrat who liked to tag, process and inventory all the corpses – officially for the loved ones to claim and mourn over of course. Celia decided it was just another form of trainspotting, nothing more than a hobby for those who loved making lists. Everyone had their own pleasures … those men, too old or weak to fight in the war collected names and statistics, spivs collected late night company. Celia collected trophies from those she killed. Nothing incriminating like obvious personal belongings and ration books or perishable like fingers or ears. A button would do or a hair ribbon as long as not blood stained. With so many victims, she liked to keep her own personal tally. It was good for a woman of her age to have a little hobby.

Luckily for her, bombs were no respecters of the human form, shattered bones, scattered limbs, charred flesh, all of which she cheerfully gathered together in rubber body bags as part of her official duties, occasionally adding a few extras along the way. It was easy … far too easy and she was already bored.

It had been fun at first, Celia's homely appearance and comforting manner put people at ease, particularly as Londoners were under so much stress, when living or dying has become a macabre nightly lottery. Her earliest victims had not been chosen randomly either, she was easily vexed and that was enough to mark them as hers. The parsimonious grocer who cheated on her cheese ration with a tiny sliver of mouldy cheddar, the bully of a housewife who pushed in front of her in a long queue for bread. But she had tired of such easily won victories. Celia liked a challenge.

After the early killing spree palled, she had chosen

victims who would be missed, stalwart vicars who kept their communities together as they rallied in the Underground station bomb shelters, brave soldiers on leave. This too only entertained her for a short time, the thrill was too short-lived, the ease in which she could escape detection was by too high a margin. Celia knew she was too clever, too cunning to betray her predation by any clumsy actions or a moment of reckless negligence. She had no fear of the hangman's noose, convinced anyone of equal intellect to her was too busy fighting the war in intelligence or scientific divisions. Such minds were too valuable to the war effort to waste, that left only the lame and halt to man the police services, she could run rings around the lot of them.

She had pondered this latest frustration all day when off duty. What could she do now to quell her restless spirit, challenge her intellect and satisfy her need to spill blood? As she drove through the dark, emptying streets to an ambulance rallying point near King's Cross station, she thought further on her revelation while in the kitchen wielding her cleaver like some legendary Amazonian she-warrior. She would kill someone of exalted status next … no more annoying housewives or irksome vicars. Celia was ready to aim high. Why not Prime Minister Churchill or one of the Royal Family and achieve something the wretched and clumsy Nazis could not? The thought spread a rare, cold but genuine smile to light up her doughy face.

The evening progressed with a relentless grim monotony, air raid sirens screeched their warning, search lights lit up the sky as the anti-aircraft guns straked the overhead death bringers in their droning craft. Celia was soon fully employed picking up and ferrying the wounded to safety, only when the night's bombing ended and dawn lit up the carnage would she help with the grim task of clearing up the bodies. Weary and filthy, her face grimy with ash, brick dust and blood, she sat with the other rescue workers back at the depot, drinking strong black tea from an enamel mug. Someone passed a small bottle of brandy around to give the tea a much appreciated extra kick.

'Any word from your cousin in the country?'

An old driver addressed her in a low whisper, glancing around in case the transaction was overheard, the black market took many forms and not just operated by spivs and criminal gangs. Celia nodded and fetched the tapestry bag from the back of her car and furtively handed out the grease paper parcels of fresh pork to the others. Better for them to remember her as a kindly woman, who helped keep hard working volunteers and their families well fed despite the risk of arrest. Better they believed she had connections with a pig farming relative in the country.

Once back home, she was unable to sleep despite her extreme fatigue, the death toll had been heavy that night, her arms and back ached from lifting so many corpses and body parts. She lit a small fire, made herself comfortable on an over-stuffed sofa and pondered over her next adventures. Getting information on the movements of important people was near impossible in war time … German spies were said to have infiltrated the population, careless talk cost lives, walls had ears. She rose, crossed the room and turned on the radio to hear what she already knew, reports of the night's dreadful bombing of London's heavily populated East End which had led to so many casualties.

The sharp light of sudden revelation made her gasp as fate and destiny revealed themselves. The opportunity to cause devastation had never been so easily given and so began a new predatory pattern in her cold, calculating mind. The much loved Queen Consort, Elizabeth would visit the Blitz-ravaged East End as she had before, boosting morale and showing solidarity with her people. What a perfect target. Celia did not care how long it would take to get close to the Queen, this would not be a victim of impulse and opportunity but careful and reasoned stalking. The risks and danger she was prepared to put herself into where phenomenal, Celia had never been so excited in her life.

By night, Celia continued her role as an ambulance

woman but worked hard not to draw attention to herself by distributing any more meat deliveries from her country cousin or murdering any ordinary people. This had lost all pleasure for her now. By day, after a short sleep, Celia would walk the two miles deeper into the East End, past crowds gawping at new bombsites and others on London streets carrying on as if there wasn't a war on. She spent many hours at corner tea rooms listening to the gossip around her, gaining local knowledge and listening to rumours. A German spy would have a field day as people cheerfully ignored the ever present posters warning to take care with all conversation in public.

After three uneventful weeks, her patience and persistence paid off. She was exhausted from a particularly gruelling on duty night when the East End was hammered with brutal Luftwaffe efficiency. Celia had heard shocked talk among the ambulance crews of a particularly disastrous hit on an air raid shelter during her hours on duty but she was not assigned to that area and knew no details. She shook off the fatigue and went back to the East End, wandering the streets, listening for news.

Celia felt a ripple of excitement growing on the streets. The King and Queen were visiting Stoke Newington that afternoon. Celia was currently in Bethnal Green, so getting to the royal appointment was easy, just a bus ride away. Her fingers reached into her handbag, reassuringly touching her weapon of choice, a sharp penknife … harmless enough unless wielded by a ruthless expert. Someone who could find a way to get close enough and melt away through the ensuing chaos unnoticed and unsuspected.

The crowds on the streets levelled by the horrific destruction were even larger and more chaotic than Celia could ever hope for, people pushing and shoving to get a glimpse of the royal couple and their entourage. The more ghoulish wanting to gawp at the scene of the night's latest terrible disaster, a direct hit on an underground shelter with the loss of over two hundred souls.

Dressed like an ordinary East End housewife, her hair

hidden by a dowdy brown headscarf, the same colour as an old raincoat she'd acquired from the wreckage of a home the night before, Celia blended in with practised perfection. She quietly barged her way to the front of the crowds, ruthless determination adding strength to her elbows and shin-kicking feet.

What police were there to protect the royal visitors were already overwhelmed and far too few in number to control the excited crowd. Celia felt another surging sense of destiny and fulfilment fill her soul with joy, everything had fallen into place to aid her deadly mission. She only had to make her kill and escape without detection to succeed. She could not fail.

The pushing and shoving became increasingly manic as the royals' black cars pulled up beside the still smoking ruins of buildings and the deep crater where the victims had lost their lives. Workers had done their best to remove signs of human loss, but Celia could smell it … the dust and debris laden air reeked with the unique blend of torn and charred flesh and boiled blood. Without knowing it, royals and subjects alike were breathing in the evaporated remains of bomb victims. Celia's experience as an ambulance driver made her believe there were still bodies unrecovered in the wreckage and the remains of many of the lost would never be recovered.

Clad in dove grey silk, the Queen stood out despite her diminutive stature, a woman with natural presence and charisma, her tears silenced and stilled the crowd as she stood next to her husband, heads bowed low in respect to the dead. Not yet, Celia whispered, the sombre spell would soon break and the crowds would surge again … all she had to do is add some element of panic and the police and royal party would be overwhelmed. She inched forward, closer and closer, relieved all focus was on the moving scene of monarch and people together in silent shock and grief.

Her fingers reached into her handbag, felt for and found the red-handled penknife, such a small instrument for creating a catastrophe to shock and traumatise this little war-torn land

and its vast, sprawling empire ... So close now, she could distinguish the Queen's delicate floral fragrance among the foul carnal stench of disaster.

Celia's grunted in pain as an iron grip seized her right elbow and superior strength steered her away from her target. Another man caught her other arm and together they hauled her away from the crowds and into a nearby alley between two ruined terraces. The police? No. Officers of His Majesty's Constabulary didn't wear such overpowering cheap cologne. The first man was short in stature, burly with no perceivable neck, his coarse features partially hidden by the brim of his hat. The other was tall, weedy but deceptively strong, weasel features with the added vanity of a carefully cultured needle thin moustache. Their outer clothing of faded tan rain coats were shabby but both men wore silk shirts and jewelled tie pins.

'We've wasted many hours following you, lady. Our boss is running out of patience, not something you'd like to provoke.'

She knew she could scream, send police and onlookers rushing to her aid against these cheap thugs but she needed to know what they wanted of her first.

'You must have the wrong person, gentlemen ... why would anyone follow me?'

'Nothing personal, lady,' replied the skinny man with a smile closer to a leer, 'but business is business and you have a commodity, our boss wants to have a share in.'

Common black market criminals. Nothing more. Celia's disappointment as the loud cheering announced the departure of the royals, grew to fury, robbed of her most spectacular trophy kill by these greedy fools. How they knew about her fresh meat supplies was of no interest now, all it would take was for one ambulance driver's wife to be a gossip. Cornered, she knew she could take them both on, unaware of her strength and murderous skills but there were too many witnesses and with the royal party gone, too many police now hanging around, keeping looters and ghouls from the

112

bombsite.

'If he makes it worthwhile, I can send plenty of 'commodity' his way, I am expecting a fresh delivery tonight. Actually, I welcome his interest, save me having to get the stuff shifted on my own.'

Surprised and relieved, the two men's mood softened and they backed off. The burly man's fat creased face broke into a horrible rictus approximation of a smile.

'That's right, lady. It's just business, we all have to get through this bastard war the best we can.'

'Indeed we do. As you have been following me, I take it you already know where I live. Meet me at my home at ten tonight and you can get the first delivery, some lovely fresh pork, really good quality. I promise you, gentlemen, your boss will not be disappointed.'

The weasel clenched his fingers into a fist and held it close to her face, 'Don't you even think of double-crossing us, missus. First sign of a rozzer and it will be a one way journey to Hackney Marshes in a sack for you.'

Celia managed a smile though her own fingers were itching to take out her knife and cut his scrawny throat from ear to ear.

'That would be pointless and stupid. I'm in this racket up to my ears, if you go down, so will I.'

That seemed to satisfy them though the thin man's small eyes were narrowed with suspicion. This encounter had been too easy. Celia walked away briskly, deliberately passing close to a group of constables to show she had no intention of giving up the spivs and returned home by bus. Inevitably, Benson was noting her return, thinking the heavy drapes of his curtains hid him from her view. *Idiot.* How could she not spot his pale, moon face and the glint of the late afternoon sun shining off his wire-rimmed glasses? Time to surprise him with the offer of tea and homemade cake at her home, a kindly invite from a neighbour, a spinster, who also lived alone and knew how lonely life could be …

Ten o'clock arrived and went, Celia became nervous

they wouldn't arrive or she would be raided by the police, alerted by a tip off from an informer. But by eleven, the spivs had turned up at the back kitchen door and carted away heavy boxes of carefully prepared and wrapped meat with the promise of payment of her share once it had been sold. Celia did not care, she would not see a penny of her of cut. No matter, she didn't need the money and new adventures beckoned on the horizon ... time to move on ...

That night, the ambulance patrol was short a driver ... and Miss Stephens never returned. Maybe she had tragically become another unidentified victim of the heavy, relentless bombing. Such a shame, the quiet, dumpy little woman was so dedicated, a hard worker and remarkably unsqueamish when it came to gathering up body parts. And she did have that oh so generous farmer cousin in the country.

ABOUT RAVEN DANE

Raven Dane is a UK based author of dark fantasy, steampunk novels and horror short stories. Her first books were the dark fantasy *Legacy of the Dark Kind* trilogy, *Blood Tears*, *Blood Lament* and *Blood Alliance*. These were followed by a High Fantasy spoof, *The Unwise Woman of Fuggis Mire*.

Her steampunk novels so far are the award-winning *Cyrus Darian and the Technomicron* and sequels *Cyrus Darian and the Ghastly Horde* and *Cyrus Darian and the Wicked Wraith*. She has had many short stories published, including one in a celebration of forty years of the British Fantasy Society and in international horror anthologies. These have included *Tales of the Lake 2*, alongside Richard Chizmar, Ramsey Campbell, Tim Lebbon and Jack Ketchum. She also had a story in Billie Sue Mosiman's *Frightmare, Women Write Horror,* which was shortlisted for a prestigious Bram Stoker award in 2016. She has also appeared in two international lists of best female horror writers.

In 2013, she was signed up by Telos Publishing for her collection of Victorian ghost stories, *Absinthe and Arsenic* and in

2015, the alternative history/ supernatural novel, *Death's Dark Wings*. All the *Cyrus Darian* books are with Telos now in new editions.

A lifelong *Doctor Who* fan, Raven was delighted and honoured to be part of the script team on a spin off film, *The Daemons of Devil's End* by Reeltime Pictures in 2017. She also contributed to the novelisation of the film, published by Telos.

Raven brought out a horror novella, *The Bane of Bailgate* in 2018.

A new novella set in a chaotic, dystopian future, *The House of Wrax*, was launched by Demain Publishing in mid-November, 2019.

AND HERE'S THE NEXT CLUE ...

Amy Myers

Mr Percy Pip had always yearned to be a crime writer. From his careful study of how to break into the market with an eye-catching potential best-seller, he realised that two obstacles lay in his path to stardom. The first was his name, which if displayed in large lettering across the dust-jacket would not instantly attract an enthusiastic readership. The second was somewhat more of a problem. He had learned that rule number 1 in achieving one's goal was to write about what you knew, but so far Percy had never committed a murder.

Percy Pip therefore took steps to remedy both of his shortcomings. Firstly, he selected a nom de plume for his new occupation. This would be part-time of course, since rule no. 2 for crime writing was not to give up the day job. When he became a household name, he might reconsider this decision but until then his employers could be reassured of his loyalty, especially as his job dovetailed nicely with his criminal purposes.

Secondly, he began to make meticulous preparations for his first murder. Unfortunately, this would have to be the first of several, since rule number 3, so it appeared from his perusal of booksellers' crime sections, was that a serial killer was an essential feature. The golden days of the lone murder, or even of two (permitted in order to keep the investigation going for 256 pages), were long since over. No, three had to be the minimum, with the necessary clues, preferably gruesome, to indicate that a series was in progress.

'What do you mean, crime scene?'

Dr Jonathan Fuller, the director of Mystery Unravelled: Crime-writing Courses Ltd., looked aghast. He had put on several successful workshops all over the country without the intervention of a corpse, and his distress hovered between his own position and wondering who amongst his current group might be a real-life murderer. Janice Dove's dead body had just been removed from the hotel, having been found in her room by his assistant Mavis Sharp, after Janice had failed to appear for breakfast. Since then the workshop's peaceful discussion of the criminal viewpoint in fiction had given way to an all too real influx of police, doctors, and scientists clad in white crime scene suits.

'Just routine, sir,' the investigating officer said reassuringly. 'Suspicious death, you see.'

'But surely it was a heart attack or perhaps food poisoning,' Jonathan croaked. 'The staff ...'

'Poisoning's possible,' was the not so reassuring reply. 'Was anyone else taken ill?'

'Not to my knowledge. After dinner at 7.30 some people prefer to go their own way or retire early,' Jonathan explained, 'but I heard nothing mentioned at breakfast about ill effects.'

Jonathan's weekend courses took place in hired conference facilities in a country house hotel in varied locations. In the current one, in Suffolk, the facilities had seemed the best yet, with his party of two dozen completely separated from the rest of the guests, although this, he realised, would focus the investigation on his own pupils. After all, Janice Dove was known from previous courses to several of the participants here. Many of them were around him now, eager, no doubt, to pick up such gems of police procedure as they could. He found himself automatically answering the inspector's questions. No, this was not the first workshop that Miss Dove had attended. Yes, she was an aspiring writer.

'Such a gift,' he added weakly. 'She showed me her latest rejection slip, on which the agent had written *a personal encouraging comment.*'

The inspector was not interested in rejection slips. 'We'll need all the information you have on Miss Dove. Do you know what she ate for dinner?'

Jonathan looked uncertain. 'I expect it was the stew. It was a buffet. We were moving around – little tables, you know the sort of thing. Most people – '

'Fish,' one of his group, Paul Merlin, interrupted firmly. 'Janice chose the fish. It had *prawns* in it.'

'She had stew,' Mavis Sharp retorted equally firmly. 'I saw this morning that Janice had been sick. It was *stew*, and plum crumble, I think.'

'Sharp of eye as well as by name, eh?' the inspector said jovially. 'You found the body, didn't you?'

'I did.' Mavis looked modest. 'Of course my profession helps.' She was the author of six lurid whodunits, one of which had actually received a review in a newspaper.

'We make a strong team. Miss Sharp is cosy, whereas I am hardboiled,' Jonathan explained, receiving a strange look for his pains.

'The two types of crime novel,' Mavis explained briskly. 'The Agatha Christie school versus the tough brigade.'

The inspector's brow cleared. 'Rebus!'

As a hat had been thrown into the ring, Mavis felt the need to distance herself from the cosier cosies. 'Of course I am in the *modern* Agatha Christie school.'

Another strange look, this time for Mavis. The inspector decided to move on. 'And you were all strangers to each other?' He cast a glance over the crowd before him.

'No.' Jonathan steeled himself to speak for his little flock. 'The venue and subject matter of these workshops change, but their value is so great that some of my students come to more than one. I believe there are about eight regulars here today.'

To Jonathan's eye they all still looked unlikely candidates for the role of murderer, and none of them so far as he knew had had any close relationship with Janice Dove, who was in her fifties and hardly likely to catch the eye of an idealistic crime writer looking for a model moll.

Among the eight three were prominent in terms of potential troublemakers, in Jonathan's opinion. One was David Patterson, an ex-policeman in his forties, who assumed his experience was an automatic gateway to publication. He wrote with enthusiasm, but the result, unfortunately, was not fiction. His stories were turgid dollops of 'I proceeded north-west in an easterly direction'.

Paul Merlin was in his early sixties at a guess, an accountant on the point of retiring, with an over-absorbing interest in what he called the psychological approach and Jonathan privately termed the sex-obsessed. He was the ferret breed of student, anxious to display his own superior knowledge while at the same time to winkle out every last drop of knowledge that might be lurking in the recesses of his instructor's mind.

Luke Hayward was twenty-nine, and a teacher with what seemed such a fanatical dislike of teaching that it was clear what drove him onwards towards the promised land of crime writing. A bad teacher, Jonathan decided, the sort who would demolish his pupils in order to rebuild them in his own image. Jonathan prided himself on his ability to pick out the achievers in his audience, a gift acquired from the auctions he conducted in his other occupation. Achievers were those whose willpower would drive them onwards, no matter what the opposition, and no matter whether they were Eton-schooled, state-schooled or unschooled. The chief achiever of the assembled company around him, including Mavis, would in his estimation be Paul Merlin, although he never underestimated the power of the non-achiever to throw a spanner in the works.

'I'm extremely sorry about Janice,' Paul told him

earnestly. 'A terrible thing to die amongst strangers.'

'We weren't strangers,' Luke immediately objected. 'We'd all met before.'

'Yes, but we didn't know each other on a personal basis,' Mavis quickly pointed out. Miss Marple always remained detached from her suspects.

'What did kill her?' Jonathan asked, after the inspector had vanished and they were being ushered back towards their own secluded workshop room for interrogation.

David almost visibly swelled with pride. 'We won't know until the autopsy report.'

'*We?*' Luke picked up sarcastically. 'Didn't know you were with the Suffolk police.'

David scowled. 'Once a policeman, always a policeman.'

'I dislike being treated as though we were all potential murderers,' Paul muttered as a gimlet-eyed policewoman opened the door for them to enter. 'How do they know she didn't take the stuff herself?'

'What stuff?' Luke pounced, as he would on an unfortunate sixth-former. 'How do you know it was poison?'

'Even if it was,' David said, 'it could have been an accident.'

Mavis drew herself up. 'It could not.'

'How—' David began.

'Because there was a distinctive supermarket plastic bag at her side full of some prickly fruit, a knife and spoon, a packet of disposable plastic gloves, and an open window and—'

'Still could have been an accident or suicide,' David interrupted, annoyed at being outranked by a woman.

'And—' Jonathan prompted Mavis to continue.

'A peppermill taped to her chest.'

There was a certain camaraderie about the Mystery Unravelled crime writing course, held three months later and on this occasion in a Hampshire manor house. Those participants who had attended the previous course, five in all, enjoyed an enviable position so far as the somewhat nervous but excited newcomers were concerned, as they were able to speak with first-hand knowledge of a real life crime scene.

David in particular came into his own, having come by privileged information gained by bribing former colleagues with beer, flattery and, regrettably, twenty-pound notes.

Even Mavis condescended to listen avidly, as they awaited lunch on the Saturday morning. 'So what did poor Janice die of?' she asked.

'Hyoscyamine,' David replied smugly. 'Datura seeds grated in the peppermill over, probably, the stew. Clever, wasn't it? I understand there's no forensic evidence to indicate anyone else was involved.'

'So it could have been suicide,' Paul said triumphantly.

'Rather a let-down,' Luke sneered, but was disregarded.

'Then why bother to tape the pepper mill on?' David grunted. 'Daft. I'm just a straightforward cop. Something like that happens in old Agatha's stuff, not in real life.'

Mavis took this personally. 'Only in this case, it did,' she snapped.

'Still suicide,' Paul maintained, anxious to maintain his lead. 'A killer couldn't guess exactly when she would die in order to creep in to attach the pepper mill.'

'The first person to find her could,' Luke said meaningfully. Mavis had criticised the best short story he had ever written. And he knew why: she intended to steal his plot.

Mavis quelled him with a look. 'I knew your thinking was wobbly, Luke, but *really*! Would I go along to Janice's room armed with a pepper mill to check if my victim were dead and then stop to tape it on in order to draw attention to the fact that it was murder?'

Luke rallied. 'Agatha might have done.'

She capped him. 'Agatha always had a rational explanation. I doubt if you do.'

David entered the fray. 'Of course, I'm just a plain cop, but in my experience, the first on the scene often *is* the killer.'

Paul switched tack to leap on the passing bandwagon. 'It's the psychology.'

'Why,' Mavis boomed savagely over him, 'should *anyone* wish to tape a peppermill on to a victim?'

'It's easy,' Paul persevered. 'In the interests of her – or of course his – art.' Two and two for a retiring accountant were permitted to make five.

'Eh?' David looked blank.

'To test us all,' Paul explained. 'If you understood the sexual perspective – '

'Balderdash,' David interrupted. 'It was a joke.'

Mavis seized her chance. 'As I explained in this morning's workshop, the death itself should *never* be a joke. A pepper mill comes perilously close to it.'

The workshop students took this to heart, and the pepper mill at the buffet lunch remained untouched either by hand or in conversation. The wine bottles fared much better. They were all emptied and five more called for, and consequently when the students reassembled for the afternoon workshop, they were some way into discussion of the intricacies of the protagonist's responsibility towards readers before Charles Beeton, one of the five regulars, was missed.

'He'll be here somewhere,' Jonathan said anxiously. 'He's probably fallen asleep.' Charles was a gentleman of mature years and girth, and after the lunch they had all enjoyed, this explanation seemed highly likely. 'But I'll check his room to be on the safe side.' When he arrived, however, he found it unlocked, but empty.

Mavis was not so lucky. En route to the ladies' room in the basement, she stumbled over Charles's dead body. Her scream could be heard by the group in the workshop, growing ever louder as she rushed back to summon help. 'Attack,' she gasped, as she reached the room, panting for breath. 'He's dead. Chest.'

'A heart attack?' Jonathan caught her words as he returned from his fruitless errand, and joined the rush downstairs, already reaching for his mobile phone.

'Attack on the heart certainly,' Luke said soberly, as he reached the body and saw what awaited them. David immediately felt for a pulse, but without success. A knife was protruding from Charles's chest, and Jonathan could not avoid seeing something else too.

Not only was there a distinctive-looking plastic supermarket bag at Charles's side, but another knife, shiny and clean, was carefully taped to his sweater.

'Don't touch the bag,' David ordered, as Luke peered curiously into it. 'Evidence.'

In his element, David took charge, seizing Jonathan's mobile to summon the police; he then deputed Mavis, Jonathan and himself to guard the body while the others should remain together in the workshop room. Any visits to the toilets would be accompanied, according to sex, by himself, Mavis or Jonathan.

The crime scene manager of the police team that speedily arrived fully agreed that the plastic bag was evidence. Inside was a pair of man's shoes, an old-fashioned plastic mac that appeared slightly stained with blood, and another packet of disposable gloves. The shiny knife too, he agreed, was evidence though its purpose naturally eluded him, as the knife that killed Charles was declaring its presence so obviously.

'What on earth was the second knife for?' Luke asked, a trifle shakily, after they had been dismissed from the crime scene and rejoined the other students round the table in the workshop room.

'The first one's easier to understand,' David said ponderously. 'Removing it would have covered the killer in blood.'

'But the second?' Luke persisted.

'I think I can guess,' Paul said, with what he hoped was quiet authority.

'Psychologically they carry a sexual implication?' enquired Luke innocently.

Paul stiffened. 'It could be,' he replied defensively. 'However, I am inclined to think these are deodands.' He looked round at their blank faces, and added modestly, 'As a solicitor, I have a knowledge of legal history.'

'I thought everyone knew what they were,' Luke immediately put in. 'They're relicts of medieval law which held that the object was a guilty party in the crime and as such forfeit to the crown, sometimes being passed to the victim's family in compensation.'

'Quite,' Paul said patronisingly. 'Not repealed until the middle of the nineteenth century, when a rail company objected to forfeiting one of their express trains. In the case of poor Janice and now Charles, the peppermill and the knife are to be held responsible for their deaths.'

'Try telling that to the Old Bailey,' David snorted. 'No way. It's a copy-cat murder. You'll see.'

They did. Or rather the Kent police did. This time, excluding Jonathan and Mavis, the number of regulars was down to three: David, who said he had a duty to be present because as an ex-policeman he could keep an eye on things; Paul, who was set on proving his deodand theory; and Luke who was set on disproving anything that anyone else suggested.

Jonathan had considered whether it would be wise to hold this course at all, but he had been heartened to find there was no such thing as bad publicity. So numerous were the applications from newcomers that he was forced to turn students away. Mavis Sharp had hesitated about instructing at another course, but on discovering that her young friend Beatrice Worthy wished to sign up she decided she would join her. Unfortunately on arrival at the Kentish hotel, she quickly discovered that Beatrice's motives for wishing to come were mixed. Firstly, she wrung Mavis's mind dry of every detail about the murders at which she had been first on the scene. Thereafter, Beatrice devoted her attention to Luke, and from Mavis's glimpse of the canoodling at the rear of the room during the Saturday workshop, she had broadened her sphere of interest.

David, Paul and even Luke (when he could detach himself from Beatrice) were all eager to outdo each other in the 'My theory about the murders' stakes, and the newcomers were equally eager to detect which of the regulars could have been the killer.

It made for an interesting forum, and Mavis, having recovered from the shock of discovering two corpses earlier in the year, was in her element. Her nose twitched continuously with the sharpness the investigating officer had commented on over Janice's death.

Discussion continued almost until dinnertime on the Saturday, and then resumed over the meal. Jonathan had abandoned the buffet approach to dinner, to everybody's obvious relief, after much earlier debate about Janice's murder. With set places, he could more easily keep an eye on everyone's presence and prevent any lone excursions.

However, after dinner, he could exercise no such control. When Luke promulgated an evening walk, Beatrice eagerly accepted. Mavis gently insisted that she should accompany them, but when she returned after powdering her nose, she was annoyed to find that they had left without her. A mistake she told herself firmly, and spent ten minutes chatting to Jonathan, Paul and David before they parted for their separate rooms.

David, through his special knowledge, had told them that the police were as baffled over Charles's murder as over Janice's, even though the Hampshire and Suffolk police forces had consulted their modus operandi files and were in constant contact with each other. Neither the knives nor the plastic mac nor the shoes had revealed any DNA or useful fibres, and thus there seemed little progress, though from time to time one or other of the witnesses was thoroughly grilled.

Jonathan himself had endured several such grillings, which was hardly surprising. After Charles's death, he had feared that the Mystery Unravelled company would be ordered to suspend all further courses, but no such injunction was laid on him although his credit and company details had been checked. What he could not satisfy the police about, naturally enough, was whether any of the participants would have reason to murder any of the others. Was there jealousy over a publishing contract? These students were nowhere near that happy stage, he had explained. Were there any romantic affairs between them? If there were, he would hardly be privy to them, he had reasonably replied. Had he, with his expert knowledge, noticed anything untoward in any of his students' characters, especially the regular ones? Jonathan hesitated over this. Did Luke's edginess or Paul's sexual obsession count? Or David's need to be involved in police work again? He decided not, and did not mention them.

Breakfast on the Sunday morning was a quiet affair with people arriving in ones and twos between 7.30 and 8.30. Some chose to go for a run first 'for inspiration', Luke had explained, since the workshop this morning would be a set exercise of a short criminal story of a thousand words. Others of the group ran nowhere, or in some cases attended early church services. They were fortunate, because it was Luke who therefore came across the dead body of Beatrice Worthy on the woodland path. His white-faced appearance back at the hotel as he blurted out the gruesome details put the latecomers entirely off their Full English breakfasts.

In the all but certain knowledge that this would surely spell the end for Mystery Unravelled courses, if only because no hotel would offer them any facilities in future, Jonathan alerted the police and the hotel manager, and bravely set off with Luke to guard the body. Mavis, rejoicing that it was not she who this time had found poor Beatrice, waited for the arrival of the police.

'Round the next bend,' Luke instructed Jonathan, stopping abruptly on the path. At this stage Jonathan too decided to wait for the police, not sure he could face a corpse again. After their arrival, however, he and Luke followed them cautiously to the scene of the crime, watching from the sidelines as they proceeded with their grim task. Even from where they stood they could glimpse the tongue protruding through blue lips, and blood and froth on the face of what had once been an attractive girl. And even from here they could see the distinctive supermarket plastic bag. They could also see something far more horrible.

Taped to Beatrice's bosom were two severed human hands.

On this occasion by unspoken accord, the workshop was abandoned. No one had the stomach for the intricacies of the psychopathic mind (fictional version) when the factual version was all too prominent in everyone's thoughts. Nor was there much stomach for lunch either, particularly for those most concerned in the investigation: the regulars.

The Kent police were assiduously interviewing every member of the hotel staff, and everyone at the Mystery Unravelled course. In addition to Jonathan and Mavis, particular attention was paid to David, Luke, and Paul as the three present at all the workshops where murders had occurred.

Again, by unspoken accord, most of the group drifted back to the workshop after lunch, as if a black cloud separated it from the rest of humanity. As it was hard for the newcomers to voice any natural speculation as to the guilty party, there was silence reigning in the room when David returned from a trip to the crime scene. There he had successfully managed to infiltrate the crime scene and circulate for ten whole minutes until ejected by the crime scene manager.

'He left his socks in the bag this time,' David told them. 'And the shoes looked much larger than last time. There was a pair of leather gloves, but no disposable ones.'

'So he went barefoot this time?' Luke asked.

'Or had spare socks with him.'

'What else?' Mavis asked, having had the scene fully described to her by Luke. 'An axe?'

Not having been first on the scene, she felt more

objective about this murder, even though it was poor Beatrice. She had her suspicions about this case. Miss Marple always did, and even though Luke was the front runner, David and Paul were still *in the frame*. That phrase pleased her as it showed that she was keeping Agatha's tradition up to date.

'Yes.' David glanced at Mavis's large capable hands. 'But she was strangled manually.'

'So it couldn't have been a woman,' Luke sounded disappointed.

'It could. Sex,' Paul announced darkly.

'Charles wasn't a sex object,' David said scornfully.

'There's sexual jealousy of the young. *And* the change of life,' Paul diagnosed.

Mavis bristled with fury. 'As I explained, Paul, in yesterday's workshop, modern medicine and technology have rendered many crime clichés unusable. Real life has moved on. HRT disposes of such problems far more efficiently than carrying out axe murders.'

'She wasn't murdered by an axe,' Jonathan pointed out in the interests of accuracy. 'The hands were taped on, not the axe.'

Paul nodded solemnly. 'I'm glad you're a convert to my deodand theory, Jonathan.'

Mavis frowned. 'You said the deodand was the object that committed the crime. But the hands were Beatrice's own. They'd been chopped off. Are you saying she strangled herself?' The awfulness of it caught up with her, and she began to weep.

Paul was not to be daunted by tears. 'No, but it's part of the psychology of the killer. We all appear quite normal to each other, but so would the psychopath who committed these murders. Two different faces, one for us, and another one for himself.'

His listeners stirred uneasily, avoiding looking at each other.

Pleased that he had made his point, Paul continued: 'After all, look at Agatha Christie and her famous disappearance. She took time off to pretend she was someone else.'

'But not a psychopath,' Mavis said sharply. 'Poor woman, she was simply – '

'Why?' David cut across the conflict. 'Why the hands at all? It's plain evil.'

'That's just what Miss Marple would have said,' Mavis said, looking at him very carefully.

It was Mavis who by chance did prove to be an achiever after all. Sharp by name and sharp by nature, as the police had said. When she called in at her local police station over a very trifling point of false claims, it was her sheer perseverance and downright bullying that drove them to look into the matter. By subsequent patient tracking of phone records they reached their quarry and then through sheer chance they discovered the murderer of Janice, Charles and Beatrice,

Mr Percy Pip was rudely awakened from a peaceful doze in which he was being presented with the Crime Writers' Diamond Dagger award, and was shattered to find upon his doorstep a CID officer plus a uniformed police constable, holding up ID cards.

'Mr Percy Pip?' And when he nodded, he heard those familiar words: 'We have a warrant here for your arrest …'

Percy's face was ashen. He had been given to understand that all policemen were either Plods and thus easily outfoxed, or drunk and disorderly with severe psychological problems. The three investigating officers he had so far met had given no indications to the contrary. What therefore had gone wrong?

'But there was no forensic evidence,' Percy babbled. 'No DNA. I was most careful. They were, I assure you, the perfect murders. All of them – '

He stopped, aware that they were looking at him in a strange way. 'We'll look into that, sir, now you've mentioned it. Meanwhile, we're here to arrest you on a fraud charge, identity theft.'

Percy Pip couldn't believe it. Caught through the mere matter of providing utility bills, driving licence, etc. to establish bank accounts, signatures, accommodation address and rented office and living space, mostly achieved through one simple house clearance. And, he remembered, a false doctorate.

'The identity theft of the late Mr Jonathan Fuller. I have to warn you....'

ABOUT AMY MYERS

Amy Myers has had short crime stories published in many anthologies and in *Ellery Queen Mystery Magazine*. She is also the author of several series of crime novels, currently the chef Nell Drury mysteries set in a country house in Kent. Before becoming a full-time author she was a director of a London publishing company. Married to an American, charity adviser Jim Myers, she now lives in Kent, where many of her novels are set. Visit her website at amymyers.net

THE TRAP

A A Chaudhuri

'I'm sorry.'

'You've got nothing to be sorry for, Seb.'

'I can't help it. I should be at home with you. Sharing my life with you. You have to believe me, baby, I didn't kill her.'

Seb's wife, Brooke, stared long and hard into his eyes. 'I know, Seb. I know you could never hurt another human being.' Her voice and gaze were steeped in a sincerity that almost took Seb's breath away.

He sighed with relief, reached across the table, placed his fingertips on hers, as if to convey how much he yearned for her touch. But just as he did the prison guard called out, 'No contact!' Reluctantly, Seb slid his hand away. The anguished look on his face told Brooke it was torture having to do so.

'I don't know what happened. How it came to this.'

It was the truth. As a respected City lawyer, with an unblemished record, not even a parking ticket to his name, Seb had never imagined that one day he'd end up in a cell at Wormwood Scrubs prison. But as he looked across the table at Brooke, in the first week of his sixteen-year prison sentence (his barrister had managed to get him a reduced sentence owing to various mitigating circumstances, including no prior record and Seb's stellar reputation at work), he traced it back to that bitingly cold January day. The day his life had rapidly begun to fall apart.

Four months ago

Seb eyed his new wife with concern. She looked so scared. As beautiful, and yet as fragile, as a China doll. She was teetering on the edge, on the brink of falling to pieces, and Seb had never felt so helpless, so sick with worry.

It was chilly inside their flat. He glanced over to the window. Saw that the snow was still falling in thick icy clumps. Over the last twenty-four hours the pipes in the area had frozen, meaning they had no heating or hot water. A shiver ran up his spine, not just because he was cold, but owing to the growing sense of unease he felt on seeing Brooke like this. All because he knew the reason for her disquiet.

They had been married for a little over three months, and so far, it had been nothing short of bliss. He loved Brooke more than life itself. And he knew that she loved him with the same ferocity. They were like two halves of the same coin. Soulmates. He couldn't imagine the honeymoon period ever being over. She constantly told him that he was the man she had been waiting for all her life, that she'd go to the ends of the earth for him, and she hoped that he knew just how much he meant to her. But Seb didn't need her to tell him this. He knew it deep down in his soul, in the pit of his stomach every time she glanced his way, making his heart melt and his insides do somersaults. It was implicit in her every look; in the small gestures she sent his way on a daily basis. That early morning coffee by his bedside. That long, lingering kiss before he went to work. The way she snuggled up to him on the sofa, showing him how safe she felt in his arms.

From the moment he'd first set eyes on her at a friend's housewarming eighteen months ago, he'd wanted to be with her. Despite knowing how wrong that was of him. All because of the hurt it would cause another. A girl he was already engaged to. A girl who also loved him like crazy, who'd always supported him, stayed true to him, someone he could trust to have his back in good times and in bad. Like when he didn't get taken on at the law firm where he trained, resulting in him interviewing at twelve other firms before he finally landed on his feet. Like when he lost his mum to cancer, the lowest point of his life, a time when he'd resorted to pills and alcohol as a means of coping. She was the one who'd been there, brought him out of his depression, stopped him from doing the worst.

Even so, where Brooke was concerned, he couldn't help himself. He simply had to have her.

It wasn't just her beauty that had captivated him. The luscious long dark hair. The almond-shaped caramel eyes, lashes that went on for miles, a bit like her legs. Sure, she had a body most women would die for, but there was also a certain magnetism about her. A unique star quality. Self-confidence seemed to radiate from her, like she knew she was special, knew what she wanted in life and nothing was going to stop her. But not in a conceited way. It came as naturally to her as the sun in the sky, and that's what had turned him on more than anything. As did the fact that they'd seemed to click instantly, as if they'd known each other all their lives. And as she'd stood chatting to some guy at Liam's party, she had happened to glance Seb's way and catch his eye, her own eyes sparkling like the brightest of stars on the clearest of nights, her face breaking into a smile that had seemed to light up the entire room. And from that moment on, he was hers.

She'd only just moved to London from Cornwall. Liam was the manager of a swanky gym in Chelsea and Brooke had recently joined there as a fitness instructor. Seb was a three-year qualified lawyer at the time, with subsidised annual membership of Liam's gym courtesy of his high-flying firm. He and Liam had become good friends over time, which is how he came to be at his housewarming one balmy evening in mid-July. At the time, Seb had been engaged to his university sweetheart, Becky, but her parents had only recently died in a car crash and she still wasn't feeling up to socialising. She had told him to go along without her. He hadn't wanted to, not in her time of need. He'd felt that it would be wrong, insensitive of him to go off and have fun, especially as she had been a rock for him in his darkest moments. But she had practically forced him out of the door. Like she'd wanted to be rid of him for a few hours, craving the space and time to herself.

Since the accident, she'd become distant. An only child, she'd been particularly close to her parents and their sudden death had devastated her. Becky was a pretty girl, with dark hair not unlike Brooke's, although she lacked that femme fatale sexiness that Brooke oozed. Had a wholesome attractiveness about her, rather than Brooke's coquettish beauty. She was intelligent and ambitious, though. And with a great job at Google, she was going places. But she was also kind, and Seb had always thought she'd make a great mum. At least, he had at the time. Back when they were a couple. But he wasn't so sure now.

Because recently, Becky had shown a dark side, a side he feared was of his own making following his whirlwind romance with Brooke, although her parents' death had perhaps added to Becky's alarming personality change. A transformation that was making him increasingly fearful for Brooke's sanity and safety. As well as his own.

'Sweetheart, what's happened now?' They were in the living room. He came closer, gestured to the folded piece of paper on the coffee table in front of Brooke. 'Is it something to do with that?'

Brooke was sitting on one of two chocolate brown leather sofas in their flat in West Hampstead, which was situated on a handsome leafy lane, close to the chic cafes, bars and boutiques of West End Lane. Brooke was leaning forwards, her fingertips resting tentatively on the single sheet of paper. Seb noticed them quiver ever so slightly, knew that whatever she'd read was the cause of her anxiety.

The flat they lived in was the same flat he and Becky had bought together after getting engaged. Nestled on the top floor of a 1920s period conversion, with high ceilings affording it an air of spaciousness and solid oak flooring throughout, it also sported a cute little balcony overlooking the exquisitely maintained communal gardens. Two months after breaking things off with Becky, he'd bought her out. Which hadn't been easy. The guilt had nearly eaten him up. It still did, occasionally. After all, she was the one who'd first seen it advertised on Rightmove. It had been her dream flat, and she'd done the bulk of the decorating, adding those little feminine touches that made a house a home, as the saying went. He, on the other hand, had provided the bulk of the deposit, giving him leverage, also because Brooke herself had fallen in love with the place and had begged him to do what he could to hold onto it. He couldn't say no to her, couldn't bear to let her down. Since coming into his life, he was under her spell, and he always wanted to please her, do whatever made her happy. Also, because, unlike him, she'd been raised by a single mum who'd never made much of an effort to make their home a happy one. She drank too much, Brooke had told him, and would bring back all manner of strange men; men who had never stayed around long enough for Brooke to call them dad.

All the same, he had still felt like a bastard for turfing Becky out. He remembered the look on her face when he'd first told her he'd met someone else, and that it wasn't just a fling. That he was madly in love with her, had to be with her, was going to marry her, and that there was nothing she could say or do to change his mind. She'd tried to reason with him, aghast that he could turn that quickly, act that rashly, break her heart without even listening to what she had to say. But he knew how he felt, knew what his gut, his soul, was telling him. He'd told Becky he'd never in a million years have expected this to happen. But it had. That was life, and his feelings for Brooke were just too strong to repel. He just hoped there were no hard feelings.

'No hard feelings? *You bastard*! I've not long lost my parents, and you're leaving me! For some gym bunny you've barely known five minutes! I won't ever forgive you for this!' He remembered Becky's words as if she'd spoken them yesterday. The coldness in her eyes had sent chills through him. She had a strong, determined character, was the kind of person who'd be loyal to the core once her trust had been earned. But once that trust had been broken, she didn't forgive so easily.

Brooke finally looked up and glanced Seb's way. Her eyes were full of trepidation, like an abandoned child lost and alone, in need of comfort, protection. Seb wanted nothing more than to wrap his arms around her. Just as he had when they'd said their vows on a beach in Mexico, fifteen months on from the moment he'd first locked eyes on her. Her hand still shaking, she slid the piece of paper towards her and off the table, then offered it up to Seb.

His stomach swirled with apprehension as he unfolded it and read what was written:

'I'M COMING FOR YOU, YOU FUCKING JEZEBEL. THERE'S NO ESCAPE. IT'S JUST A MATTER OF TIME.'

Big bold capital letters written in black font.

There was no way of proving who had written it, but Seb had a good idea. As did Brooke. This wasn't the first time they'd received threatening messages.

Since they'd been married, Brooke had received anonymous emails from a sender known as Miss Devoted. The content was always broadly the same. Messages like:

HE'S TOO GOOD FOR YOU, YOU WHORE
YOU STOLE HIM FROM ME, AND I'M GONNA GET HIM BACK
DIE YOU BOYFRIEND STEALER
IF I WERE YOU, I WOULD'T BE ABLE TO SLEEP AT NIGHT
I BET YOUR MOTHER WAS A SLUT LIKE YOU

It had to be Becky. But they had never replied. For fear of goading her further, falling for whatever trap she might be laying for them. Giving her the satisfaction of knowing she had got to them. The last thing they had wanted was to show Becky they were scared or intimidated by her. By ignoring her messages, they had hoped that, with time, the emails would stop, that it was all talk, a bluff, nothing more than that, and Becky would give up and move on. But today was the first time they'd received a handwritten note. Seb recognised Becky's handwriting, so he was certain it was her who had sent it. It seemed that ignoring her had only served to rile her further, and with this latest threat, things were getting way out of hand. Something had to be done.

'What if she comes here when you're not around, Seb? What if she tries to kill me?'

Tears flooded Brooke's eyes, and Seb was filled with a burning rage that consumed him from head to toe. He felt a certain kind of madness, like an untamed animal that couldn't keep still, pacing the kitchen floor, almost feeling like he wanted to kill Becky for terrifying Brooke, making her so miserable. He was disgusted with himself for thinking such thoughts, but he couldn't help himself. Seeing her so scared, so distraught, sent him somewhat crazy. Her pain was his pain and he needed to do something about it.

'Enough is enough! I'm going over there now,' he said, crouching down beside her, taking her hands in his, softly caressing them as if they were made of silk. He brought the back of her palms to his lips and kissed them tenderly.

He knew where Becky lived. He'd needed to send some of her things onto her a month or so ago. Smaller things she'd forgotten to take when she'd first moved out.

Brooke looked at him gratefully, managed a half smile, blinking back tears.

'No, I'm worried she might try to attack you. And I don't want you doing anything you'll later regret. I suspect that's what she wants, what she's gunning for. She wants to spur a reaction in you. And what if she succeeds? Lands you in trouble, succeeds in tearing us apart? I couldn't bear for that to happen.'

Brooke was right. The way Seb felt right now, he might do something he'd come to regret. He needed to calm down, think more rationally.

'OK, maybe you're right. We need to get the police involved. Get them to have a word, sort her out.'

'The police?' Brooke questioned.

'Yes. You said so yourself, we can't go on like this.'

Brooke sighed. 'I guess you're right, we have to put an end to this somehow. Once and for all. The woman's clearly gone mad. I mean, I feel sorry for her, losing her parents like that, and it can't have been easy losing you so soon after. But it wasn't our fault. It was fate, these things happen. You can't help who you fall for. We didn't plan to fall in love.'

Seb smiled. Brooke was not only beautiful and smart she was kind and thoughtful too. He loved her for these qualities as much as for her looks and charm.

'Pass me my phone.'

Seb was about to hand Brooke her mobile when an image of Becky's anguished face flashed before his eyes. It was probably Brooke referring to Becky's parents' death that had sparked the memory. Of that fateful evening when the police had knocked on their door to inform Becky that her parents had died in a car crash. Unlike him, who had a brother and sister, two blood relations to cling to when his parents passed on, she had no one left. And only a month or so later, he'd left her too. Perhaps he needed to give her another chance, perhaps he needed to call her, try to reason with her. He told all this to Brooke. She listened patiently, then got up and caressed the side of his face.

'That's what I love about you. You're so thoughtful, so caring. And I think you're right. I think you should try and talk some sense into her, give her another chance. But I'm not sure calling her will work. Perhaps you should go and see her, face to face.'

They agreed that Seb would go and see Becky the next evening, a Sunday, at her place in Ealing, where she'd moved after their split. But when Seb turned up the next day, around 8.30pm, there was no answer when he pressed the buzzer for her flat. He tried her phone, but she didn't pick up. It was frustrating but there was nothing he could do about it. As he turned and walked away in the direction of his car parked a little way up, he heard a door open and a voice call after him. 'Are you looking for Becky?'

Seb swivelled around. Saw a girl, perhaps in her early thirties, sporting a blonde ponytail, standing on the doorstep. She was only wearing cotton pyjamas and must have been freezing on such an arctic night.

'Yes,' Seb said, walking back over.

'I'm Sharon, her flatmate. She's out with a friend for dinner. Just the Pizza Express on Bond Street, near Ealing Green.'

'Do you know when she'll be back?'

Sharon shrugged her shoulders. 'Beats me. Are you a friend of hers? Want me to pass on a message?'

Seb said it was ok, he'd try another time and left it at that. He didn't want any trouble. God knows what Becky had told Sharon about him. He thanked her for her time, told her to go back inside else she'd risk catching her death. He thrust his hands deep inside his coat pockets, started walking back down the street once again towards his car, resigned to the fact that he'd have to try again tomorrow, when his mobile started ringing. It was Brooke. Frantic. So frantic she could barely get the words out.

'What is it?' he asked.

'She sent me a video!'

'Video?'

'Yes. Of us, having sex that time on the balcony. When it was almost dark and we thought no one was looking. Fucking twisted bitch must have been watching us. I feel sick, Seb. I don't know what to do! Where are you? Have you seen her? What did she say?'

Seb explained that Becky was out to dinner at Pizza Express, and that he was heading home. But just then, his anger got the better of him.

'This has to end,' he said. 'I'm going to wait for her to come home, make it clear that if she doesn't stop, we'll call the police, and she could end up doing time.'

'What if she's got a knife or something?' Seb heard the panic in Brooke's voice. 'Maybe it's best if you go to the restaurant. That way there'll be witnesses.'

'I doubt she'll attack me, sweetheart,' he said gently. 'If she's at dinner with a friend, she's unlikely to have a knife on her. I won't go inside her flat. I'll have it out with her on the street here. She can't do anything to me out here.'

'But you'll freeze to death.'

'I'll give it an hour, wait in the car, keep a look out for her, don't worry.'

'OK, let me forward the video to you.'

'Yes, do. I want to have all the facts to hand before I confront her.'

'Are you going to send her a message? She'll know I'll have forwarded it to you.'

'I wouldn't worry, it's probably what she wants. To provoke a reaction in me.'

Five minutes later, settled in the warmth of his car, Seb kept one eye on the street outside, the other on the video playing on his iPhone. He remembered that night in mid-September. They'd been in the throes of an Indian summer. It had been a blisteringly hot day, but the evening air was cooler and they'd sat outside on the balcony, sipping chilled white wine. Everything had been perfect. Brooke had been wearing nothing but a flimsy negligee and they'd been looking forward to their big day in a month's time. He'd looked at her, his heart swelling with love, told her how much he loved her and that's when she'd got up from her chair, turned to face him, then straddled his hips, leaned in and kissed him on the mouth. It was risky, but so goddamn hot all the same, and he hadn't been able to help himself. He'd watched her raise her nightie over her head, letting it drop to the floor. They'd had sex then and there. But someone had been watching. Someone had recorded their lovemaking. And he knew who that someone was. Becky. He wondered if she still had a key to the flat. If she'd let herself in that night? Filmed them from a secret hiding place in the living room, intending to use it one day as ammunition against them. And now it appeared that day had come.

IF YOU DON'T LEAVE HIM, THIS IS GOING VIRAL.

Seb stared at Becky's accompanying message, again sent

via the name – Miss Devoted – as he waited for her to appear. As he did, he felt the anger rise up in him. He knew it was probably what Becky wanted but he couldn't help himself. He started typing a text message to her:

You've gone too far this time, Becks. I won't let you hurt Brooke. I'll do anything to stop that from happening.

Seb pressed send. Hoped that his threat might do the trick. If not, tomorrow he'd call the police. He was done trying to reason.

An hour passed and there was still no sign of her. It was only 9.30 pm, and he guessed she could still be at the restaurant. He'd had enough, was afraid him sitting there alone in his car at night was starting to look suspicious. He'd already caught the attention of a couple of passers-by who'd eyed him warily, no doubt wondering what he was up to. Perhaps it was best if he had it out with her in public, as Brooke had suggested. With witnesses around. It was a shame to have driven all this way for nothing. He could but try.

Seb turned on the ignition and made for Bond Street, Ealing, where Pizza Express was situated, ringing Brooke along the way to update her. It was only a five-minute drive, but Seb wasn't fortunate enough to find a space nearby. He ended up parking alongside Ealing Green. Parking was free at this time of the night, thank God. He got out, sprinting to Bond Street, darting across the road, dodging a van coming too fast in the process. The driver gave an irate honk of his horn, but Seb was unfazed. Desperate to catch Becky before she left the restaurant.

But it appeared she already had. He peered through the window. No sign of her. Then went inside, apologising to the manager for the intrusion but explaining that he was looking for someone and that it was urgent. Since Becky had gone psycho on him, he'd deleted all her photos. Now he wished that he hadn't. All he could do was describe what she looked like and hope for the best. The manager seemed to remember a customer fitting Becky's description, but said she'd left perhaps forty minutes ago with her male companion. Seb wondered if she'd gone back to his place. Poor sod didn't know what he'd let himself in for, Seb thought.

Just over an hour later, having driven the streets for a while, just to clear his head, Seb snuck into bed next to Brooke. She turned over, stroked his face, told him she felt calmer now that he was back and lying next to her, but also that the time had come to call the police. He'd tried his best, she'd said, but tonight was the last straw, and they couldn't risk Becky releasing the video and jeopardising his position at work. Not to mention hers.

The following morning Seb got showered and dressed for work as usual. Brooke wasn't due at the gym until later. She had an 11.30 am pump class, but nothing before that. Coming into the kitchen, he found her sitting at the table, staring at her phone. She looked like she was in shock.

'Not another message?' Having woken up calmer, Seb was suddenly fuming.

Brooke looked directly at him. 'She's dead.'

Seb was confused. 'Dead? Who's dead?'

'Did you kill her, Seb? Is that why you were so long? Please tell me you didn't.' Brooke's voice was barely audible.

Seb came closer and Brooke instinctively flinched. Like she was afraid he might hurt her.

And then he realised what she was saying. 'Are you telling me Becky is dead?'

Brooke gave a faint nod, then held out her phone. Seb took it and looked at the screen, showing an article on the BBC News website: *Body of a woman found on Ealing Green*

Seb's heart began to race as his eyes scanned the headline, then drifted down to the main article, which gave the victim's name. Brooke was right. Becky was dead. Her body had been found last night on Ealing Green. She'd been identified by her hysterical flatmate, Sharon Barker, who'd called the police around midnight, worried that Becky hadn't come home, and wasn't picking up her messages.

Seb's stomach dropped, his feet nearly giving way. He made it to the nearest chair and sat down, stared at the article as if staring long and hard enough might cause the contents to change. But they didn't, of course. He thought about Sharon. Who would no doubt tell the police about the stranger who'd come looking for Becky last night. She'd give the police a description. As would the manager of Pizza Express. And possibly those who'd spotted him sitting in his car outside her flat.

He looked up at Brooke. 'I did not do this.'

For a moment he feared she didn't believe him. But then she came over, crouched down at his feet, and took his hands in hers. 'I know baby. It must have been the guy she was out with. He'll be the prime suspect, not you.'

Relief engulfed Seb. Locked in disbelief and panic, he'd forgotten about Becky's dining companion. Brooke was right. The police would question him, the last person to be seen with her. He had nothing to worry about. He had to be her killer, because he sure as hell wasn't.

But later that day, sitting at his desk in the office, he got a phone call from reception. Telling him the police were waiting in the lobby, and that they wanted to speak with him.

Fear choked Seb. His tie was suddenly like a noose around his neck, and he realised what was coming. The text message he'd sent Becky. They'd obviously found her phone, seen the message, traced it back to him. Not to mention his earlier missed call to her. He told himself to stay calm. He hadn't done anything wrong, and therefore he had nothing to fear.

Even so, his palms were sweaty as he shook hands with the DI and his assistant, then showed them to a vacant interview room on the ground floor.

Sitting across from him at the table, he felt like one of his own clients being cross examined in the witness box. They questioned him on his relationship with Becky, asked him whether they'd still been on good terms. Seb was tempted to lie. Then again, if they had her phone, they would have seen his text message to her, possibly already traced her spiteful emails to Brooke under the name Miss Devoted, including the one attaching the video of them having sex.

So, he told them everything. They listened in silence. Then produced a sealed bag, containing a mobile phone. Becky's phone. The DI removed it, then thrust it in Seb's face. The screen displaying his text message of last night.

Seb explained how he'd gone to Becky's flat the previous night, intending to reason with her, but that she hadn't been in, so he'd waited in his car for her to return, and in that time, Brooke had forwarded to him the video of them having sex on their balcony at home, sent to her by Becky earlier, along with a threatening message. Blackmailing her. He explained how, in a fit of rage, he'd sent Becky the text they'd just shown him, then gone to Pizza Express, hoping to find her there. But he hadn't found her. And so, he'd driven around a bit, just to cool down, then gone home. That's all he did. He didn't kill Becky and he was truly sorry that she was dead.

'Shouldn't you be questioning the man she had dinner with?' he asked. A bit too smugly, he realised afterwards.

'We have, and he has an alibi. There's a bus stop on Bond Street. CCTV shows him kissing Becky goodbye outside the restaurant, before waiting at the stop, and getting on the number 7 bus ten minutes later. CCTV also captures Becky crossing the main road, presumably to take the path across Ealing Green back home, which is where the footage stops. Close to where you say you parked your car last night.'

Having regained his composure, Seb's hands were clammy again. It was cool in the room, but Seb felt stifled under the DI's interrogation. Beads of sweat formed across his brow, and the back of his neck.

'This is crazy,' he said. 'Ask my wife, she'll tell you what time I got home.'

'We have, and she says it was just before 11pm.'

'That's right.'

'The victim left the restaurant around 8.50pm, giving

you plenty of time to kill her before driving home.'

'But you must know from speaking to the manager that I didn't turn up to the restaurant until just after 9.30pm. Forty minutes after she'd left.'

'Yes, that's very convenient.'

Seb knew what the DI was thinking. That he had already killed her, then staged his visit to the restaurant, making it seem like he'd just missed Becky. It wasn't a huge window of time. But it was enough.

'Forensics found foreign DNA on your ex. Would you be willing to take a DNA sample, Mr Wilder?'

'You can't get a sample unless you arrest me.'

'Which is why I'm asking you to give one voluntarily. The victim's dining companion has already done so, and he's in the clear. If, like him, you have nothing to hide, you won't mind giving us one.'

They had him. If he said no, he looked guilty. But he wasn't guilty. He'd been nowhere near Becky last night. He had nothing to hide.

'Sure, no problem.'

They'd come prepared and took a swab from his mouth then and there, before leaving a somewhat shell-shocked Seb alone in the meeting room. Shocked because he found it hard to understand how things could have gone so crazy in the space of 48 hours.

The rest of the afternoon passed in a haze. He couldn't focus, even though when he'd called Brooke to tell her what had happened, she'd reassured him things would be OK because he was innocent. He prayed she was right and that the swab results came fast so he could stop sweating and get on with his life.

Later, as they sat at the dining table, having a late supper around 9pm, the buzzer in the hallway went.

Seb jumped. Who would be calling at this time of night, on a cold January Monday evening? He could only think of one possibility, and his meal was suddenly travelling back up his gullet. Brooke told him to be calm, that she would go and investigate.

It was the police. Seb knew he was in trouble. They'd have called if all was well.

The same two men he'd seen earlier appeared at the door, both wearing stern expressions. Then the DI informed Seb that the DNA found on Becky matched Seb's.

Seb felt sick. He ruffled his hair, glanced at Brooke, who instantly covered her mouth with her hand, said surely there must be some mistake. But there wasn't. The DI read Seb his rights and took him away. His life as he knew it was over. Someone had set him up. But who? And why?

Back in the present, as Seb looked at Brooke across the table in the visitors' room, he asked her that very question.

'It's eating me alive not knowing who killed Becky. I just feel that if I knew, it would at least be of some relief to me. Stop me from going completely mad. Sometimes I worry that I blacked out. That I actually killed her, in some sort of psychotic trance. That I'm blaming it on someone else, when all along it was me.'

Seb looked into Brooke's beautiful eyes, which were suddenly animated, like she wanted to say something, like it was on the tip of her tongue.

'What is it? You look like you want to tell me something.'

At that point, Brooke leaned in. Said in a whisper, 'It's OK, I know you didn't kill her, that you didn't black out.'

Seb smiled. A look which told Brooke her sweet devotion meant the world to him. 'How can you know that for sure?' he asked.

Brooke leaned in further still, her eyes still sparkling. 'Because I killed her.'

Seb swallowed hard. 'What?' he just about managed.

'Becky was my half-sister. We shared the same father. My mother was a cleaner at the law firm he worked at when they first met. Before he met Becky's mother. They had an affair, and she got pregnant with me. She was desperately in love with him, and had thought he loved her. But when she told him she was pregnant, he ditched her on the spot. Said it had been fun, but that he didn't see her as marriage material and she should do herself a favour and get rid of me. She was devastated but had me all the same. Never got over it. Became severely depressed. Killed herself eventually, after she found out he'd married Becky's mother. I was only three. Got shoved into foster care, went through families like hot meals and suffered a ton of abuse along the way. But I stayed alive, somehow, even though the shrinks I've seen over the years seem to think I have *issues*.' Brooke gave a little grunt. 'What do they know? When I turned eighteen my mum's solicitor contacted me, said Mum had left a small sum of money in her will to be given to me when I came of age. She also left a handwritten letter. In it, she spilled the beans. Told me exactly who my dad was and what he'd done. That he never wanted his own child. I did my research, found out Daddy was some hot shot senior partner in the City, happily shacked up with some property heiress, and that they had a daughter. Becky. Who'd been given everything a child could ever want. I watched and waited, played for time. Watched the progress of your relationship with Becky. She had the perfect life. A life I'd been denied. A loving family, good schooling, parents who'd wanted her, and a devoted boyfriend. And I was determined to make her, and our bastard father pay.'

Seb could hardly believe what he was hearing. Her story was a sad one, he couldn't blame her for being jealous of Becky, for hating her father. But to act on it, to do what she had done, was unforgiveable. The actions of a psychopath. And then another thought occurred to him.

'Did you kill Becky's parents?'

Brooke grinned. He had his answer. 'What can I say? Faulty brakes. People never check them enough.'

What a fool he had been. Seduced by this stunning, yet severely deranged woman. Who had deliberately targeted him as a means of getting back at Becky, destroying her life, the life she felt should have been hers.

'You set me up,' Seb said. 'It wasn't fate that brought us

together. You wanted her dead, and you used me to do it. Why not just kill her the way you killed her parents? Make it seem like an accident.'

'I got away with two murders, but I couldn't risk getting away with three. Plus, where's the fun in that? I wanted her to suffer.'

'You sent those emails, the handwritten note, the video, to yourself? How did you do it?'

A sly self-satisfied nod. 'I'd seen Becky's handwriting before. It was pretty easy to forge. The emails I sent were from an internet café in central London, using a bogus address. And the video? I sent that from the same café that Sunday morning. When you were at the gym. As for the sex tape, that was pretty fun to make, wouldn't you agree?'

'Did you follow me as soon as I'd set off for Becky's that night?'

'Yes. I was sitting in my car two streets away from you when you called and told me exactly where Becky was. It could have gone horribly wrong. But luckily it didn't. You always did whatever I asked of you. And you waiting there for an hour gave me time to catch that bitch on the green, kill her, and plant your DNA all over her. Before heading home.'

Seb was shaking now. He caught the prison guard's eye. 'I'll tell them everything. Tell them what you said.'

Brooke grinned. 'Don't be dumb. Do you really think they'll believe you? There's no way of proving any of it. Mother never mentioned my father on the birth certificate, and I've long since destroyed her letter. They can't trace the emails, or prove who sent the letter. And I made sure my DNA was nowhere to be found on Becky's body. Unlike yours.'

Brooke got up.

'Did you ever love me, Brooke?'

'No. Like a typical man, like my scumbag father, you ditched someone who cared about you without a second's thought. How could I love someone so shallow?'

She had a point, and Seb felt sickened by his actions.

Brooke made to leave but Seb called after her, 'Where are

you going, Brooke?'

'Back to our home, of course. To the flat I'm free to do with as I please. What's mine is yours, right?'

'I don't think so.'

Brooke looked at him, puzzled, then gave a snide chuckle. 'Have you gone mad in here already?' She surveyed the drab surroundings. 'I can't say I blame you.'

Just then, the prison guard was at her side. He grabbed her arm. 'You're under arrest, Mrs Wilder.'

She looked at him, at first startled, then enraged. 'Get your hands off me!'

Seb didn't move from where he was sitting. He looked past her and said, 'Did you get all that?'

Confusion swathed Brooke's face, and then she slowly turned around to see the same DI who'd arrested Seb standing by the exit door.

He nodded. 'You're free to go, Mr Wilder.'

Another perplexed look. And then the penny dropped. 'You were wearing a wire? You trapped me into talking!'

'You're not the only one who's capable of laying traps, my sweetheart.'

'But how did you know it was me?'

'A witness came forward after reading about the trial in the newspapers. Saw the photo of my distraught wife outside the Court. Said they'd spotted you on the green that night. They'd been dealing drugs and were too afraid to talk, but had since got clean and grown a conscience. It caused the police to look back over Becky's so-called emails to you. And, low and behold, they traced the IP address back to an internet café in Bloomsbury. It was a mistake to use the same café and the same portal. Very amateurish. The owners identified you from the photo the police showed them. All they needed then was a confession.'

Brooke appeared lost for words. Her mouth dropped open as the DI cuffed her hands and Seb stood up and walked around the table, stopping to give her one last look.

'You can't have known I'd talk,' she said.

'No, that was a risk. But you're a sociopath, a pathological liar. You're proud of what you've done and enjoy torturing people. Including me. I was hoping you'd take the opportunity to brag and torture me further. Particularly when I conceded I might have done it. Up to that point, I'd always maintained my innocence, and you couldn't bear to let me take the credit for your actions.'

Brooke wriggled like a wild animal caught in chains, her eyes demonic. Seb felt like a fool for not seeing her for what she really was beneath the angelic façade she portrayed to the world.

'I should never have left Becky for you. I caused her death and it's something I'll never forgive myself for. But at least now, justice has been done, and she and her family can rest in peace.'

Seb turned and walked away, never once looking back, despite the barrage of expletives being hurled his way by the monster he had married.

ABOUT A A CHAUDHURI

A A Chaudhuri is a former City lawyer, turned thriller writer, who lives in Surrey with her family.

Once a highly ranked British junior tennis player, competing in the national championships and a member of the national squad, she went on to tour the women's professional satellite circuit as a teenager and achieved a world ranking of 650.

After returning to full-time education, she gained a BA Honours 2:1 in History at University College London, and a commendation in both the Graduate Diploma in Law and Legal Practice Course at the London College of Law, before training as a solicitor at City firm Norton Rose and then practising as a commercial litigator at two other City firms, Kendall Freeman and Travers Smith.

She left law in 2008 to pursue her passion for writing and in 2010 passed the NCTJ fast-track newspaper journalism course, in respect of which she was awarded The Oxford University Press Public Affairs Award for the most outstanding public affairs central government paper.

In 2013 and 2014 she self-published two women's fiction novels under the name Alexandra Sage: *Love & Limoncello* and the sequel *Love & Loss*. *Love & Limoncello* has sold more than ten thousand copies to date, reaching number 53 in the Amazon Kindle Bestsellers List in October 2014.

The Scribe and *The Abduction*, published by Lume Books in July and December 2019, are her first crime book series, plunging readers into London's glamorous legal world and featuring series' heroine, Maddy Kramer, fiction's first female City lawyer amateur sleuth, who teams up with charismatic DCI Jake Carver to solve a gruesome series of murders and a puzzling abduction.

Both books have hit the bestsellers lists in the UK, Australia and Canada, with bestseller tags in Australia and Canada.

The Scribe and *The Abduction* were published as audio books by Isis Audio on 1st January and 1st March 2021, both read by David Thorpe.

She has also contributed an original short story 'The Encounter' to crime anthology *Given In Evidence* published by Lume Books in May 2020, has written many articles and short stories for The Crime Writers' Association.

In February 2021, Alex signed a two-book contract for two standalone psychological thrillers with Hera Books, the first entitled *She's Mine*, was published in August 2021, the second in 2022.

Besides being an avid reader, she enjoys fitness, films, anything Italian and a good margarita!

https://www.facebook.com/AAChaudhuri/
https://twitter.com/AAChaudhuri/
https://www.instagram.com/A.A.Chaudhuri/
https://www.linkedin.com/in/a-a-chaudhuri-55a83524/
http://aachaudhuri.co

THE CAVEMAN DETECTIVE

Rhys Hughes

He had been bitten by an insect and a fever followed. As a result, Og lay on a bed of leaves for a week. He had been cared for, given food and water, and as he slowly recovered, he bewailed the fact that he was physically unable to contribute to the welfare of the tribe as much as he felt he should. He was far too weak to hunt or even forage.

His strength would return, but in the meantime he wondered what role he could play. He loathed inactivity. On the very last day of his fever, the big idea came to him and he embraced it at once. He would help the tribe with his mind instead of his muscles.

Og's mind was an unusually developed one for the time and place. He had made the connection between the insect bite and his illness, solving a mystery that had troubled people for long ages. His mind was a tool, soft when contrasted with a stone axe, but no less sharp. This tool would be a boon to his people. But in what way?

Og decided to devote the period of his recuperation to solving crime. Why not? All tribes had their share of assaults and petty theft was rife and the abduction of women was common. Although he didn't know it, Og had resolved to become the very first detective the world had known and the first case he would solve would become the very first solved case in the whole history of criminology.

He idly wondered what this case might be.

As it happened, no sooner had the first day of his new

vocation begun than his services were called upon. Or rather, he managed to nose his way into an incident that had occurred during the previous night. While in his fever, oblivious to his surroundings, a murder had taken place, but it was a murder that had baffled everybody.

The strongest member of the tribe, a man called Gub, had been killed while sleeping alone in a sealed cave, and furthermore the cave had been secured *from the inside*. The cave was the size of a large room and doors and locks hadn't been invented but Og understood that this was a locked room mystery. What were the details?

Plenty of people were eager to tell Og everything they knew about the bizarre incident. Gub sealed his cave every night by rolling a big boulder across the entrance. This rock was too heavy for any other member of the tribe to move. Only Gub had the strength.

Gub was something of a loner, as much of a loner as anyone could be in his situation. He had no woman companion and lived in his cave on his own. He rarely invited anyone inside it.

He was liked by most people but a few individuals saw his desire for solitude as an expression of arrogance. It never occurred to them that he might simply be a bit shy. They decided he had a high opinion of himself and didn't want to mix with the rabble.

Og knew better. Gub was humble and unassuming.

Last night, Gub had gone to bed as usual, rolling the boulder over the entrance to the cave to secure it against intruders. Everyone else went to bed in their own caves and they all slept deeply apart from Og who tossed and turned in his fever. Nobody reported hearing any strange sounds that night. Everything seemed very tranquil.

It was a moonless night and the stars shone with fantastic clarity over the Neolithic scene but no one was awake to appreciate them. This was a region of low cliffs full of caves that the Wutsong Clan had chosen to be their permanent home. The settlement was rarely attacked by bears or any other wild beast and rival tribes had never tried to invade it. There was no reason to think that going to bed might be dangerous. Why did Gub take precautions? Blocking his cave mouth with a boulder every night was an eccentric thing to do. What did he fear?

At dawn the following day, Zop rose and went about waking up every tribe member in the traditional manner.

This was Zop's task and the way he did it was by standing outside the caves and banging on his large drum. The beating of the drum skin served also to summon people for breakfast.

They sleepily stepped out from the cave mouths, yawning and rubbing their eyes, and gathered around the fire pit, but Gub never showed, which was an unprecedented occurrence. He loved his big breakfasts, especially if they involved figs, honey and nuts.

Zop returned to his cave to bang the drum again, louder this time, but the boulder remained in place. Something was definitely wrong. After ten minutes of futile drumming, Zop called for assistance. Two men came to help him roll back the boulder and open the cave, but even with three of them, the effort involved was extreme.

Gub truly was a man of exceptional strength. Or rather, he *had* been a man of such strength, for now he was dead. It would be necessary to talk about him only in the past tense from this moment on. He was clearly and horribly dead, with the terrible fang of a sabre-toothed tiger embedded in his chest and protruding from his back.

The tooth had evidently broken off when the beast bit him. It was the only wound on Gub's body but it was an absolutely fatal injury. The fang once extracted proved to be as long as Gub was tall. It was presented as evidence to Og when he asked to see it.

How had a sabre-toothed tiger managed to get past the heavy boulder and into Gub's cave without being heard by anyone? Why had it bothered to roll the boulder back into place after the deed was done? Why hadn't it eaten the dead body of its prey? It made no sense and Og already doubted whether the case could ever be solved.

'But I am the only detective in the world and if I don't try to find the answer nobody else will,' thought Og.

He still felt weak and sat on a fallen tree to rest.

Then he decided to question Zop.

He found the drummer preparing to head off into the forest to look for berries and gather mushrooms. 'One moment, if you please,' he said, and Zop turned with an exasperated smile.

'What do you want, Og?'

'When you banged your drum outside Gub's cave the first time, did you hear any noise from within?'

'How could it? I was banging the drum.'

'Ah yes, of course.'

Og felt dismayed. He had already shown how amateurish he was as a detective and the fact he was the world's first was scant consolation. He watched sadly as Zop turned his back and loped off down a path into the trees. Then he wandered weakly through the settlement. Every member of the Wutsong Clan was busy at tasks, mending cloaks or sharpening flints or painting pictures on cave walls or inventing musical instruments, and Og spoke to all of them at great length and learned nothing new, but only Var refused to say anything in reply.

That was strange too, because Var was normally very sociable. Maybe he was in shock because of the death of Gub, although they hadn't really been close friends. Yes, it must be that.

Og went to look at the tooth that was propped up against the boulder that had guarded poor Gub's cave.

Then he frowned and reached out to touch it.

The tooth was so long that the beast it belonged to would have been too large to fit through the cave entrance.

Og imagined himself as the sabre-toothed tiger but the sensation was unpleasant. He went into the cave.

The morning sun was in exactly the correct position to

illuminate the interior, which normally would have been in darkness, and Og noticed an interesting thing indeed. A thick vine with one end tied to the boulder but where was the other end? He followed the length and saw it went around another big rock in the corner of the cave and ended near the spot where the unfortunate Gub had chosen to sleep.

Og stooped to pick up the end of the vine and saw that it was frayed. It had snapped or been cut with a rough edge. Then the sun moved a little and the cave was in shadows again. There were only a few minutes each day when the sun shone directly into it.

No wonder nobody had noticed the vine until now!

He stepped back outside the cave and examined the tooth closely and he thought he detected something odd.

But he needed to be sure, so he went to find Var and ask him for the loan of the crystal the fellow had found a few months ago. Var had found it after a landslide had exposed the middle of a nearby cliff and he took it from the rubble because it looked nice, but after he brought it back to the tribe and people had played with it, they discovered it magnified objects if you peered through it with one eye.

Var was in his usual place, weaving baskets from reeds.

'You are quiet today,' Og said.

Var merely nodded, tight lipped and wary.

'I also happened to notice that you didn't eat any breakfast. You were there but you didn't take a bite.'

Now Var shrugged and blinked his eyes.

'Are you ill?' Og asked.

Var shook his head and seemed unhappy.

'You don't have to put on a brave face. Look at me. I was ill for many days and I don't mind admitting it.'

Og waited in vain for Var to answer him.

'Very well, I won't intrude upon your time any longer. I just wish to ask if I may borrow your crystal?'

Var nodded and in fact seemed relieved.

He kept the crystal in a pouch by his side and he passed

it to Og, who went back to Gub's cave and looked at the tooth in much finer detail with the aid of the magnifying apparatus.

He began at the tip of the fang but saw nothing. Then he progressed to the base and saw a few fibres there. The fibres exactly matched the colour of the thick vine. Og was stunned.

His first breakthrough in the murder case!

Pondering deeply, he understood that Var was in trouble, but that the investigation had to be conducted on strictly rational lines and that it was bad to jump to conclusions. More evidence was needed. He returned the crystal to Var and while doing so he deliberately stumbled and trod on the basket weaver's foot as if by accident.

Var opened his mouth wide to yell and Og peered inside.

One of Var's teeth was missing.

The left canine tooth, the one that resembles a fang.

'Oh dear,' said Og sadly.

And he pointed at the stub of enamel.

'I broke it last night on the stone inside an avocado,' said Var, 'but I said nothing because it was bedtime. Then when I woke and learned that Gub had been killed by a sabre-toothed tiger and that its fang was stuck in his body, I became very frightened.'

'You assumed you would be blamed for his death?'

'Naturally. They would accuse me.'

'Of being a were-tiger, a man who can transform into a sabre-toothed tiger on certain nights. Are you one?'

'I am not,' said Var, 'but who will believe me?'

'Nobody at all,' Og admitted.

'The ironic thing is that my tooth didn't actually fall out last night. It was broken but still attached to my gum. This morning, when Zop banged his drum, the vibration finished the work started by the avocado stone and the tooth tumbled from my jaw.'

'May I ask where you obtained the avocado?'

'Zop gave it to me.'

'Why did you bite into it? Surely you knew there was a stone hidden in the creamy green flesh?'

'But I didn't. I had never eaten an avocado before. Zop knew that and told me it was a delicious treat. He was keen for me to try one. I guess he forgot to warn me about the stone.'

Og rubbed his chin.

The word 'stone' had affected him strongly.

But he wasn't sure why.

'What do you intend doing now, Var? You can't keep a missing tooth secret forever. Everyone knows you had a full set of teeth yesterday and it won't be difficult for them to make a connection between the murder and your mouth. What is your defence?'

Og waited for Var to argue his innocence or outline a cunning plan of escape, but the basket weaver was at a loss for good ideas. Var knew how to weave baskets or find crystals and that was the sum total of his talents. Gub had been slain and Var would get the blame. He would be speared to death before he had a chance to again turn into a sabre-toothed tiger. The tribe took no chances with its safety.

'The situation is most unfortunate,' said Og, 'but I have a feeling you aren't guilty and I will try to solve the case quickly so that nothing drastic happens to you. Keep your mouth shut.'

'Thank you,' said Var.

But it was too late for the basket weaver to avoid trouble, for Zop was back from his foraging expedition and had been listening to this exchange from the cover of some bushes.

He strode forward with a pointed finger.

'You are the culprit. You are the murderer of Gub! You turned into a sabre-toothed tiger last night but you kept the mind of a man. So then you had both strength and intelligence.'

'Not true. I remained a man all night,' said Var.

'Liar! With your human intelligence you knew that you had to roll the boulder back after the deed, and with your animal strength you were able to do that unaided. But you bit him too hard and your tooth snapped off. I consider you to be a deadly menace.'

Og raised his arms high.

'Calm down everyone! This is a baffling case but I feel I'm close to a solution now. Var is innocent. Nobody turned themselves into anything. I think the solution was less magical.'

'Pah!' spat Zop. 'You are still suffering the deliriums of fever. I will call all the members of the tribe and tell them about Var's missing tooth. Let us see what they say about it.'

'That evidence is only circumstantial,' said Og.

'But I have more evidence and you shall hear about it when I call the Wutsong Clan to a general assembly!'

'Is that really necessary?'

But Zop had already walked away and was going to fetch his drum. It was very rare that a general assembly was called. The last time was more than a decade ago when a meteorite landed in the settlement and knocked off the head of Yab. The assembly had decided that the gods were angry with him for some reason or other.

Og and Var exchanged mournful glances.

Soon the steady throbbing of Zop's drum was sounding in the distance as he strode the circumference of the region of caves, calling all members of the tribe to stop whatever they were doing and hurry to the fire pit, the place where tribal business as well as communal meals was chewed over. Var sighed and then smiled at Og.

'There is no point trying to flee. There are others who can run faster. I will submit to my fate. But you have been nice to me and thus I want you to have the crystal to keep forever.'

He passed it to Og, who gripped his shoulder.

'Don't talk like that.'

'Why not? I am doomed,' said Var.

'No, you are not. The general assembly will turn into a trial and I will be your defending counsel. I will prove to the Wutsong Clan that you are not responsible for Gub's death.'

'But someone must have killed him.'

'Yes! And I think I know who. You will see. Come!'

And he led Var to the fire pit.

The fire was still smouldering and the embers glowed. A few sticks at the edges of the pit were smoking.

Most of the tribe had already gathered there.

They booed Var when they saw him.

'What is this?' protested Og. 'You have pre-judged a man before his trial has begun? You are savages!'

The compliment was acknowledged. 'Yes, we are, thank you. But you won't help him by flattering us.'

Zop was sitting on his drum and now he stood and spoke.

'Look inside the villain's mouth!'

Var opened his jaws without prompting, because he didn't want them to be forced open, and everyone filed past to peer inside. Shocked sounds were emitted from those who did.

'Obviously a were-tiger!' someone cried.

Og struggled to make himself heard above all the shouting. 'But why would he want to kill Gub? He had no reason. There is no motive for this murder. A conviction would be unsafe.'

This silenced the crowd and Og felt he had their full attention at last but Zop spoiled everything by saying:

'Listen to me, my friends! I went to find mushrooms in the forest and while I was there the ghost of Gub appeared and spoke to me. He told me that Var was jealous of the fact that Gub was famous for his strength. Var felt that *he* ought to be more famous because he was stronger, but only if he turned himself into a sabre-toothed tiger. So that's what he did. He felt no need to eat Gub because the point of the murder was to show which of them was the strongest. Var is guilty!'

The tribe greeted this speech with shouts and stampings of feet. It was well known that ghosts were real, nobody could doubt that, and Zop had provided clinching proof that Var was the one who ought to be punished for this crime. The crowd surged forward to take hold of Var. They would drag him to some cliff edge and then throw spears at him, but Og moved to position himself in front of Var.

'Wait! Do not act rashly! Listen to me first!'

Only by holding high the crystal and letting it flash in the sun was Og able to arrest the forward motion of the surge of vengeful tribesmen. The sparkle hypnotised them for a few seconds. They stood still and swayed as the rays refracted and reflected.

Og seized his chance. 'Gub was an anxious man. Why else would he lock his cave securely every night? Do you really suppose he was scared of a were-tiger? If that had been the case, he would have killed Var with his own hands while Var was in human form. No, Gub was frightened of something else, something more difficult to fight than pure force. He was afraid of guile and cunning. And that is how he was murdered. Not with a bite from a fang but by treachery.'

Zop was furious. 'This is utter nonsense. Why do we waste our time with the ravings of a febrile lunatic?'

'My illness is over,' replied Og, 'but yours will never be cured, dear Zop, because you have a disease of the mind. It is you who was jealous of Gub's strength. You are the one who decided to prove that ingenuity was greater than brawn. You killed him!'

Zop laughed hysterically and urged the crowd around him to laugh too but they were intrigued by Og's words.

'You planned the crime very carefully. You chose an innocent victim to take the blame. You gave him an avocado, knowing that he had never eaten one before, and you didn't warn him about the stone. You guessed he would break a tooth on it. But the tooth didn't fall out. No matter, you had a backup plan for that. Next morning you drummed especially loudly outside Var's cave in order to shake the tooth out. And you also drummed with extra vigour outside Gub's cave, just in case the rock hadn't broken all the way through. A devious plan!'

Zop turned himself into a dramatic actor and began gesticulating and making faces at his audience. 'What rubbish! I never heard anything this absurd in my entire life. What was that you said about a rock? What does a rock have to do with anything at all?'

'There was no sabre-toothed tiger,' declared Og.

'But we saw the fang!'

'There was no fang,' insisted Og.

'You must be joking!'

'It wasn't a fang but a stalactite.'

The communal intake of tribal breath was deep. Og waited for the full implications of his words to sink in.

Then he clenched his fist and shook it at Zop.

'Very few people knew what the interior of Gub's cave was like, but you must have been one of them. You found some excuse to go inside at the one time of day when the sun shone into the cave. You looked around and made a mental note of the geological formations there. A big rock in the corner and several long stalactites hanging from the roof. One of these stalactites was suspended directly over the place where Gub usually slept. That's when you had the idea.'

'These are insane ravings! I refuse to listen!'

'On the day before the fateful night, you tied one end of a vine to the boulder that Gub always rolled over the mouth of his cave. You looped it around the big rock in the corner and tied the other end to the base of the chosen stalactite. You probably stood on your drum to reach. You knew that when Gub rolled the boulder it would pull the vine taut and the base of the stalactite would snap off.'

'This is ludicrous. I demand you keep silent.'

'And if it didn't break all the way through, your fierce drumming the next morning would finish the task. You would be one of the first on the scene when the cave was opened and it would be you who would identify the stalactite as the fang of a sabre-toothed tiger. Once you planted that idea in the minds of everyone else, it became obvious to them that it was indeed a fang. You helped them to fool themselves. But when Var told me about the avocado stone, the word 'stone' wiped the word 'fang' out of my mind. Then I began to know.'

'Gub was bitten to death by a were-tiger!'

'No, he was stabbed by the falling stalactite that you had arranged to kill him. Var is innocent. You are guilty. Later you cut the end of the vine so that the stalactite was no longer connected to the boulder. That was an attempt to hide evidence, but I saw several vine fibres on the base of the stalactite using this amazing device.'

Og held up the crystal to his eye and his eye was magnified to a huge size and the tribe muttered in awe.

Some men stepped forward to seize Zop by the arms. He struggled but he was soon overpowered. Og regarded the tribe and nodded. They were totally convinced by his arguments.

'But where do stalactites come from?' someone asked.

'Good question,' replied Og.

They waited for him to answer it, but he shrugged and said, 'I am the first detective ever. Give me time.'

Now Var stepped forward. 'A detective ought to have special clothes to let everyone know who and what you are. Why not wear this leaf here as a hat? It suits you admirably.'

Og had to admit that the large leaf was very comfortable on his head. Then he did something almost inexplicable. He reached down and picked up a smoking stick from the fire pit. It was a stick with a long stem and a knob of smouldering wood at the other end. He put it between his lips on an impulse but took it out to speak.

He addressed the crowd in his most impressive voice. 'Stalactites are things we know nothing about. There are many things we know nothing about, but it is our duty to learn and keep learning. Geology is definitely one subject we ought to study with diligence and I propose that we begin right now. For example, I suggest we divide rocks into three groups for the purposes of classification. In the first group we will have the igneous rocks and in the second group we shall find the metamorphic rocks. Most stalactites will belong to the third group.'

'What is the third group?'

Og kept the crystal pressed to his eye and with the hat on his head and the smouldering pipe in his hand he addressed the entire tribe as he gave his carefully considered answer.

'Sedimentary, my dear Wutsong.'

ABOUT RHYS HUGHES

Rhys Hughes was born in Wales but has lived in many different countries. He graduated as an engineer and currently works as a tutor of mathematics. He began writing fiction at an early age and his first book, *Worming the Harpy*, was published in 1995. He is nearing the end of an ambitious project to complete a cycle of exactly 1000 linked short stories. His most recent book is the novella *My Rabbit's Shadow Looks Like a Hand* and he is hard at work on a collection of crime stories called *The Reconstruction Club*. Fantasy, humour, satire, science fiction, adventure, irony, paradoxes and philosophy are combined in his work to create a distinctive style.

FACELESS KILLER

Christine Poulson

You know how they talk about the faceless masses, well, for me it's not just the masses that are faceless, it's everyone, and yep, I mean everyone. I wouldn't know my own mother if I passed her in the street. I don't even recognise myself in the mirror. The police couldn't understand how I could see the man who went past me and – not see him. When they asked me, would you know him again, would you be able to identify him, I had to say no …

But I'm getting ahead of myself. Let me take you back to that day last summer.

It starts as just another working day at the cathedral where I'm the head mason. No-one there knows about the face blindness, or prosopagnosia as it's also known, and there's no reason why they should. It's not as if I can't manage. For instance, on that day as I pass the tourist desk, I know it's either Kate or Rachel on duty, but it doesn't matter which. I'm friendly with both.

'Morning!'

'Morning, Lorna.'

I think that was Kate.

It's a bit more difficult when someone's wearing a cassock. But when the figure says, 'Hot enough for you, Lorna?' it can't be anyone but Fred, the Head Verger. He leaves no cliché unturned. Fred's been here forever. He locks the place up at night, polishes the silver, lays out the vestments.

The next person wearing a cassock is the Dean. It's easier with her because she's, well, she's a big woman, and she's wearing preaching bands – those white strips of cloth at the neck. That means she's one of the chapter and there still aren't that many women, so I know it's her.

'Hi Lorna, good weather for viewing the tower. It is today?'

I tell her I've got to deal with some paperwork first and get the key. Then I'm meeting Richard up there. He's the Canon Treasurer.

It's a long haul to the top of the tower. After I've climbed the spiral staircase that goes up through the thickness of the wall, I stop on the gallery for a breather. It's where we store the crib – the shepherds, the three wise men, the baby Jesus – and broken chairs, that kind of thing – there's literally a kitchen sink! It's like being back-stage in a great theatre. The cathedral is a theatre, really, God's theatre … the music, the spectacle. If you walk along to the end of the gallery, there's a wonderful view of the nave and when someone's practising on the organ, it's as close to heaven as you can get. Today I catch a whiff of cigarette smoke and wonder where it's coming from.

You wouldn't think people would drop litter in a cathedral, would you? They do! I've just picked up a bit of a paper when I hear footsteps hurrying down the staircase from the tower. Someone in a cassock emerges and straightaway disappears down the staircase to the nave. They whisk out of sight so quickly that I don't have time to register anything except the cassock. Of course I wouldn't have recognised them anyway.

I've been on the tower for about half an hour when Richard arrives.

'On a clear day,' he says, 'you can see every parish in the diocese, but with this heat haze …'

'It is awfully humid.'

'Weather's bound to break sooner or later. We're due a thunderstorm.'

My mind goes a blank and there's an awkward pause.

Richard says, 'So. What did you want to show me?'

'We need to get on the scaffolding. I've brought you a hard hat.'

He looks doubtful. 'Well, if it's really necessary. I don't care for heights.'

He follows me and we climb over the wall.

'Look at the erosion over there,' I say. 'That parapet: the stone's crumbling – it's dangerous.'

You might wonder how it's possible to fall in love with someone when you can't remember their face from one time to next. But when he's so close that I can smell the soap he uses, my stomach flips over. And his hand – when he puts his hand on the wall, close to mine … I'd know it anywhere: well-shaped, the nails trimmed short. I want to put my hand on his. An image flashes through my mind: we're lying together on the top of the tower, wrapped in each other's arms – oh Lord –

'Sorry, what?' I've missed what he said.

'The stone, it's so flaky.'

'What? Flaky. Oh, yes. When they did that restoration work in the sixties they didn't have the technology …'

Sometimes I think he feels the same about me. He's so kind – always interested – but then he's kind to everyone …

'I can see it's going to be a big job,' Richard says.

'Just one more thing I want you to see at this end. Now if you can just look at where I'm pointing.'

'I wish you wouldn't lean out like that, Lorna.'

'That's funny … there's a shoe down there … about six or seven metres down to the right, just at that junction with the gully …'

And then I realise what I'm seeing. And it's not just a shoe.

'You've very pale, Lorna.' The Dean plugs in a kettle. 'Strong sweet tea, that's what you need.'

The police brought up the body and asked me and

Richard and the Dean if we could identify it. A young man in a suit: the others didn't know him, so I thought it was a safe bet to say that I didn't either. And now we're in the Dean's office.

'Poor troubled soul,' Richard says.

'You mean, you think he did it on purpose?' I ask.

'The cathedral does tend to attract people in dire straits. If only he'd spoken to someone, we might have been able to help.'

'But how did he get up there?' the Dean says. 'The door at the bottom of the tower's usually locked. It *was* locked when you went up, Lorna?'

'Yes, and the scaffolding's alarmed, so he couldn't have got up that way either. But – I did see someone up there. They came down from the tower while I was on the gallery. I didn't see their face. I was at the other end, looking down into the nave. Just saw that they were wearing a cassock.'

'I wonder who that was and if they saw anything. I'll check if any of the vergers are aware of the door having been left open or if there's a key missing.' The Dean sighs. 'There's going to have to be a police enquiry and an inquest. And we'll have to set our own inquiry in motion to find out how this terrible thing could have happened.'

There's always been a Choral evensong in the cathedral and there always will be. Even when the cathedral took a direct hit in the second world war – half the cloister went – they managed to keep it going. As I sit listening to those pure young voices, I can't stop thinking about that young man. And I wonder again about the man that passed me on the gallery – so far no-one among the cathedral staff has admitted to being up there.

The service is ending. And then I don't see exactly what happens, but one moment choir are processing out as usual and the next Simon, the choirmaster, is on the floor. The Dean and I reach him at the same time.

'Don't know quite what happened,' he says. He tries to get up and winces. 'I must have twisted my ankle.'

The Dean sends one of the boys to get Fred and the first

aid kit and sends the rest of them off to the Robing room. We help Simon to his feet and Fred arrives, a serious look on his face.

'The police have come back, ma'am,' he tells the Dean, 'and they're asking for you.'

Fred and I help Simon over to the choir stalls.

'Rice,' Fred says. 'R. I. C. E. For sprained ankles. Rest. Ice. Compression. Elevation. It was on my first aid course.'

Simon shakes his head. 'That's not necessary. It was a shock more than anything, I'll just sit quietly for a while.'

Fred says, 'Didn't you trip over something in the vestry the other day? I should take more water with it if I were you.'

The jocular tone grates on me, so what Simon feels ...

He frowns. 'It could happen to anyone ... these uneven floors.'

Fred says hastily, 'Yeah, sorry, course it could. Well, if you're OK, I'd better do my rounds.'

He's about to go when the Dean gets back and tells us that the police have identified the dead man. 'His name is Harry Glendale. He works – worked – in a bank in the town.'

'Glendale?' Simon says, staring at her. 'Harry Glendale. But it must be – I know him! He used to be a chorister here.'

The DCI is standing with me on the gallery and for the second time he takes me through what I saw.

'And this man didn't speak?' he asks.

'No. I told you. He was in a tearing hurry and he didn't see me. It was a matter of moments.'

'You said he was wearing a cassock? That narrows the field.'

'It's not just the cathedral canons and the vergers who wear them, there are the lay vicars – they sing in the choir – and the vicars from the local parishes. It might not even have been someone connected with the cathedral – or even a clergyman.

Anyone can put on a cassock.'

'But not just anyone would know how to get hold of a key. You said you were sure the door was locked when you came up.'

He lets the silence stretch out.

He says, 'I get the feeling there's something you're not telling me, Lorna. If you did recognise him ...'

And that's when I should tell him about the face blindness. I'm about to, I really am. But I open my mouth and – it's been my secret for so long – what comes out is quite different –

'No, I didn't recognise him. Really. But I've just remembered. I smelt cigarette smoke up there. Could that have been – whoever it was. Do you think they saw the accident ... or ...?'

'We don't believe it was an accident. Or suicide. Harry Glendale was already dead, or pretty near, when he went over the edge. So you do see, it's vital that we identify this mystery man in a cassock.'

It's after eight o'clock when I get home. I'm putting the kettle on when the doorbell rings and it's Richard. The Dean's sent him round to see if I'm alright. I offer him a cup of tea and then I think, 'what the hell,' and suggest a gin and tonic.

'Can't think of anything I'd like better,' he says.

I get a tray of ice cubes out of the fridge.

'How was your interview with the police?' he asks 'They accepted it OK? That you couldn't identify the man you saw?'

'I can't find any lemon. Will lime do?'

'Fine, thanks. It can't be a condition they come across very often.'

'And there's only one can of tonic water. We'll have to – *What* did you say?' I turn and look at him, a gin and tonic in either hand.

'2.5% of population. isn't it?'

'You mean, you *know?*'

'Well, yes …'

'But how—'

'Last winter. You blanked me in the street. Then five minutes later I met you again in a shop and I'd loosened my scarf, so then my dog-collar was showing. You gave me a lovely smile and that was when I guessed. I had a friend at university who had it.'

'And you didn't say anything? Who else knows?'

'No-one! Not through me. You don't think I'd … Lorna, I wouldn't dream of—'

I take a large gulp of gin and my head swims.

'I didn't tell the police,' I say. 'About not being able to recognise anyone.'

'But Lorna …'

'You can't imagine what it's like. I was bullied at school – people thought I was stupid – in my first job – my apprenticeship – the lads played practical jokes on me.'

'You should have told the police.'

'I just want to be like everyone else. Is that too much to ask?

'But in this one respect you're not like everyone else, are you? Would it really be such a bad thing if people knew? Lorna, I'm not the only one you've ignored in the street. If people knew, they might not think …' His voice trails off.

'Yes?' I say. 'What might they not think?'

'That you can seem … well, a bit aloof … standoffish.'

The blood rushes to my face. I'm too mortified to speak.

'It's nothing to be ashamed of,' he says. 'Oliver Sacks had it, did you know that? Lorna, do at least tell the police. You could be putting yourself in danger. That person you saw – maybe they had something to do with this young man's death – and if they think you can identify them – I've already heard some gossip -'

'I can't believe that you've known all this time – and that you didn't say anything – and now you're telling me that other people – I feel such a fool—'

'Oh, Lorna, never that.' He moves towards me, I can smell the soap he uses, and he's looking into my eyes and 'Lorna,' he murmurs, and for a crazy moment I think he's going to kiss me.

Then he says, 'That's my gin you've been drinking.'

'So it is.'

'I think I'd better go.'

'I think you better had.'

As soon as the door shuts behind him, I burst into tears.

I fumble in my pocket for a tissue and bring out a bit of paper. I can't think what it is and then I remember that I picked it up off the floor of the gallery. I smooth it out and I see for the first time what it is.

'A safe deposit receipt,' the Dean says. It's the next morning and we are in her office. Her shoulders are slumped and she seems tired. 'Wilkins and Watson. The cathedral hasn't had dealings with them for years. Perhaps it's something to do with Harry Glendale. I'm seeing the police soon. I'll hand it over then.' She hesitates. 'I'd better tell you, Lorna – they are holding Simon for further questioning. He's admitted to being up the tower. He went up there to smoke a joint.'

I can't believe my ears. 'He did what?'

'He's got multiple sclerosis. The cannabis helps with the joint pain. I've known about it for a while: the MS, I mean, not the cannabis. After he fell over last night, he decided he'd rather people know than get the wrong idea and perhaps think he's been drinking. So I have his permission to tell you.'

'He's in the clear then? Now that the police know why he was up there?'

'Well, no. The police accept that he was smoking a joint, but they also think that he arranged a meeting with Harry Glendale.'

'But why would he ...' I begin. Then the penny drops. 'Oh. Oh no. Because this man used to be a chorister and Simon was the choirmaster, they think that ... But Simon's married! He has children!'

The Dean sighs. 'Oh, my dear ... as if that ever ... but you're right. In Simon's case it's absurd, but we can't expect the police to take our word for that.'

I think about this, then I say, 'Simon isn't the only one with a secret. I didn't recognise the man I saw up there because – 'I hesitate, and then I take a deep breath, and plunge in. 'Because I suffer from prosopagnosia: face blindness. I wouldn't have recognised him, because I can't recognise anyone. Even you. I mean I know you're you, because I'm in your office, and because of the way we're talking and because there aren't many women in the chapter – but as far as your face goes, you could be anyone.'

Of course, she's lovely about it. She tells me not to worry and she'll mention it to the police. I know they'll want to talk to me again, but in the meantime, I go to my office and get on with some paperwork.

I'll have to crack on with the survey of the tower, if we're going to get the grant application in on time. The police have taped off part of it, but I can still get to the scaffolding. Of course, I'm not fool enough to go up on my own, not when there's a murderer on the loose. I take Nathan, one of the apprentices, with me.

It's even more humid than the day before and the sky is overcast. We get in a couple of hours work before Nathan says he needs a pee. The sky's getting darker and darker and it looks as if it'll start tipping down any minute, so I let him go and tell him I'll be down myself very shortly. I'm just doing a final measurement when my mobile rings. I hear Richard's voice and my heart dips a curtsey.

'I've just seen Nathan,' he says. 'I don't think you should be up there on your own.'

'I'm just about to pack up.'

'And have you seen the sky? The heavens are going to open any moment.'

Right on cue there's a distant roll of thunder.

I'm expecting Richard to end the call, but instead he says, 'I spoke out of turn yesterday. I'm sorry.'

'No, I'm sorry too. You were right. I'm not going to keep it a secret any more. I've already told the Dean.'

'Oh Lorna, that's great.' There's silence and then he says, 'I wonder, could we, I've been thinking—'

'Yes?'

'Lorna, will you have dinner with me?'

'Yes!'

'Tonight?'

'Yes!'

'I … I don't think I can wait until then. Stay there, Lorna, I'm coming up.'

'That would be—'

There's a click as Richard ends the call and I find I'm talking to myself – 'that would be lovely. Very lovely. Oh my goodness.'

I'm standing there in a daze of happiness, when my reverie is broken by a big fat raindrop landing plop on my forehead and I remember that 1 haven't packed up. I'm bustling about, raindrops spattering around me on the stone, when behind me the tower door creaks open.

'That was quick!' I say. 'You must have raced up those stairs!'

There's silence except for the drumming of the rain.

I turn and look. A man in a cassock is standing in the doorway.

'Richard?'

The man's moving towards me, his eyes fixed on mine. I can't read his expression, but suddenly I'm frightened. This isn't Richard. The man's wearing gloves, white gloves, the kind the vergers use for handling the plate.

He says, 'Why haven't you told the police yet? I know you saw me. I suppose you want a piece of the action in return for keeping quiet? Is that it? Well, think again!'

I back away, but there's nowhere to go. I feel the edge of the parapet sticking into my waist. He's coming closer.

I snatch off my hard hat and swing it, putting all my weight behind it. It flies out of my hand and makes contact with his head. He staggers sideways, slips on the wet stone and falls heavily against the parapet.

Turns out I was right about that parapet. It collapses under his weight. With a hoarse cry, arms flailing, he disappears over the edge.

That was six months ago. Fred's trial for the murder of Harry Glendale comes on next week. His cassock caught on some crenellation, so he only fell about five metres and got off with a broken leg.

The safe deposit receipt was for two large boxes of seventeenth century communion plate, solid silver, worth hundreds of thousands of pounds. Must have been stored in the bank during the air-raids. Fred had been selling it off piece by piece for years. Harry Glendale found out and was blackmailing him.

Everyone at the cathedral knows now. About me, I mean, and my face blindness and it's fine. As for me and Richard, I can't wait for tomorrow when I walk up the aisle to join him at the altar. We've agreed that he'll reach for my hand and squeeze it.

Just to let me know that I'm marrying the right man.

ABOUT CHRISTINE POULSON

Before Christine Poulson turned to writing fiction, she was an academic with a PhD in History of Art. Her Cassandra James mysteries are set in Cambridge. *Deep Water*, the first in a new series featuring medical researcher Katie Flanagan, appeared in 2016. The second, *Cold, Cold Heart*, set in Antarctica, came out in 2018, and the third, *An Air That Kills*, in 2019. Her short stories have been published in Comma Press anthologies, *Ellery Queen Mystery Magazine*, Crime Writers' Association anthologies, the *Mammoth Book of Best British Mysteries* and elsewhere. She has had stories short-listed for the Short Mystery Fiction Derringer, the Margery Allingham Prize, and the CWA Short Story Dagger.

SLASH

Samantha Lee Howe

'The mind is its own place, and in itself, can make a
Heaven of Hell, a hell of Heaven.'
- John Milton

'And it's a wrap,' said the director.

Lucia Santana walked off the set. Another Italian/American horror film down and she was still nowhere near as popular as her co-star Franco Benicia. She wondered again how she had been talked into doing this film. It had been the worst script Lucia had ever had to work with. Written and Directed (and Produced and Edited and Scored … he even probably painted the sets!) by the same man – never a good thing – but the money offered had been respectable enough and she just couldn't turn it down with no other work in the offing. These films, dire though they were, had a huge following. Years after the *Giallo* period, Lucio Fulchi and Dario Argento had followed in the footsteps of other ground-breaking Italian creators but even as the horror genre was diminishing the independent film industry was still trying to recreate their works. Hadn't Franco found international fame from doing them? That kind of success could get her out of Europe, and hopefully into better roles in the United Kingdom.

'Lucia?' Franco said behind her. 'Want to come for a drink in my dressing room? Now that we've finished? We deserve to celebrate.'

Lucia looked over her shoulder and smiled but her eyes remained cold. She had no intention of being alone with Franco, his reputation for not accepting 'no' was well known, and she wouldn't be another notch in his bedpost.

'My boyfriend is waiting for me,' she said softening her rejection. An out and out refusal had seen his last co-star thrown off set never to work again. Lucia wanted more opportunities and no enemies and so had she tread very carefully with both the director and male lead.

Franco shrugged, 'Another time then?'

'Of course!' Lucia said. 'Great working with you!'

She hurried away. Aware of his eyes on her back, she found herself wondering if his stare was poisonous. She didn't look back for her own peace of mind.

In her dressing room, Lucia cast off her character's blood-stained clothing. All that effort to make it look as though she really stuck a knife in the heart of her on-film attacker and the whole thing was blown out of proportion with the excessive amount of *faux* blood used. The clothing was soaked and so was her skin beneath, which was stained so red that even Argento would have admired the effort it took to get off afterwards. Lucia took a shower and scrubbed her skin until she was no longer sure whether the pink stains were just from her efforts or still the remains of the obnoxious sticky concoction.

She stepped out of the shower, a flash of the horror and gore she'd witnessed rushed behind her eyes. Lucia found herself swaying. Sometimes in this world it was hard to separate life from the art.

Lucia pulled on a glittery gold jacket over her bra. She had decided not to go to the afterparty Not with the letchy director and Franco both there. It was bad enough avoiding one of them, let alone both when they were drinking and on their worst behaviour. Let them have the lesser stars for their sexual fodder. She was beyond that now, hadn't she already paid her dues? So, Lucia had arranged to meet friends, there was no boyfriend on the horizon and there only ever was when she needed an alibi. Lucia's own preference was one that was deemed unacceptable in a beautiful Italian actress – not if she wanted to sustain any kind of credibility anyway: she liked women. Men did nothing for her.

The phone on her dressing table rang as she buttoned up her double-breasted jacket and tugged the shoulder pads neatly in place. She ignored the ringing for a moment, tempted to disregard whoever was calling. She was tired and ready for some much-deserved Champagne but the caller was persistent and she felt compelled to answer. She picked up the receiver.

'*Si?*'

'Lucia? It's Manny. How did the shoot go?'

Lucia deep signed. Manny Fishburne, her American agent, was about to get the full blast of Lucia's wrath. If only he'd told her the truth, she'd have been prepared to fend off the two creeps so much better.

'The director *and* the leading man – you know exactly how it went Manny!' she said.

Manny took a long slow drag of something, a cigarette or maybe a joint, Lucia didn't know which as his breath hissed out and she imagined the released smoke floating over the mouthpiece.

'What? At the same time? Did you—?'

'No. I did not! What do you take me for?' Lucia said. 'I don't do casting couch; you need to protect me better.'

'Yeah. Well. No harm then,' Manny said. 'I knew you could handle yourself.'

'I shouldn't have to deal with this at my level,' Lucia said. She pouted but then realised that such a physical gesture would be lost as Manny couldn't see her.

'Every woman has to deal with this shit, whatever level,' Manny said. 'You think Sophia Lauren hasn't had her fill? Name anyone you think hasn't and I bet I have a story to prove you wrong.'

'It's not right.'

'It ain't. But it's the industry you signed up for.'

Lucia fell silent. She wanted to lose it with Manny. Yell. Scream. Threaten to sack him. But she knew what he'd say. 'Lucia have you taken those pills I gave you? You know you have to keep calm …' Why did she even bother trying to talk

SLASH

about the issue with a man? He'd never understand, nor would he help her. Things had to change. She couldn't do this again, and maybe Manny wasn't the right manager for her anyway. Despite all his empty promises, she was still no closer to the British or American studios.

'So – how did the filming go?' Manny asked again.

'Fine,' she said but the full force of her disappointment hung between them like the smoke from the dry ice the director had insisted on using in almost every shot of this awful film.

'Good. 'Cos I got an opportunity for ya,' Manny said.

'Another B movie?' she asked.

'No. Something way better. I got you an audition in London. All expenses paid.'

The plane took off and Lucia picked up her Campari and lemonade. She was struggling to believe all that had happened in the last 24 hours. Manny had sprung it, despite all her doubts. There she was, flying first class to London from Rome. He hadn't told her much about the job – the script would be given to her when she arrived. It wasn't the lead, he'd explained, but this was a stepping stone in the right direction. And the director had seen and admired her in other roles.

Lucia was nervous, knowing so little, but Manny had assured her that the producers weren't going to compromise her, and they thought highly of her. The comparison made her think again of unhappy times when things had gone wrong. She sometimes felt *damaged* by it. Especially at the beginning, when her father had managed her. Those days ... the decisions he made on her behalf ...

Lucia's mind closed this thought down as fast as it came. No, she wouldn't remember that now, and though it was hard to trust that things wouldn't go wrong again, it was easier to believe she was cared about when she found herself here, in first class.

Later, when she collected her luggage and swept easily through passport control, Lucia found a man waiting outside in the Arrival hall, holding a plaque with her name printed in expensive-looking gold lettering.

'I'm Carl, your chauffeur, Ms Santana,' he said. 'I've been instructed to take you to your hotel.'

Lucia tried to hide her excitement at having her own chauffeur – surely only the big-name stars were treated this way? How many times had she struggled to the studios on public transport at stupidly early times in order to be made up and on set just as the director strolled in?

After that the London trip was a whirlwind. She was whisked off to a beautiful hotel and given a stunning suite all to herself.

As Carl deposited her luggage in the room, he informed her there was a dinner reservation in the hotel restaurant. Lucia was worried this was some kind of ploy by the director or producer, it was all too good to be true. But when she arrived downstairs, fashionably late by 15 minutes, she found a whole table full of people, including the leading lady, a famous face she was very familiar with. Lucia had spent her whole career trying to follow in her footsteps.

'Carlita St Clair …?' she said.

'*Si*. Come and sit beside me. We Italian sisters need to stick together!'

Lucia couldn't believe the welcome she was receiving.

'Benjamin, the director, has told me all about you. You have done so well to catch his eye,' Carlita said.

Lucia's ego was duly boosted and from then on she would have done anything at all to keep in Carlita's good graces and to impress her. But it wasn't necessary, Carlita was easy company and so relaxed with the other actors, and she introduced Lucia to them as though the younger actress was her own protégé.

'Where is the director?' Lucia asked.

'He never joins in with these dinners,' Carlita explained. 'He thinks it's unprofessional.'

'You've worked with him before?'

'Many times,' Carlita said.

'And he isn't ... he doesn't ...?'

'Oh goodness no! We're in London now, you don't need to worry about being molested by some *strisciamento*.'

Lucia's eyes were round and shining as she enjoyed the delicious dinner and the expensive wine: all of it paid for by the studio. Lucia was incredibly happy for the first time since she had stepped foot onto a set. Manny had really done her a great turn this time. Yes. He finally was worth the percentage she paid him, and maybe wasn't so bad after all.

After dinner the talent all dutifully went off to their own rooms. If there was anything between any of them, Lucia didn't see it. She was so unused to this civilized behaviour that it all felt like a dream, or a well-constructed script to lull her into a false sense of security.

Her phone was ringing as she reached her room. Lucia hurried inside and answered to find Manny on the other end of the line – calling long distance from Los Angeles.

'You having a good time?' he asked.

Lucia thought this a strange thing to say but soon poured out all that had happened.

'Good,' said Manny. 'These are good people. Listen ... they want to shoot with you tomorrow. I didn't tell you you'd got the job already on your own credit. Thought you'd be nervous.'

'Tomorrow? Actually shooting the film? But I haven't seen a script.'

'It'll be adlib. Kind of a warm up for the real thing.'

'Oh so this is an audition then,' Lucia said disappointed.

'No. You're in. This is the real deal and you're filming and getting paid from tomorrow.'

Manny told her how much. A week's salary was more than she'd earned for the whole of the last film. Lucia had to sit down.

'You're taking your pills, aren't you?' Manny asked.

'Of course,' Lucia said.

When she hung up, she lay back on the bed, wondering about how wonderful this all was. She was finally going places.

So what if she wasn't the lead. Carlita's draw would help bring Lucia to British screens and fandom more than anything and anyone else had so far.

'I'm on my way …' she thought.

Lucia left the make-up department wearing a smart skirt suit, flat shoes and simple make-up. Her normally luscious black hair was swept up and away from her face and tied back in a severe knot at the nape of her neck. As a finishing touch the make-up artist, Ally, had given her a pair of clear glasses.

'What am I? A librarian?' Lucia asked.

'No. A normal woman, a teacher maybe or an office worker,' Ally smiled. 'It'll all become clear.'

She still hadn't seen a script but she felt oddly comfortable in the dowdy clothing. This was going to be a serious role. At last! She might even win an Oscar for it … *No*, she corrected herself, it was a British film so more likely a BAFTA …

But any accolade would be amazing. She didn't care at all. All she wanted was her name on those credits and the recognition she deserved.

Lucia walked onto the set and found herself in an office situation.

'I'm Ben,' said a voice behind her.

Lucia turned and saw the director for the first time.

Ben was holding out his hand. Lucia took it and they shook.

'We are going to do some … role play here …' Ben explained. 'You are a secretary and you work for this man. His name is Victor. Your character is slightly infatuated with Victor. But he's not what he seems.'

Lucia took a step back, her eyes swept over the set. The camera man and the sound technician were conversing in the corner, and Ally from make-up was waiting at the door to touch up her hair and make-up as necessary.

'I …' Lucia said.

'What's wrong?' asked Ben.

'Is this … is this a … *porn* film?'

Ben laughed. 'Oh no. Goodness no! Think of it as a love story that has gone wrong. You see your character is in love with Victor, but he is in a relationship with Lauren – Carlita is playing her. You're jealous. This is unrequited, you see?'

Lucia gave an awkward laugh. 'I'm sorry. I've just been put in awkward positions before …'

'I'm more into method acting. You know, you submerge yourself into the role and give me what you feel the character would do in a situation. Then, we'll go over the script and talk about how to bring these feelings and emotions into it.'

'Yes. Of course!' Lucia said.

Her face broke into a smile brought on by her relief that she had not been duped again. All sorts of murderous thoughts had gone through her head as she briefly considered what she would do to Manny if he'd set her up.

Even so, her heart was still palpitating as she took up her position after brief instruction from Ben.

They ran smoothly through a scene then, walking through what action should take place for the camera as Lucia met her co-star for the first time, an unknown actor, but striking to look at. She barely heard his real name as she sank herself down into the illusion that he was Victor and she was Diana, his secretary. Ben even referred to her as Diana after that, and so did the crew as they set the scene around her and Victor.

For the first time in her career, Lucia began to genuinely find the actor on set with her attractive. Even as thoughts that he was out of her league pushed into her subconscious. She barely noticed how well the costume she was wearing made her feel she was Diana and all that was boring and dowdy about her came out of her mouth.

'Action!'

Lucia walked onto the set carrying a coffee mug for her boss. Victor didn't look up as she placed the cup down on his desk before him.

'If that's all?' she asked.

Victor nodded.

'Cut!' said Ben. 'Did we get all that?' he asked the cameraman.

Lucia looked up and over the set, she felt as though she was staring out from the screen of a television looking back at the audience. How strange this method acting was. How surreal. She almost didn't want to return to her normal self.

'Take a break,' Ben told her. 'But stay in character both of you please. Everyone, this is Victor and Diana for the rest of the day.'

'Would you like a drink, Diana?' said a voice beside Lucia. She saw then an elderly woman standing beside a trolley on wheels on which was placed several cups of coffee and some fruit snacks.

Lucia was about to say she preferred her coffee black but then she considered how 'Diana' would drink it. Diana would have cream. And perhaps she'd have sugar too.

The catering woman obliged. Lucia felt pleased with herself. She was sure she was going to learn so much from working on this film and Ben's suggestion of method acting was a good one. Hadn't actors like Dustin Hoffman made a career out of 'becoming' a character? It was rumoured he'd lived as a woman for his role in *Tootsie* and the film industry grapevine said his best role was yet to come. Lucia wanted that same success and recognition for her talent too, because she'd known all along she was destined for more than those awful slasher films.

'New scene,' Ben said. 'Diana. This is the morning after. Victor got you drunk the night before and used you for a one-night-stand. But you woke up thinking this meant he loved you. Then, you find him with Lauren. You see him propose to her. How do you feel? What do you do?'

Ben walked away and left Lucia to think about all he'd said. What would Diana feel? She'd be hurt. She'd cry!

They played the scene out with Victor and Diana. The tears were easy but Ben called a halt to the filming halfway through what Lucia felt was a breakthrough performance.

'I don't believe it because you don't believe it,' Ben told her. 'I want to see what Diana feels and I want to see what Diana does. This man used her. Is she going to let him get away with that?'

Lucia took up her mark and the scene began again. Victor alone in his office smiled as she came in, but it wasn't a warm smile. It was the smile that said 'I used you and I don't care'. Lucia felt that primitive hatred she had for men like Victor and she did feel the stirrings of Diana's emotions shifting inside her. It wasn't just her usual analysis of what she thought the director wanted, but something else, as though she could connect with this poor boring girl who had given away her most precious gift.

'Cut!' said Ben. 'That's enough for today. Diana – go back to your hotel – think about things. Victor, come with me, I need to talk through what I want from you.'

Lucia was tired after filming but she was also elated. To not have to scream like a banshee. To not be running around a set, pretending to be chased. To not be covered in blood …

Only a few of the actors attended the dinner that evening, even Carlita had called off, claiming to be learning her lines. Lucia envied her for having a script. Improvisation was so much harder when you had so little direction. Transforming into someone else in such a short time was also not easy.

As the few actors around that evening dispersed to the hotel bar, Lucia found herself alone with Victor.

'I'm sorry,' she said. 'I forgot your real name with all this method work today.'

'That's okay. Call me Victor, it will only help for tomorrow.'

Lucia nodded but her confidence had slipped back with her failure so far to satisfy Ben's demands that she 'become' Diana.

'Cheer up,' Victor said. 'It will all fall into place.'

'I don't know,' Lucia said. 'It's not how I usually work.'

'Then let's rehearse a little more, Diana …' Victor suggested.

Victor ordered two large brandies and against her better

judgement Lucia let him accompany her to her suite so that they could rehearse in private. Lucia sat down on the sofa while Victor placed one of the glasses of brandy in front of her.

'I was new to method acting too,' Victor said. 'But I've been working with Ben for a while now. I'm better for his instruction. And I promise it will get easier. In a way, you just have to lose yourself into the character. It frees you from your usual inhibitions.'

Then Victor began to talk to Lucia as though she was his secretary. They played out the role of her bringing him coffee, the coffee of course was the brandy, and then Victor invited Lucia to drink with him. As Victor pressed the glass into her hand, Lucia thought, *why not?* For once she would try to be free. No one would know about it, after all. It would all remain between her and Victor and she could bring the experience to the table during filming the next day. After all, maybe some things were worth sacrificing for your art.

When she woke a few hours later, Lucia reached out her hand to Victor's side of the bed. She felt the warm spot that he had recently vacated and a strange disappointment came over her that he hadn't remained for the night. She latched on to the emotion, knowing full well that this is what Diana would feel, and she turned over, swallowing the hurt and then anger and blending it with Diana's character. Who was she anyway? A drab spinster that someone like Victor could never love. Yet there had been tenderness in the act that suggested otherwise. Lucia told herself she was Diana and she closed her eyes and forced sleep. But her sleep wasn't restful, haunted as she was with memories of the past. She'd done things she'd rather forget. And her father …

The next morning Diana woke. She was groggy and irritable. She recalled her tormented dreams following her encounter with her boss, Victor. *Oh no!* She hadn't really slept with him, had she? Her judgement had been so impaired by the alcohol and she'd had this stupid dream that they were both actors, playing their parts in a film. She wished.

Diana stumbled out of bed and into the shower, throwing on her drab work clothes as she glanced at her cheap watch. In the bathroom she found a pill bottle with the name *Lucia Santana* on the side. Confused, she dropped the pills into the bin.

She was late, but surely Victor wouldn't comment on that fact. Not after last night?

She felt a little nauseous. How much did they actually drink? How had it even come about? Oh yes, Victor's girlfriend, Lauren, had dumped him. Then he'd invited Diana to have a drink. There was always hard liquor in Victor's desk but he'd never asked Diana to share it with him before.

When she walked into the office, Diana felt embarrassed. She could see Victor, standing by the door and he was talking to someone else who was in his room, but who Diana couldn't see. She decided taking his morning coffee in would be a good excuse to face him for the first time, especially as he wasn't alone. There could be no awkward exchange of words. And although Diana suspected Victor might regret their encounter, she wanted to hold onto the fact that he might feel otherwise. For, as long as he never told her there was nothing between them, then she could hope there was.

The coffee was steaming in her hand. As she passed her desk, Diana saw the pile of letters waiting for her to take into Victor's office for his attention. She picked up the envelopes and walked towards Victor's door.

There she saw Victor sink to one knee; a small box sat on his open palm as he held it out.

Diana paused. Her heart missed an excited beat and then a long-nailed hand reached out and took the ring from the box. There was a squeal of delight as Diana pushed the door open and saw Lauren, sliding the ring onto her finger. A perfect fit.

'Leave it on the desk,' Victor said barely looking Diana's way and dismissing her as if she were nothing.

He threw his arms around Lauren, picked her off the ground and swung her around. They danced around the room oblivious of Diana still standing in the doorway.

A range of emotion swept over Diana. Tears of anguish began to fall and then she saw Victor for what he was. A brutal selfish man who had used her to take his mind off Lauren. How stupid she'd been. How ridiculous were her dreams of them being actors, thrown together for the first time? Diana didn't even like men that way ... But she had been blind to his deceit, desperate for his lurid attention anyway.

Her eyes fell on the sharp letter opener that Victor always kept on his desk and then to the cup of scalding black coffee in her hand. She threw the coffee at Lauren, the black liquid connected with her beautiful face, burning her cheeks in an instant. Lauren screamed and before either she or Victor could react, Diana picked up the letter opener and plunged it into Victor's faithless heart.

There was more screaming and chaos around her. Diana found herself pulled away, even as she yanked out the knife and aimed another strike at Victor.

'My god! What's happened?' shouted Ally running from her post by the door to the office set.

'She's lost her mind!' Ben said.

Victor stood by the table still, blood pooling over his crisp white shirt, even as someone threw water over Lauren's red and blotchy face.

'Get an ambulance!' yelled Ben.

The sound engineer and cameraman held onto the writhing body of Lucia as she screamed and spat and foamed at the mouth.

'It's only acting!' Ben yelled in her face. He ran his hands through his hair and then as Victor stumbled against the desk, he hurried forward to catch him.

But Lucia's aim had hit true, up and under the ribs with the practiced skill of an actress who had spent too many years working on *giallo* movies and had somehow absorbed how a killer would really strike.

Victor's heart stopped long before the ambulance arrived.

'This is your fault, Ben,' Lauren wailed as the ambulance crew looked at her burns and Victor's body was taken away in a black body bag. 'You told him to sleep with her.'

Ben sank down into the chair behind Victor's office desk. His head fell into his hands. 'It was all for the art. I didn't know she'd really *become* Diana!'

In a padded cell, Diana, formerly Lucia Santana, rocked back and forth. She knew her lover, Victor, was dead and that Lauren was probably scarred for life. But it wasn't her fault. It had all started with her father … For a moment she recalled the dark and how, in the middle of the night, she'd feared the covers being lifted She shook her head pushing back all recollection down into the deepest recesses of her broken mind. Now she was Diana, she could truly forget about *him*, and think only that she got her revenge on the man that used her. A crime fitting of a Hollywood star, and one whose name would go down in history for taking 'method' as far as she could.

ABOUT SAMANTHA LEE HOWE

USA Today bestselling author Samantha Lee Howe began her professional writing career in 2007 and has been working as a freelance writer for small, medium and large publishers ever since.

Samantha's breakaway debut psychological thriller, *The Stranger In Our Bed*, was released in February 2020 with Harper Collins imprint, One More Chapter. The book rapidly became a *USA Today* bestseller.

In June 2020, Samantha signed a three-book deal with

One More Chapter for her explosive spy thriller trilogy, *The House of Killers* (Book 1 *The House of Killers*), *Kill Or Die* (Book 2) and *Kill A Spy* (Book 3) were all released in 2021. Pitched as *Killing Eve* meets Jason Bourne this is a nerve shredding, enemies to lovers tale that is simmering with obsession and espionage.

In August 2020, Samantha signed a deal with production company Buffalo Dragon for the option and screenplay for *The Stranger In Our Bed*. The feature film went into production in November 2020 and should be released 2021/22.

To date, Samantha has written 20 novels, 3 novellas, 3 collections, over 40 short stories, an audio drama, a *Doctor Who* spin-off drama that went to DVD, as well as the screenplay for *The Stranger In Our Bed*.

A former high school English and Drama teacher, Samantha has a BA (Hons) in English and Writing for Performance, an MA in Creative Writing and a PGCE in English.

Samantha lives in South Yorkshire with her husband David and their two cats Leeloo and Skye. She is the proud mother of a lovely daughter called Linzi.

THE GOOD NEIGHBOURHOOD

Paul Finch

Terri was just going to bed when the knock sounded on her front door. She'd turned the lights off in the lounge and the hall, and was in the process of mounting the stairs, a cup of tea in one hand, a paperback in the other.

She halted, puzzled. Had that been an actual knock, or did she imagine it?

Another knock followed.

Terri descended to the hall but didn't proceed further. Apart from the fact she was wearing only pyjamas and slippers, it was after eleven o'clock at night. Who came to your front door at that hour? In truth, who came here at all? She didn't remember the last time anyone had knocked on her door whom she hadn't been expecting. But even then, she didn't automatically assume the worst. Chertsey Vale was a good neighbourhood. Lots of nice detached houses, manicured front lawns, decent cars on the driveways. She lived in one of several leafy cul-de-sacs where the biggest (if not only) disturbance was the arrival of teams of noisy gardeners in May and June.

At present, though, it was only March. And of course, nearly midnight.

She placed her tea and paperback on a shelf in the hall and padded along the carpet, halting by the porch door. This hadn't been closed properly in years as its lock was broken, and she felt so secure around here that she'd never bothered to get it fixed. And it wasn't as if the actual front door didn't provide all the safety she needed, a heavy, solid fixture made from oak, though she'd often wondered if it was a weakness that it didn't have a peephole in it. There was a tall, narrow window on the left-hand side, but that was frosted, plus to look through that she'd have to get right up to it, which would mean that whoever was outside would see her and then know that she was in.

In all likelihood, of course, they knew that anyway. As a third knock attested.

If no one answered the first time you knocked on a door, you'd assume they hadn't heard it. The second time, though, you tended to realise that, for whatever reason, most probably because they were out, no one was going to come. To do it a third time, therefore, implied not only an awareness that the occupants were present, but a *requirement* to see them.

Terri still wasn't inclined to open up, even with the safety-chain in place.

'Who is it?' she called, waiting by the porch door.

'I need to speak to Teresa Bates. Sorry about the lateness of the hour.' It was a muffled reply, but clearly female.

That didn't necessarily reassure Terri. She remembered a horror film she'd seen not too long ago, in which some people were murdered by a gang in their holiday home, but only after a lone woman came to their front door late at night, pretending to be lost.

'Okay,' she replied. 'But who are you?'

A hand appeared at the side window, flattening some rectangular object, an open wallet maybe, against the distorted glass. It was difficult to see, but while the lower half of it appeared to be carrying lines of official-looking type, the upper half had a flat silvery object in the centre.

'Detective Sergeant Julie Tyler,' the voice said. 'I'm sorry to be here so late, Miss Bates, but I need to speak with you as a matter of urgency.'

Terri disabled the alarm and opened the door to the couple of inches the chain permitted.

The woman outside was young, probably in her mid-twenties, and slim, with shoulder-length fair hair and a rather pretty face. She was gloved and wore a beige mac over slacks and a white blouse.

'You're a police officer?' Terri asked.

'DS Tyler.' The caller showed her identity again, before flipping the wallet closed and shoving it into her pocket. 'I'm with the Serial Crimes Unit ... we're part of the National Crime Group.'

'Oh my God,' Terri breathed, not at all liking the sound of *that*.

'I usually find it's best if conversations like this happen indoors, away from prying eyes.'

Terri agreed. It was late now, and Duncot Drive tended to go to bed early midweek, but if the conversation was protracted, curtains would start to twitch, and that was all she'd need. Too many of the neighbours thought her an odd fish as it was.

Still though, she was unsure. 'I'm sorry, but I have to know what it's about.'

DS Tyler's face was blank, inscrutable, but when she said, 'Liam Haggerty,' that was all Terri needed to hear.

She removed the chain, allowing the officer entry, before glancing warily around outside. A car she didn't know, a blue Ford Puma, sat by the kerb at the end of her drive. Beyond that, the other houses and gardens lay in darkness. A few shreds of last autumn's leaves drifted on a gentle breeze. Shivering, she went back inside, ensuring to close the front door properly so that its latch *snicked* into place.

Terri felt self-conscious in the presence of Detective Sergeant Tyler. It wasn't just that Tyler was younger and better looking than she was; Terri had been a catch in her day, though she'd put weight on recently, she rarely bothered with makeup anymore and really ought to do something with her straggling black curls other than get her hairdresser to hack them short every two months. It was more that the young policewoman had a cool, efficient aura. She did a dangerous, high-pressure job, and yet here she was, even though it was the middle of the night, smart, relaxed, cool as you like, while Terri was blundering around in her pyjamas, looking scruffy and tired. Even the dressing-gown she'd pulled on was her old, tatty one, which looked more like a bit of old carpet.

At least the lounge was tidy. Though mess was rarely a problem when you lived alone.

'Do you want to sit down,' DS Tyler said.

Bit of a cheek, Terri thought. *Being asked to sit down in my own house.*

But the police would always be the police, she supposed. And oddly, now that she thought about it, there was something vaguely familiar about this particular officer. Not that an explanation sprang immediately to mind. They were hardly the same age group, Terri now in her late thirties, so it could not have been a social thing. But it scarcely mattered at present.

'Please tell me what it is,' Terri said. 'Has something happened to Liam?'

The policewoman regarded her with studied interest. 'You're aware who I'm talking about?'

'Of course.'

'Yes … of course.' Disdain flickered in Tyler's face, but she suppressed it. 'How well do you know Liam Haggerty, Miss Bates?'

'Only through the letters we've exchanged.'

'I'm sorry to have to ask you this, but were those romantic letters?'

'No, not really.' This question made Terri even more uneasy. 'Just the usual thing.'

'The usual thing?'

'I offer friendship and support. For those who are alone and have no one to turn to.'

'I see. You are aware what Liam Haggerty did?'

'Yes.'

'I mean, it's not every criminal who receives a mandatory full-life sentence.'

'I know what he did.'

Tyler glanced fleetingly away. That look again. Disdain, disgust even.

'Were *you* on the case?' Terri asked. 'Is that what this is about?'

'I was involved in the investigation, yes.'

That's where I know her from, Terri told herself. The woman had probably been on television. Perhaps coming out of court on a newsreel. Maybe being interviewed.

'And let me guess,' Terri said, 'you think I'm some kind of weirdo for having made friends with him?'

'It's a case of each to their own. I'm no one to judge.'

Then why are you doing it, Terri thought tetchily.

Tyler surveyed the lounge. 'Curious. I see no religious items. No crucifixes or statuettes.'

'I'm sorry?'

'We usually find that women who befriend convicted murderers fall into two categories. Groupies, who are attracted to bad boys but fall in love with them from a safe distance. Or sympathetic ears, who are acting through misguided religious motives.'

'Misguided?'

'Well, you say you want to be his friend … you say he's all alone. But some would argue that's exactly what he deserves. Others would argue he deserves a whole lot worse.'

Terri shook her head. 'I can't speak for anyone else, but no … seeing as you ask, I'm not religious. I'm a humanist. That means I value all human life instinctively and for its own sake, without needing some imaginary God to tell me that it's worthwhile.'

Tyler seemed fascinated. 'And does this philosophical stance draw some kind of line when it comes to the value of the persons Liam Haggerty murdered. There were six of them, in case you'd forgotten. Three men and three women. All shot to death during aggravated burglaries. Completely unnecessarily, as even though they were what we'd classify as high-end targets, they were all elderly and none of them was likely to have put up a fight.'

Terri held her ground. Not exactly proud, not even defiant, but attempting the same patient, dignified response with which she'd greeted her hostile neighbours when one of the daily rags had first broken the story that she was in the habit of 'filling her time by writing cheery letters to imprisoned killers'.

'Sergeant, I'm sure this is not why you've come all the way here so late on a Wednesday night. To tackle me for trying to bring some light into the darkness of Liam Haggerty's life.'

'No, you're right, it isn't.' Briefly, Tyler seemed contrite. 'I'm sorry, you'll have to forgive me … I live day-to-day in a less forgiving world than yours. No, what I'm actually here for is to inform you that, earlier today, Liam Haggerty escaped from Belmarsh Prison.'

'He … *what?* Liam escaped …?' Terri's words petered out as though she couldn't believe she'd uttered them herself. Slowly, the room commenced spinning. She swayed, dazed, before plonking herself down on the couch. 'Oh … oh my God.'

'I know. As I say, I'm sorry to be the one to have to tell you this.'

Terri glanced up, nauseous. 'When did he escape?'

'Early this afternoon.' DS Tyler also sat on the couch, but at the other end of it. 'Around two o'clock. He was injured in a fight in the kitchen. He was on his way to hospital when he broke free.'

'And they haven't recaptured him yet?'

'Well, no. That's why I'm here to warn you.'

Terri looked even more shocked. Before trying to force a laugh. 'Warn *me*? Oh, I sincerely doubt that … that *I'm* in any danger. I mean …' But the policewoman's expression remained grave. 'Am I?'

'Miss Bates, someone has already died.'

'Oh, no …' Terri felt faint again. She put a hand to her mouth in case she was sick.

'One of the prison officers escorting him. His skull was crushed against a kerbstone.'

'My God!' Terri shook her head. 'But I've seen nothing on

the news.'

'It's embargoed at present.'

'Heaven ... good God in Heaven!' Terri stood up sharply. More by instinct than design, she lurched towards the hall door. 'I was about to say would you like a cup of tea, but I think I need something stronger ...'

'I wouldn't fuddle yourself with drink just at this moment,' Tyler advised.

Terri glanced back.

'I'm not saying Haggerty *will* come here,' the policewoman said. 'But he might. And it's a *real* might, I'm afraid. He has your address after all, and Belmarsh is less than half a day away.'

'But he and I made friends.'

'That may be his motivation.'

Terri sat down again, this time in the armchair.

Tyler's expression softened a little. 'I'm sorry, I'm not trying to alarm you. But unfortunately, these situations where nice middle-class ladies like yourself strike up friendships with men serving time for violent crimes ... they rarely end well.'

'I feel I *know* Liam ...'

'Trust me, you don't.'

'I certainly know that he has no reason to harm me.'

'Apart from the fact he's now in desperate straits. He'll be looking for money, food, perhaps a warm bed for the night. And if you, his supposed friend, can't provide any of that, then heaven knows how he'll react.'

Terri considered this glumly.

'It might even be,' Tyler added, 'that he just plain resents you.'

'Me? Surely not? I mean, why ...?'

'Because he's a psychopath, a madman. Look, Teresa ... can I call you that?'

'I prefer Terri.'

'Look, Terri ... I know it's a difficult pill to swallow, but these men really are different from us. *Everything* about them is different. All they know is hate. They have no empathy, no feelings of pity, charity, kindness. They accept no responsibility for the terrible things they've done, or for their failures in life. It's always someone else's fault, and that someone will always pay if the chance comes along ...'

'And you're not trying to alarm me? Dear Lord!'

'Well, I'm hoping the fact I'm here now will reassure you a little.' Tyler stood up, suddenly business-like. 'At least you'll have company tonight.'

Terri frowned. 'Excuse me?'

'That's the other reason for my visit. To stay with you until we can get a firearms officer to guard the house, which will probably be first thing in the morning. Or until Haggerty is recaptured, which might be sooner.'

Terri was amazed. 'Let me get this straight ... I'm under police protection?'

'For the moment.'

'But you yourself aren't carrying a gun?'

'I know what you're going to say next: and because we never recovered the murder weapon, Haggerty might now have retrieved it himself. Well ... that's why we're mobilising firearms units. But it's only a precaution. We don't believe that Haggerty's armed. He's on the run, and his priority will almost certainly be to get clean away.'

Terri nodded as she took this in. She too stood up, fastening the strap of her dressing-gown, making an effort to get herself together. 'If you don't recommend anything stronger, how does that cup of tea sound?'

'Smashing,' Tyler said. 'But first we need to check that all your windows and doors are locked.'

Terri nodded again. That made sense.

'I see you have an alarm. Does it cover all entry points?'

'Only the front and back doors. This is a good neighbourhood. I've always felt safe here.'

'In that case let's make sure everything's secure ourselves.'

They went about it together.

'You say Liam escaped around two o'clock this

afternoon?' Terri asked.

'There or thereabouts.'

'So, theoretically ...' Terri had to suppress a shudder.

'Yes, I know,' the policewoman said. 'He could already be here.'

'Oh God!' Terri yelped. 'There's someone down in the garden!'

She was in her bedroom, which faced out to the rear of the property, and, having gone around the house checking everything, was in the process of getting dressed when she'd just happened to glance through the window.

With a thudding of feet, DS Tyler came along the landing and entered the room. She found Terri fastening her jeans and pulling on a sweatshirt but staring down into the garden.

'Don't stand where he can see you!' the policewoman hissed.

At her suggestion, they'd already turned all the lights off inside. This didn't reduce the possibility that if Haggerty showed up here, he'd try to break in, she said, but at least he wouldn't be able to work out where everyone was.

Terri lurched to the right side of the window and stood out of sight, while Tyler went to the left. From here, they peeked down together. The back garden lay tranquil in the moonlight. It was squarish, about forty yards by forty, and mostly lawn, with a rockery against the left-hand hedge and the woodshed in the far-right corner, though this latter stood under a couple of elm trees and was partly concealed by shadow.

'What did you see?' Tyler asked.

'I'm ... not sure.' Terri's voice was querulous. 'A dark shape, I think. It flitted out of sight around the back of the shed.'

They watched on as silent seconds passed.

'You think it's him?' Terri asked.

'I don't know. I don't see anyone.'

'Shouldn't you radio this in?'

'We don't carry radios in CID anymore. But I've got my phone.' Tyler dug under her mac. 'Stay here, keep watching.'

Terri held her position as the policewoman went out onto the landing. Half a second later, she heard her muffled tones. It was difficult to distinguish the words, but Tyler sounded apologetic, and Terri knew why. Most likely she didn't believe that her charge had seen anything. They already had her down as a headcase, probably the last sort of person they'd want to rely on as a witness.

'Support units will be here in five,' Tyler said, tucking her phone away as she came back into the room.

Terri was worried by that. 'I *thought* I saw someone. I could've been mistaken ...'

'Doesn't matter. Better to be safe than sorry.'

The policewoman resumed her former position, and they scanned the garden again. Still, nothing moved down there.

'Five minutes,' Terri eventually said. 'Funny how that can seem like a long time.'

'Don't worry. We're locked up tight. If it *is* Haggerty, he can't get in here.' But then the policewoman's mouth turned crooked, her posture straightening. 'He *can* get away, though. Which is not really what we want. Not when the cavalry's on the way.' Thoughts raced visibly through her head as she moved to the bedroom door. 'You stay here, Terri.'

'Wait,' Terri said, but Tyler was already halfway downstairs. She'd evidently decided that hiding indoors was some kind of dereliction of duty. Terri hurried down after her, urging her to reconsider, but the policewoman shook her head.

'I'm going out via the front door. Be sure to close it behind me and lock it.'

'For God's sake!' Terri protested. 'Just wait till help arrives.'

'I can't do that. Haggerty's already killed one person since he got free. If he stays free now ... and kills someone else, it's on me.'

That made a kind of sense, Terri realised. But was it brave or simply reckless?

'Do you have *any* kind of weapon?' she asked. 'A pepper spray or stun gun?'

'We don't routinely carry stuff like that in plain clothes.'

'You need something.' Terri dashed to her under-stair closet, rummaged through the clutter inside it, and extricated a three-foot timber shaft, painted black and white, with a handle at one end and a curved, flattened head at the other. 'Here … take this.'

Tyler looked amused. 'A hockey stick?'

'I take it they didn't play when you were at school? If they had done, you wouldn't query its usefulness as a weapon.'

The policewoman took the item and hefted it, still smiling. 'Better than nothing, I suppose.' Then she turned the catch on the front door. 'Don't come outside for anything.'

'But if something happens to you …?'

'Help's on its way. It'll be here imminently.'

The door closed behind her, the catch again *snicking* as it caught.

Terri stood alone in the darkness, still stunned that all this could have happened. Outside, there was a *clunk* and *squeal* as the wrought-iron gate at the side of the house was opened. Hurriedly, she moved through into the kitchen and lifted the Venetian blind. Nothing stirred in the back garden, moonlight reflecting from the lush turf, the silent row of ornamental stones in the rockery, the shadowy upright shape of the woodshed. When DC Tyler appeared there, Terri expected that she'd give the shed wide berth, veer across the lawn to the far hedge so that she could peer down the narrow gap at the back of it without getting too close. That would be the sensible thing.

Except that DC Tyler didn't appear.

Terri grew tense as she waited.

It was no more than twenty yards from the side gate to the back of the house. It should not have taken more than two or three seconds, but still there was no sign of her. When a full minute had passed, Terri decided there was a problem. But as per the policewoman's instructions, she wasn't going outside. Not when there was an alternative. She hurried up the stairs, at the top of which, on the right, there was a small square window. She felt fairly safe unlocking and opening this one as it was so high up, though she had to open it wide in order to lean her head and shoulders out and peer downward.

The side passage lay directly below her. And was empty.

She glanced to the right and saw that the wrought-iron gate at the front of the passage stood ajar, so Tyler had clearly opened it. When she glanced left, she could only partially see the rear garden, never mind the shed at the far end of it, but there was no indication of movement down there either.

Her uncertainty morphing into concern, Terri hurried around her three bedrooms to get better vantage on the whole neighbourhood. Her own bedroom window still showed the back garden lying serene, but when she got to the second bedroom, which looked out at the front, she stopped rigid.

There was no sign of the policewoman, while her blue Puma still sat at the kerb. But some fifty yards to the right, a solo figure – a man, by the shape of him – with back turned and hands in pockets, was walking away along Duncot Drive.

Terri watched, her spine tingling. He could be anyone, of course. But there was no one else around, nor even a hint of light from any of the other houses.

When the man turned the corner at the end of the street and vanished, the midnight stillness returned a hundred times over.

Terri stood cold and stiff, the skin on her back crawling, before she jolted into action.

Dashing back through the house into her own bedroom, she looked down again at the rear garden. Still nothing. However, her eyes were now attuning to the dimness and she could see more of the shed. Suddenly, the mere fact that it concealed a tiny portion of the garden made it seem sinister. She hadn't even seen the policewoman approach it, but *someone* had gone around the back of it. Had it been him? The man she'd just seen? Had he then committed another serious crime? Was that why he'd now made a speedy exit? And was the evidence of that crime down behind the shed, or even inside it?

Terri continued to watch, but nothing else happened. Eventually she reached the only conclusion possible. She was going to have to go out. There was no other way.

She could have called 999, but a police unit was already en route. They were taking their time getting here, but that was often the case, and ringing the emergency number wouldn't bring them any faster. Another alternative would be to sit tight and wait, but how would that look if DS Tyler, who'd come here to help, was lying injured, while Terri Bates, the criminals' friend, simply hid and did nothing?

Even then though, it was difficult unlocking the front door and stepping outside.

She'd pulled an anorak and gloves on, but the midnight March air gripped her like an icy claw. The neighbourhood had never been more silent. There wasn't even that usual hum of occasional distant traffic. When she glanced left and focussed on the open gate, she almost had second thoughts. Tyler had told her to stay indoors at all costs.

But then again, this was Liam they were talking about. And everything they'd said about his no-doubt disturbed state of mind notwithstanding, she still felt certain that *she* was in less danger from him than almost anyone else. Besides, hadn't she just seen him leaving the area?

Before approaching the gate, she scanned the front garden for any kind of weapon. At first glance there was nothing even as useful as a hockey stick, but then her eyes fell on the rake, which lay in a corner of the lawn.

A rake.

On a scale of one to ten in terms of ridiculousness, that would clock in at about a hundred.

But again, it was better than nothing.

Firstly, she double locked the front door, ensuring to pocket the key in her anorak, and then, grabbing up the rake, ventured to the gate. When she glanced down the passage, all she saw, as before, was a slice of rear garden and a sliver of wooden shed.

She waited and listened. There was no sound.

It was tempting to call out to DS Tyler, to ask if she was okay. But Terri couldn't help wondering how she'd react if she did that and then heard the sound of heavy feet coming racing back along Duncot Drive towards her. That imaginary prospect was so overpowering that she swung sharply around and stared back along the road.

Nothing and no one.

But this was no guarantee that she was alone. Well pruned though it all was, most of the neighbourhood's front gardens contained bushy vegetation of some sort or other, while there were hidden niches around the sides of garages and carports, even around the cars themselves. Lots of hiding places. Lots of means by which someone could steal up on her without her realising.

But enough with the flights of fantasy.

Levelling the rake like a rifle with a bayonet, Terri advanced down the side passage. All the way, her nerves were like cello strings, but no one jumped out in front of her at the far end, and though she glanced continually over her shoulder, no one stepped into view behind. When she entered the rear garden, it was the same as ever. Placid, peaceful, bathed in gentle moonlight. A place where nothing bad could happen.

Even so, when she approached the shed, she did so cautiously, constantly glancing back to ensure the entrance to the passage remained empty, and only crossing the lawn in a wide half-circle. From the perimeter hedge, she could see all the way down the gap at the other side of the shed. At the far end of that, there was a break in the undergrowth where someone could pass with relative secrecy into the garden of her sniffy neighbours, the Mortons. But she could see through that as well, and nothing out of the ordinary was lurking down there. Even so, the darkness and silence of the neighbourhood was weighing on her, and when she approached the shed, knowing that she'd need to look inside it before she could go back indoors, it was with extreme trepidation.

And with good reason.

Because as she reached for the ring-handle, she heard the first sound that she herself wasn't responsible for. A light, hollow *thud*. Just one. Nothing more than that. But it sounded distinctly as if it had come from inside the small wooden structure.

Terri halted, stood stock-still, and then began to backtrack. At any second, she expected the door to explode open.

'Liam,' she breathed, almost aloud. 'Oh my God ... why have you done this?'

Now a second *thud* sounded, louder and more localised. And it drew her eyes up to the shed roof, where the neatly divided, black and white face of the Mortons' cat, Bilbo, was looking lazily down at her.

Terri sagged where she stood. Her knees threatened to buckle.

And a hand alighted on her shoulder.

She swung around, shouting, hefting the garden rake like a poleaxe.

DS Tyler looked even more amused than before. 'I'll swap you that rake for this hockey stick.'

Terri tottered sideways with relief. 'What ... what happened?'

'What're you doing out here?'

'I thought something had gone wrong. I didn't see you come into the garden.'

'I was about to go down the passage at the side of the house,' Tyler said, shouldering the hockey stick. 'I opened the gate, but then it struck me that if I went into one of your neighbours' gardens first, I'd spot him before he spotted me.' She shrugged. 'It didn't work. There's clearly no one here.'

'Not now there isn't,' Terri replied. 'Because I've just seen him leaving.'

The policewoman frowned. 'Where?'

'The far end of Duncot Drive. He was walking quickly. You know, like he'd looked around and there were no opportunities.'

'You're sure?'

'I'm sure I saw someone.' Terri hesitated. 'I can't guarantee it was him.'

'Come with me.' Tyler hurried back down the side passage, leaving the hockey stick propped against the side of the house.

Terri followed tentatively. 'What are we doing?'

'Going after him. I don't think you'll need that rake, by the way.'

Terri left the rake in the passage, next to the hockey stick. 'I thought the idea was to lock ourselves in?'

'We *will* be locked in.' Tyler headed down the front drive. 'But in the car. If I can locate him now, I can redirect the support units ... better we catch him on the streets than at your house, eh?'

Terri couldn't argue with that. She climbed into the Puma's front passenger seat, while Tyler slid behind the wheel, dug her phone out and speed-dialled someone.

'Sir ... it's Julie. Listen, we've got a possible sighting of Haggerty. Heading down Duncot Drive towards the junction with ...' she glanced at Terri, 'what's the next street?'

'Yellow Brook Road.'

'Yellow Brook Road. I've got Miss Bates in the car with me. I didn't want to ignore this lead, but I didn't want to leave her on her own either ... so we're going to drive around for a bit. Sort of scour the neighbourhood. Yeah ... okay. I'll keep updating you.'

She put the phone down, hit the ignition and threw the Puma into gear.

'How long will the others be?' Terri asked.

'That's down to the local boys.' Tyler swung the car through a three-point turn and gunned it towards the junction with Yellow Brook Road. 'But it's midweek, which is usually quiet. Don't see why they won't get here when they said they would.'

'Five minutes has passed now. Easily.'

'He's giving them a nudge. We'll likely meet them somewhere on the estate.'

Terri explained that the man had turned left, so they went that way first. Perhaps inevitably, there was no one on

Yellow Brook Road. But neither was there on Rookery Close, nor Linwood Crescent, nor Turing Lane, nor any of the other interconnected tree-lined avenues that made up Chertsey Vale. It wasn't exactly a cookie-cutter neighbourhood, but as they prowled slowly and quietly, it struck Terri for the first time how much each thoroughfare looked similar to the next: neat suburban homes, two cars on every drive, kids' toys scattered on front lawns, lines of trimmed privets.

'*There!*' she shouted, pointing. Tyler hit the brakes. The road lay empty, but Terri knew that she'd just seen a running shape disappear into an alley leading between two of the houses ahead on the left. 'It was a man, I'm sure!'

Tyler drove forward, halting on level with the alley, though all they could see from the car was that it led off towards a single streetlight and beyond that, blackness.

'Where does that go?' Tyler asked.

'Ultimately, Carrington Park.'

Tyler put her foot down, and within eighty yards took a left-hand turn, the signpost to which read 'Carrington Lane'. This road too was bereft of life, though on the right side of it there was an iron railing, beyond which stood a crowd of leafless but tight-grouped trees. Tyler drove on until they came alongside the exit from the cut-through. Directly opposite, on the other side of the road, was a gateway into the park. It stood wide open. The Puma's engine rumbled as they sat there, the policewoman contemplating.

'You're not thinking of going in?' Terri said. 'Not alone?'

Tyler dug her phone out again. 'Even *I'm* not that daft.' She placed another call. 'Sir … it's Julie again. Can you put it through to Division that Carrington Park might be worth a look? My witness thinks she saw someone going in there. Yeah … okay. I hear you.'

She cut the call, put the phone away and knocked the Puma back into gear.

'What did he say?' Terri asked.

Tyler started driving. 'Me and you are going back to yours. Sitting tight, just like before. Local units are en route.

They're being diverted to the park.'

Terri glanced behind as they turned away from the wall of fencing and darkened trees. Elsewhere in the night, there was still no sound of approaching sirens, no sign of swirling blue lights. But then she supposed that no copper worth his salt would want to alert a suspected fugitive that they were closing in on him.

Poor Liam, she couldn't help thinking. Though she couldn't resist feeling angry with him too. Facing a full-life sentence was surely the most onerous thing imaginable, as he'd intimated to her in several of his letters. But craziness like this was no solution. And now he was paying the price for it. Lurking out there in the night like a frightened animal.

A frightened and rather *dangerous* animal, she reminded herself.

It didn't pay to get too dewy-eyed about Liam.

The police didn't think he was armed, but that hadn't stopped him crushing a man's skull.

Terri bit her lip so hard that it almost drew blood.

On a kerbstone.

DS Tyler applied the handbrake but made no effort to get out of the car. She didn't even switch the engine off.

Terri looked at her. 'Is something wrong?'

Tyler nodded along the drive to the wrought-iron gate. 'Didn't we leave that open?'

Terri saw that the gate was now closed. A vague chill went through her. 'I don't know. Could your colleagues have been here? Perhaps they had a look around the house?'

'We redirected them to the park, remember?' Tyler turned the engine off and unbuckled her seatbelt. 'When we get out, just go straight to the door and straight inside, yeah?'

'If you think he's here, isn't it better to keep driving?'

The policewoman climbed from the car. 'I *don't* think he's here. Frankly, I think we're jumping at shadows. But let's take no more chances.'

She headed up the drive, veering towards the side gate. Terri meanwhile, went to the front door, inserted the key and turned the lock. The door swung open and she looked back – and saw Tyler running towards her.

'Inside!' she hissed.

'What is it?'

'*Inside!*'

Terri allowed herself to be pushed through into the porch. Tyler followed, slamming the front door behind them, ensuring the catch was in place and attaching the safety-chain.

'Can you double-lock this?' she said, breathless.

Terri complied nervously. 'I thought you said we were jumping at shadows?'

But the policewoman was pale-faced even in the dimness of the hall. 'I thought that, yeah. Maybe I *hoped* it. But … we left the rake and the hockey stick in the side passage, didn't we?'

'Of course.'

'There's only the rake there now.'

'Oh no …'

'And I can't see any of my colleagues wanting to fool around with an old hockey stick. You definitely locked the whole place up?'

'Absolutely.'

'I didn't hear you disabling the alarm when you came in just then.'

'I didn't put it on.'

Tyler pulled a face at that. 'What are your neighbours like?'

'What do you mean?'

'If there was a sound of breaking glass, would they respond?'

'Yes, I think so. They don't like me very much, but as I say … this is a good neighbourhood.'

'Okay, well we still need to check around.' Tyler switched the downstairs lights back on, and led the way as they circled each room, thankfully finding every window and the back door still intact, and no sign of forced entry. 'Your neighbours are a pain in the arse, then?'

'Well, you know …'

'There was some kind of newspaper article, wasn't there?'

Terri shrugged, hot-faced. 'Load of tittle-tattle. Rabble-rousing nonsense in one of the red-tops. I'd love to know who tipped them off.'

The lights upstairs were still off, but feeling better now, they ascended the staircase in single file, the policewoman at the front.

'One thing I've learned in all my years in this job,' she said over her shoulder, 'there's always someone who'll talk.'

'You mean someone at the prison?'

'Or some solicitor somewhere, or even some copper. Easy money, isn't it?'

They reached the landing, Tyler switching the upstairs lights on. Terri made to enter her bedroom, but Tyler's left arm shot out, blocking her progress. Terri looked around and saw the policewoman's right hand pointing at the square window at the top of the stairs. Which hung wide open.

'Hell …' Terri breathed, though she wasn't quite as alarmed as Tyler. 'I opened that earlier to see how you were getting on.'

'And you left it open while we were out?'

'That's twenty feet from the ground. He can't have climbed up there surely?'

'Terri … a twenty-foot climb would provide no obstacle even for an average burglar, and this guy is very far from average, wouldn't you agree?'

They pivoted around, eyeing each and every open doorway. Until Terri glanced into her own bedroom, and another bolt of ice passed through her.

An extendable steel ladder lay alongside the bed. It was old and dirty and stained all over with globs of dried emulsion, just the kind of thing a housepainter would use, and most likely keep stored in his garage between jobs. Instinctively they both understood why Terri had spotted Haggerty walking away.

He'd been looking for a way to gain entry, and during their absence, it seemed, he'd found one.

The policewoman backed towards the top of the stairs, hauling Terri with her. But when they reached it, with light now shining down the stairs from the landing, they spotted something they'd missed on the way up: a set of muddy footprints descending, darker and more pronounced near the top, fading as they neared the bottom.

Terri thought first about her own feet; she'd been plodding about in the garden. But it hadn't been wet. And in any case, by the looks of these marks, the feet had been large.

'Jesus ...' Tyler breathed, 'he's *downstairs.*'

Terri was initially unable to reply. Her thoughts whirled chaotically.

The policewoman scanned her immediate surroundings, and spotted a trapdoor several feet overhead. 'Is there a fold-down ladder up there?' she whispered.

'Yes,' Terri said, also in a low voice. 'But we don't want to go into the loft, surely?'

'Better than downstairs.'

'Downstairs, we can make a run for your car.'

'We'd have to unlock the front door. He'd have plenty of time to intercept us.'

'But we've already looked downstairs ...' Terri's voice was turning shrill; she had to lower it again. 'We looked, and he wasn't there.'

'Obviously, he was hiding.'

'We checked everywhere.'

'In the under-stair closet?'

Terri's mouth dropped open. Neither of them had checked the under-stair closet.

'Remember the Lubbington family murders?' Tyler said quietly. 'He broke in while they were out. And hid under the stairs till they came home.'

'My God,' Terri breathed.

'Old habits die hard with these guys.'

Terri glanced again downstairs, but all she could see was

the empty hall.

'He didn't attack the first time because he didn't know who and how many of us there were,' Tyler whispered. 'But he's probably worked out by now that we're a couple of women. That'll encourage him. And he's not going to let us leave this place given that we *know* he's here.'

Terri nodded, swallowed and, reaching out almost gingerly, took a prop down from alongside the jamb to her bedroom door. It had a rubber button on one end and a hook on the other. She reached up with the button, hitting the press-stud on the catch to the trapdoor, and when it swung down, used the hook to connect with the aluminium ladder folded in the darkened recess above. Unfortunately, the ladder didn't descend quietly, its articulated joints clattering and banging, but there was nothing they could do, even when Terri fancied that she was hearing movements downstairs. When the ladder's feet struck the carpet, Tyler urged Terri to get up it first. Still, it seemed appallingly noisy, more thuds and clatters ringing through the interior of the house. Again, Terri didn't know if it was the ladder, or the sound of heavy feet ascending the staircase.

At the top, she threw herself up through the square aperture, reached down behind her, and grabbing Tyler by the collar of her mac, lugged her bodily upward. The policewoman brought the ladder with her, and pulled the trap closed with a thumping crash.

For good measure, she jammed the prop through the rungs of the re-folded ladder, ensuring that it couldn't be yanked downward again.

'Why bother with that?' Terri panted. 'He could use the decorator's ladder ...'

'And if he does, we hit him with everything we get our hands on. He's *not* coming up!'

But for the moment at least, whoever it was down there, they didn't seem to be trying.

The women knelt in darkness, listening, sweating hard, the dust settling over them like an itchy second skin. Silence reigned, a mysterious and very protracted silence.

'I was sure I heard someone down there,' Terri whispered.

Tyler put a finger to her lips, but sufficient landing light leaked up around the edges of the trapdoor to show her taut body posture gradually lessening. Eventually, she signalled by pointing that they should move deeper into the loft, which was actually more like an attic in that it had a floor and two windows at the gable end. Sitting side by side, these two dusty panes formed a single arch and looked like a pair of villainous eyes. Ever since Terri had lived here, they'd reminded her of the house in that film, *The Amityville Horror*. At present though, they were facing away from the moon, so only minimal silvery light intruded, and the women had to negotiate their way around the stacks of boxes and disused furniture by touch alone. Despite this, Tyler was just approaching the windows, filching her phone from her pocket, when a coat was dislodged from a rack, and behind it, the weak light fell on a tall figure.

It was partially cloaked in shadow, but quite clearly a man.

For half a second, she was locked in place, every muscle rigid. Then, she squealed and lurched away, caroming into Terri and sending her staggering and falling.

'It's okay,' Terri said hurriedly. 'It's a mannequin. You know, like in department stores.'

Tyler was so shaken that she continued to retreat until she came up against the narrow strip of brickwork between the two windows. In the half-dark, the figure certainly *looked* real, though it didn't help that its back was turned, concealing its fake plastic features, or that it wore a hoodie top, ensuring that its fake plastic hair was also hidden.

'You … you have a mannequin in your attic?'

'It was my mother's.' Terri dusted herself down as she got back to her feet. 'She was a seamstress. She acquired it from a shop in town so that she could hang clothes on it.'

The policewoman shook her head as if the mere thought of that was appalling to her. However, just as quickly as she'd taken fright, she relaxed again.

'Do you think he'll have heard that kerfuffle?' Terri asked.

'Bound to, but he knows we're up here anyway.' Tyler stripped her mac off and laid it on the dingy floorboards under the windows. 'Question is ... will he consider it worth the risk trying to battle his way up here, or will he cut his losses and run?'

'I can't believe this is happening.' Terri took her anorak off too, draped it on the floor and sat on it, her back to the wall. 'It's come on us so quickly.'

Tyler slumped down next to her. 'I bet you're sorry you wrote those letters now, aren't you?'

'That's a cheap shot.'

'You mean it *hasn't* got you into terrible trouble?'

Terri said nothing but drew her knees to her chest.

'Just out of interest,' the policewoman asked, 'how many killers have you written to over the years?'

'Only a handful.'

'Anyone else I know?'

A second passed, before Terri said: 'Jason Woodrow.'

'The guy who abducted those two little girls from their back garden up in the Midlands? Raped and smothered them both! Jesus Christ, Terri!' Tyler shook her head again. 'Funny friends you keep. Who else?'

'Francis Dewson.'

'The arsonist? Burned down an OAPs' home up in Hartlepool. Twenty-four dead and counting.'

'You make it sound so wrong ... just writing letters to them.'

'All full-term lifers. What on Earth are you trying to prove?'

'I'm not trying to prove anything ...'

'I just can't understand what you gain from this.' Fleetingly, the policewoman's tone became angry, intense. 'I mean, take Liam Haggerty! That last couple, Mr and Mrs Whitehead ... who he attacked in their cottage in Surrey. They were savagely beaten before he executed them. The SIO reckoned they'd already given him the combination to the safe, because there was so little in it. The extra violence was either because the bastard thought there was somewhere else where valuables might be hidden ... or for revenge because it wasn't a decent enough haul. Jesus Christ, Terri. John Whitehead was sixty-five years old, his wife, Dora, was sixty-two ... yet you've never seen anything like the crime scene we found there.'

'I can't explain it.' Terri shook her head tearfully. 'They're loners, outsiders ...'

'Like you, you mean? No one loves them and no one loves you, so that makes you two of a kind? No doubt these guys come on all soppy and regretful in their letters to you, but let me assure you, Terri, you and Liam Haggerty are *not* two of a kind. You think he's here to thank you for your kindness? If so, why didn't he knock on the door with a bunch of flowers?'

Terri hung her head, tears seeping onto her dusty cheeks. 'My God ...'

'God isn't going to save you tonight. Not before the Tunbridge Wells police do.'

'Speaking of which ...' Terri looked up again. 'Don't you think you should call them? Direct them back to the house?'

'That's what I was about to ...' Tyler stuck her hand into her coat pocket. And then into another one, and then into the pockets of her slacks. 'Damn it! That wretched, bloody mannequin scared the crap out of me.' She started groping around on the floor. 'Phone must be around here somewhere.'

She produced her torch and switched it on, playing its beam across the floorboards. Alongside them sat a cardboard box so crammed that it bulged at the seams, its top flaps hanging open. She dipped into it, still searching, rummaging hard.

'What is all this stuff?'

'Bric-a-brac,' Terri shrugged. 'Maybe a spider or two.'

'*Jesus!* Body parts!'

'Body parts?'

'Mannequin body parts!' Tyler threw something heavy

onto the attic floor, the torchlight picking out the pale, slick contours of a fake arm. A foot and half a leg followed. 'We've got all sorts in here …'

But Terri was shaking her head. 'That can't be right.'

'What can't?'

'We only ever had *one* mannequin.'

The penny seemed to drop painfully slowly. Several seconds passed before Tyler swung around to look at her. Their faces both wan, glinting with sweat.

When they turned to look up at the mannequin, it was too late.

Because the mannequin had turned around first.

Its face was hidden under the dark hood, but its gloved hands clutched the hockey stick.

'Run!' Tyler shouted, jumping to her feet. '*RUN!*'

Terri *did* run, blindly, haring across the attic, crashing into and over things all the way, only vaguely aware that two shadowy figures were tussling violently in her peripheral vision. When she reached the trapdoor, she fought frantically with the prop jammed through the folded sections of ladder. At first, it wouldn't come free. She looked back; the struggling figures were no longer in sight, but she saw the curved end of the hockey stick silhouetted against the windows as it rose and fell, each time impacting with a *whump* and a *whump* and a *whump.*

Hysterical, Terri battled with the prop again, and at last it came loose. She stamped on the trapdoor and it swung downward, kicking the ladder after it, the segmented device unfolding all the way to the landing floor.

She sensed rather than saw the shape coming at her through the darkness, and screamed as she commenced her descent. She was halfway down when the hockey stick struck the top of the ladder and came clattering after her. She fell sideways to avoid it, landing on her hip on the carpet, the hockey stick touching down just to her left. It was stained all over with red.

Numb with terror, Terri clambered to her feet and ran

recklessly down the stairs. As she did, the ladder began rattling and banging again. It was only as she reached the front door that she remembered she'd double-locked it.

And that the key was in her anorak pocket.

In the attic.

Sweat flying, she spun around and gazed up the stairs. The hooded figure at the top was gazing back down. She could see enough of his face to note that he'd grown a beard, but his eyes were still hidden from her.

'Liam … for God's sake!' she shrieked. 'Liam, we can talk about this!'

Slowly, one foot after another, he descended.

'Liam, in the name of heaven. Don't I mean anything to you? Why did you escape? Why on Earth would you come *here*? You should have realised the police would expect it. *For God's sake, Liam!*'

She fled along the hall towards the kitchen. The intruder was still only halfway down, but vaulted athletically over the banister, landing in a crouch just behind her.

Terri no longer screamed or shouted. As she dashed into the kitchen, she didn't even veer towards the back door, because there'd be no time to unfasten its top and bottom deadbolts or its central lock. Instead, she dragged a stool from under the breakfast bar, pushed it across the tiles and climbed up on it to reach a box on one of the top shelves.

But there was no time even for this.

She wailed in despair as two strong arms enfolded her from behind, lugging her backward off the stool, swinging her around and propelling her out into the hall.

'Liam, talk to me!' she wept.

Hot breath rasped in her ear as he carried her through into the lounge and flung her forcefully onto the armchair.

Terri lay sprawled and splayed, peering up white-faced at the towering, bearded form.

'I don't understand,' she whimpered. 'I loved you … that's all I've ever done, *loved* you.'

'And there was me,' came an amused-sounding voice

from the hall, 'fooled into thinking you felt sorry for a lost soul.'

As the owner of that voice sauntered in, Liam yanked his hood back.

Terri lay blinking with shock, still paralysed with fright, but perplexed as well.

Firstly, the man was not Liam Haggerty. Secondly, the woman who'd stepped in from the hall was DS Julie Tyler. Considering she'd just been beaten to death, she looked astonishingly fit and well. There wasn't a mark on her.

'Sergeant …?' Terri stuttered. 'Sergeant Tyler?'

Tyler put a fingertip to her lips and sampled what looked like a blob of blood. 'Funny stuff, this theatrical gore. Tastes a bit like raspberry.'

Terri's gaze switched haplessly from one to the other.

The man was younger than Liam would have been, equally as big in the chest and shoulders, but heavier in the neck and jowls. His mop of hair and bushy, untrimmed beard were carroty red, whereas Liam's of course was dark. She glanced at DS Tyler again, the woman still licking the last specks of crimson from her fingers.

'Who …?' Terri said hoarsely. 'Who in the name of God are you?'

Tyler shrugged. 'Well, it should be screamingly obvious that this isn't Liam Haggerty. And I must be honest, I was a bit worried from the outset that you might realise I wasn't Detective Sergeant Julie Tyler. I mean, she exists … but she doesn't look anything like me. Much more like you.' The woman smiled. 'Older, heavier, well past her best.'

Terri struggled to sit upright. 'What is this? In the name of Christ?'

'You genuinely didn't recognise me, Terri? At no stage?'

'I …' Again, Terri remembered that there'd been something familiar about the woman.

'You ought to. You being a murder groupie, I'd be amazed if you hadn't spotted me in a couple of photos here and there. The real name's Donna Whitehead.'

'Whitehead …?'

'This is my older brother, Gerald.'

'Gerald ...?'

'These cogs turn slowly, don't they?' Gerald snorted, his voice slow and monotonous.

'Yeah, but she's getting there,' his sister replied.

Terri shook her head with incredulity. 'You're related to ...'

'We're the son and daughter of your latest fixation's most recent victims,' Donna Whitehead said. 'It was *our* parents' house in Surrey that he last broke into. It was *our* parents he terrorised into opening their safe. It was *our* parents he beat and tortured because he still wasn't satisfied. It was *our* parents he then shot through the head from point-blank range while they were tied up. It was *our* parents whose murders completely screwed our lives up ... almost drove Gerald here to suicide. Three years ago now, and he hasn't worked since.'

Terri continued to glance from one to the other, mesmerised. 'Liam? Liam hasn't escaped from prison at all, has he?'

Donna Whitehead smirked. 'You actually believed that story about a news embargo? Jesus, I knew you must've been pretty dumb to fall for that creep in the first place, and then to not even recognise a make-your-own police warrant card. But to believe they wouldn't put the story out that a mad-dog killer had escaped from jail ...'

'This whole thing was ...' Terri was breathing easier now, but still astounded. 'This whole thing was ... a pantomime?'

Donna mused. 'No. 'Pantomime' implies fun. I don't think you've had fun, have you? Let's call it a lesson. Because now *you* know the meaning of fear. Now *you* know what it's like to have your home invaded, to be forced to confront your own mortality in a state of absolute certainty that you're about to die ...'

'I could report you for this!' Terri blurted. 'For breaking and entering. For impersonating a police officer.'

Donna smiled again. 'First of all, it'd be your word against ours, and there are two of us and one of you. And just in case, please don't let your gullibility extend to imagining that we haven't already got perfectly secure alibis sorted out for tonight. Secondly, do you think they'd actually care? A silly bitch like you, who gets aroused writing letters to lunatics and then shits her knickers at the possibility one of them might turn up. You're pathetic, woman. You're a sad, lonely joke. They'd laugh you out of the first police station.'

Gerald sniggered, clearly liking the image.

Terri regarded them helplessly. Evidently, they'd covered every base. Even though Terri had dumped her own gloves in the kitchen on returning to the house, Donna Whitehead, she now realised, had never once taken hers off all the time she'd been in here. Gerald Whitehead was also wearing gloves. They'd evidently planned this thing intricately. Most likely there'd be no evidence they'd ever been in the house.

'I think our work is done for tonight, Gerald,' the woman said. 'We've kept this nice lady up long enough.' With a last withering smile, she turned and left the room.

Gerald treated Terri to a dull, bovine grin before trudging after his sister.

Terri remained where she was. Only when she heard a key turning in the front door did she rise shakily to her feet. That wretched Whitehead woman had even had the cheek to go through her anorak up in the attic and bring down the key! She didn't miss much.

As the front door slammed again, Terri went to the lounge window and drew back the curtain. They were outside, chatting and chuckling as they headed down the drive towards their Puma. They were a confident twosome, by the looks of them. But then their mother and father had been wealthy, so most likely they'd been raised that way. But sometimes, detailed planning and overweening confidence didn't always go hand-in-hand.

Terri left the lounge stiff-shouldered, diverting first into the kitchen, before walking back to the front door. When she too strode down the drive, they were already in the car, Gerald behind the wheel, Donna in the front passenger seat. So engrossed were they in self-congratulation that they didn't realise she'd opened the rear door until she was already installed in the back.

'Hey …' Donna Whitehead began.

'Shut up!' Terri jammed the revolver's muzzle against her cheek. 'You've said your bit, now I'll say mine. Don't worry, I won't be as boring about it as you were.'

The Whiteheads sat rigid, stunned. The mere sight of the Bulldog .44 had knocked every inch of merriment out of them.

'You say I miss stuff that's right under my nose?' Terri said. 'How about you, Donna? Like … how can I afford to live in a house this size, in a neighbourhood like this, given that by day I'm a sales assistant in a backstreet shoe shop. Like why would the sad, scared little woman you thought I was go outside when it looked like you were in trouble … with or without a garden rake?'

'You *were* scared,' Donna said tremulously. 'Don't give us that.'

Terri mused. 'A little maybe. Who wouldn't be? When your boyfriend's been in jail for three years, and then suddenly you hear that he's coming home with all the hounds of hell on his fucking trail, you're never quite sure what state of mind he's going to be in. Not when the only communications you've exchanged with him were letters written in code. Not when you took great pains to write to other convicted killers too to provide cover for your relationship with him, not to mention your own involvement in his string of offences … only to then learn that it was making him jealous as hell. What's up, guys? You look shocked. Find it hard to believe I'm a nifty little getaway driver when it suits me?'

'Th … this is bullshit,' Gerald stammered.

'Does this look like bullshit?' Terri swung the gun right, sticking the muzzle into his ear. 'This isn't the weapon Liam used on your mum and dad, by the way. That was a Browning Hi-Power 9mm, and I chucked it in the Medway. This was Liam's spare. It's never been used before and it's completely untraceable. Which is a good thing, I'm sure you'll agree. As it's now *yours*.'

Gerald frowned, his brow creasing with fear. 'Mine?'

'Oh yeah …'

She swung the Bulldog left again, blasting Donna in the side of the head. The explosion was deafening and dazzling, blowing out the window and spraying the interior upholstery a livid, glimmering red. Gerald Whitehead had no time to react, not before she'd swung it back, and blasted a gaping hole in his skull as well.

Carefully as she could but wasting no time, Terri leaned forward.

'Poor, poor fella.' She folded Gerald's nerveless fingers around the Bulldog's grip and trigger, and gently patted them closed. 'Those damn suicidal tendencies. But why'd you have to do it *here*?'

She took her gloves off as she climbed from the car, tucking them out of sight and closing the door. Backing into the road, looking around and seeing that no other house lights were visible yet, she extricated the cotton buds from her ears.

And screamed.

ABOUT PAUL FINCH

Paul Finch is a former cop and journalist now turned best-selling crime and thriller writer, and is the author of the very popular DS Mark 'Heck' Heckenburg and DC Lucy Clayburn novels.

Paul first cut his literary teeth penning episodes of the British TV crime drama, *The Bill*, and has written extensively in horror, fantasy and science-fiction, including for *Doctor Who*.

However, he is probably best known for his crime/thriller novels, of which he has sold a million to date, specifically the Heckenburg police-actioners, of which there are seven, and the Clayburn procedurals, of which there are three. The first three books in the Heck line achieved official best-seller status, the second being the fastest pre-ordered title in HarperCollins history, while the first Lucy Clayburn novel made the *Sunday Times* Top 10 list. The Heck series alone has accrued over 2,000 5-star reviews on Amazon. Paul is currently with Orion, for whom he is writing a trilogy of stand-alone titles.

Paul is a native of Wigan, Lancashire, where he still lives with his wife and business partner, Cathy.

AFTERWORD

Towards the end of 2020 I was invited to become a patron of the advocacy charity, POhWER, a charity that helps people who, because of disability, illness, social exclusion and other challenges, find it difficult to express their views or otherwise get the support they need. As a newly appointed patron I was determined to find ways to help support POhWER's very important work. I was happy of course to talk about my relationship with them, share their news and to support their work in my social media. I had plans to take collection boxes out with me when I made public appearances but with another pandemic lockdown imposed in late December this became impossible.

The idea to create an anthology of crime stories came to me in early 2021. It was an obvious solution and I could use my skills as an editor and writer to help make this happen.

I consulted with Helen Moulinos, the CEO, of POhWER, and she loved the idea. I then had to write to some of the lovely authors I knew and beg for their help. Within these pages I'm sure you've found the result of the incredibly generous donation of a story from each of these amazingly talented writers. I am absolutely delighted with all of these stories and I feel the anthology as a whole is very strong indeed for their contributions.

And so, my afterword therefore must be about thanks to everyone who has taken part and become involved in making this anthology happen.

First, huge thanks to all of lovely authors: listed alphabetically: A A Chaudhuri, Raven Dane, Caroline England, Paul Finch, Rhys Hughes, Maxim Jakubowski, Awais Khan, Paul Magrs, Sandy Murphy, Amy Myers, Bryony Pearce, Christine Poulson and Sally Spedding. Extra thanks goes to

Maxim for helping me make some of these new contacts. Thanks also to David J Howe and Stephen James Walker of Telos Publishing for agreeing to publish the anthology – all royalties will be going to POhWER.

Thanks to Helen Moulinos whose tireless dedication to the charity has been a source of inspiration to me and thanks to my good friend Penny Bodger-Yates for introducing us.

And finally, thanks to you, dear reader, for buying this anthology and supporting the endeavour. If anyone wishes to make a donation to POhWER, then please head to their website at www.pohwer.net/ everything donated will go to a great cause.

Samantha Lee Howe
18 August 2021

Also Available From Telos Publishing

CRIME

THE LONG, BIG KISS GOODBYE
by SCOTT MONTGOMERY
Hardboiled thrills as Jack Sharp gets involved with a
dame called Kitty.

MIKE RIPLEY
Titles in Mike Ripley's acclaimed 'Angel' series of
comic crime novels.
ANGELS AND OTHERS
JUST ANOTHER ANGEL
ANGEL TOUCH
ANGEL HUNT
ANGELS IN ARMS
ANGEL CITY
ANGEL CONFIDENTIAL
FAMILY OF ANGELS
THAT ANGEL LOOK
BOOTLEGGED ANGEL
LIGHTS, CAMERA, ANGEL
ANGEL UNDERGROUND
ANGEL ON THE INSIDE
ANGEL IN THE HOUSE
ANGEL'S SHARE
ANGELS UNAWARE

HANK JANSON
Classic pulp crime thrillers from the 1940s and 1950s.
TORMENT
WOMEN HATE TILL DEATH
SOME LOOK BETTER DEAD
SKIRTS BRING ME SORROW
WHEN DAMES GET TOUGH
ACCUSED
KILLER
FRAILS CAN BE SO TOUGH
BROADS DON'T SCARE EASY
KILL HER IF YOU CAN
LILIES FOR MY LOVELY
BLONDE ON THE SPOT
THIS WOMAN IS DEATH
THE LADY HAS A SCAR

TANITH LEE
DEATH OF THE DAY

GRAHAM MASTERTON and WILLIAM S BURROUGHS
RULES OF DUEL

EVGENY GRIDNEFF
A STINK IN THE TALE

TELOS PUBLISHING
Email: orders@telos.co.uk
Web: www.telos.co.uk

To order copies of any Telos books, please visit our website
where there are full details of all titles and facilities for
worldwide credit card online ordering, as well as occasional
special offers.